Love Heals

TARA CONRAD

HIS ONE HER ONLY

Contents

This book is dedicated to those who have been made to feel like less than, marginalized, or rejected because of who they love. Know that your love is valid, your identity is worthy, and your presence makes the world a better place.
May this book serve as a reminder that you are not alone and that your story matters.

Leopold

"I'm a hot mess. A loser with nowhere to go and no one who gives a shit if I live or die," I say through the tears that are pouring down my face.

Tony opens his arms, and I collapse into them. Shamelessly, I bury my head against his chest as he closes me in the safety of his embrace.

"I'd care," he says softly.

Snowflakes float through the air while I fall apart in Tony's arms. He holds me against him, rocking me gently, providing me a safe place to cry until numbness finally washes over me, and I lift my head.

"I'm sorry," I say, wiping my face with the back of my hand. "You caught me at a bad time. I'll be okay." I look around for my box cutter. When Tony leaves, I intend to finish what I started.

My vision's blurry from all the crying I've done, and I don't spot it fast enough. Tony bends over, reaching for the metal glinting from the streetlamp's light.

"Are you looking for this?" He holds the blade up.

"Can I have it back?" I reach out for it, but Tony pulls his hand back. "That's mine for work."

"Didn't you just tell me you no longer have a job?" he asks, grabbing my wrist. Blood trickles down my arm, staining the pure white snow a crimson hue.

"Yeah," I say and attempt to pull my arm back.

Tony tightens his grip while he examines my arm. "It doesn't look too deep, but you'll need a bandage."

Pulling the elastic of my coat sleeve over my wrist, I say, "It'll be fine."

"You're right. That wound will heal." He slides my box cutter into his pocket. "I'm more concerned about the wounds on the inside." I turn my head, ashamed to look at him. "Leopold," Tony says my name softly. "Please look at me." When I don't respond, he takes his finger and gently turns my face toward him. "Come home with me—"

"No way." I hold my hands up, cutting him off, and take a step back. "The last guy who said that to me... Let's just say I almost paid with my life. I'm not about to make that mistake twice."

"There's no way I'm leaving you out here," Tony says. "Do you have anywhere else to go?"

"No," he whispers. "I'll take my chances on the street."

"I can't leave you out here. Do you have anyone you can call? You can let them know where you're going," I propose. "I'll give them all my contact info. That way, someone you trust knows where you are."

"I don't have any way to call them." Tony reaches into his pocket, pulls out his phone, and hands it to me. "What do I say?"

"Whatever you're comfortable with. I'll give you some privacy." Tony motions off to the side. "When you're ready for me, let me know."

"Wait," I call, stopping him. "Why are you doing this?"

Tony studies me thoughtfully before answering, "The first day you walked into my restaurant, I was drawn to you. I looked forward to seeing you and was sad when you left." His tone sounds sincere, but clearly, I'm a poor judge of character. "Kameron and I used to walk this path all the time. I've avoided coming here since he died, but I couldn't tonight. Something in here." He places his hand over his heart. "Told me I had to come here." Tony points to the phone. "Call whoever you want," he says and steps away.

I type in Ramiro's phone number and wait while it rings. Part of me hopes he doesn't answer because I don't know what to tell him. How do I say I screwed up again? Do I tell him I tried to end my life?

"Hello?"

"Ramiro? It's me, Leo."

"I didn't recognize the number and almost didn't pick up," he says, chuckling. "Did you finally get a cell phone?"

"I'm borrowing one from a friend." A fresh wave of tears begins to fall.

"Is everything okay?" he asks, but I don't answer. "Leo, what's wrong?"

"I don't even know where to start." I hiccup. "I'm such a screw-up."

"What happened?" Ramiro asks calmly.

"I've been trying so hard, but I lost everything." I turn away from the phone as my body tries to expel the contents of my empty stomach. Between my sobs and dry heaving, I can't take a deep breath and fall to my knees.

"Leopold," Tony calls as he rushes to my side. "It's okay. I've got you." He helps me to my feet and walks me to a nearby bench, lowering me to sit. Then, he puts the phone on speaker. "Hello?"

"Who are you?" Ramiro asks defensively.

"Tony. I'm a friend of Leo's."

When I got the job promotion, I told Ramiro all about him. So, thankfully, he's familiar with Tony's name. Although it doesn't seem to help right now. "What's going on? Is Leo okay?"

Tony looks at me, and I nod, giving my unspoken permission for him to tell Ramiro what happened.

"Leopold's received a lot of bad news," Tony explains. "His boss passed away, causing him to lose his job."

"I'm so sorry," Ramiro says.

"It gets worse," I say quietly. "I don't have a place to live anymore."

"What do you mean?"

"I couldn't make rent, and I got evicted." A tear slides down my face and plops onto the screen of Tony's phone.

"Why didn't you call me?"

"Everything happened all at once. They locked me out, so I—"

"What do you mean they locked you out? They didn't give you any notice?" Ramiro asks, raising his voice. "This is my fault. I haven't been there for you like I should. Let me get you a hotel room for the next few nights until we figure something else out."

"I've invited Leo to stay with me," Tony interjects. "I understand he's had some bad experiences, so if he agrees, I'll give you all my contact information so you know where he is. You can check on him whenever you'd like."

"A bad experience is an understatement," Ramiro says. "I'd feel more comfortable if he was in a hotel."

"I'd rather he not be alone," Tony insists, and I'm sure this is where he'll tell Ramiro what I did. Instead, he says, "Christmas is tomorrow. Leo shouldn't be alone in a sterile hotel room for the holiday." Tony takes my hand in his and gives it a reassuring squeeze.

"What are your thoughts, Leo?"

I chew on my lower lip as I struggle with indecision. My thoughts are so jumbled right now I can't decipher one from the next. I'm cold and exhausted. Resigned to whatever happens, I mumble, "I'll go with him." My eyelids droop closed.

"You have my number on your caller ID," Tony says.

"Yes. Give me a second to get a pen so I can write down your address." There's a quiet pause before Ramiro comes back. "I'm ready." Tony gives him the address as well as the number of the front desk. "Keep your phone on you all at times," Ramiro instructs. "I expect you to call me when you get to his house so I know you got there safely."

"I don't have a phone," I interrupt.

"Shit. I forgot."

"He can use mine," Tony offers.

"I don't like that Leo's dependent on you for his ability to make a phone call. No offense," Ramiro adds.

"There's a twenty-four-hour mart a few blocks from my house. We'll stop, and I'll buy him a pre-paid phone."

"No," I say quickly. "I have no way to pay you back." My body shivers, and my teeth chatter.

"I'll send him the money," Ramiro offers.

"We can figure that out later," Tony says. "It's snowing, and Leo's freezing. I want to get him home before he gets hypothermic."

"Are you sure about this, Leo?"

"Yeah. I'm sure."

Reluctantly, Ramiro hangs up, and I pass the phone back to Tony.

"No," he says. "I told your friend you'd keep my phone until you have one of your own."

"You don't have to do that." I try again to give it back.

"I gave both of you my word, and I intend to keep it," Tony says. "Let's get moving before you freeze out here."

After we emerge from the subway, we stop at a small, well-lit bodega where Tony purchases me a pre-paid iPhone. With the bag in hand, we walk the last few blocks to Tony's Park Place building in silence.

When the doorman sees us coming, he pulls the glass door open. "Happy Christmas Eve, Anthony."

"Same to you, Wendell." He motions to me. "This is my friend, Leo. He'll be staying with me for a while."

"Pleasure to meet you, Leo," Wendell says, offering me a friendly smile.

"You too," I respond, being sure to keep my hands inside my pockets so he doesn't see the blood.

After we pass through the door, Tony leads me to the front desk, where he introduces me to Joe. He takes my personal information and Ramiro's for my emergency contact.

"Would you like a keycard, sir?" Joe asks.

"No th—"

"Yes, he would," Anthony interrupts.

A few minutes later, Joe holds out a black and silver card. I hesitate to accept it until he says, "This is for you."

I look to Tony, who nods. Pulling my hand from my pocket, I tentatively reach for the card. When Joe sees my bloody hand, he gasps. "Do you need medical attention?"

"This? Um..."

"He had a small accident at work." Tony glances at me, and I smile at him with a small but appreciative smile. "Nothing serious."

"I'm glad to hear that."

I take the offered card and slip my hand back into my pocket, hoping not to draw any more attention to myself.

"Thanks, Joe," Anthony says. "Merry Christmas."

The elevator dings, signaling its arrival, and we step inside. As soon as the doors close, I turn to face him. "You didn't have to give me a key to your apartment."

"I didn't have to, but I wanted to." After a quick ride up, the doors open. "There's only two apartments on this floor," Tony says as I follow him down the ornate hallway. He swipes his card and the door lock clicks.

Tony's apartment has a minimalist, modern design. Pocket doors that are currently open connect the spacious living room to a modest-sized kitchen with a wall of floor-to-ceiling windows overlooking lower Manhattan.

"It's late, but I'm starving. Would you like something to eat?" he asks.

"I don't want to be a bother."

"You could never be a bother," Tony says. "You can get cleaned up while I cook if you want."

Shivers travel down my spine as memories of Krew saying eerily similar words push to the surface. "I'm okay. There's no need to go through any trouble," I mumble.

Tony changes the subject. "Come on, I'll show you to your room."

The walls of the guest room are creamy white, and the curtains are light grey. The room isn't overly big, but the high ceilings and the corner windows give it an airy feel. The furniture is minimal, a king-sized bed with a crisp white bedspread and a chest of drawers.

"I'm sorry it's a bit bare," Tony says. "It was recently renovated, but I haven't gotten to decorate it yet."

"It's beautiful," I reply.

Tony smiles. "You can help me pick out the décor and bedding you'd like after the holiday."

"That's not necessary. I'm not staying—"

Tony holds his hand up, stopping me. "Let's not put a timeframe on it tonight, okay?"

"Okay."

"We do need to talk about what happened." I look down. "Do you want to do that now or after you get cleaned up?"

"Can I shower first?" I ask, hoping to buy myself some time.

"Of course. Wait here. I'll get you something to change into." Tony leaves for a minute. When he returns, he has a pair of sweatpants and one of his T-shirts. "I'll be in the kitchen if you need anything," he says, then leaves me to shower.

I sit on the edge of the king-size bed and bring his clothes to my face. They smell of lavender, lemon, and a woodsy cedar—of Tony.

The room has two doors. One is closed, and the other is cracked open, so I go there first, finding an attached bathroom that rivals the size of the bedroom. The walls and floor are adorned in luxurious grey and white marble, making the room feel elegant. Fluffy light grey towels hang meticulously from a wall-mounted bar. Stripping off my damp, dirty clothes, I carefully adjust the water before stepping beneath the soothing cascade.

A stream of red flows down the drain, a stark reminder of my suicide attempt. Holding up my arm, I look at the cut. It's deep, but hopefully not enough to warrant stitches. I'm pretty sure it's going to leave a scar.

Tony already reminded me that we're going to have a conversation about what happened. He's going to want answers about why I was trying to end my life. Up until now, I've been able to dodge most of his questions about my past, but I'm afraid that time is up.

Not wanting to use too much water, I shower quickly and pull on Tony's clothes. Despite their loose fit, wearing his things brings a rush of desire, igniting an unmistakable attraction to him. Before I go back out to the kitchen, I set my new phone up and call Ramiro.

"Hello?" he answers on the first ring.

"It's me."

"I was beginning to get worried."

"I took a shower and got into some dry clothes," I murmur.

"I'm sorry I wasn't there for you." Regret laces his voice. "I should've been more present—"

"You're not responsible for the messes I make. I'm an adult. What happened is all on me."

Once a loser, always a loser. You'll never be good enough.

"Do you feel safe with Tony? At least until after the holiday."

"Yeah, I do." I relay the building information to him and explain he can also contact them to check on me.

"I've already called Phil and left a voicemail. There're a few things I want to say to him," Ramiro says, an angry tone in his voice.

"You don't need to do that."

"I very much do," Ramiro responds. "Evicting someone in

their program without trying to help. Hell, without warning is wrong."

There's a knock on my door.

"Come in," I call.

Tony opens the door but makes no move to enter. "The food's ready whenever you are."

"Ramiro, I have to go. Tell Jacinta and the girls Merry Christmas."

"Hang in there, Leo. We'll get you back on your feet."

He might get you on your feet, but you'll screw up again. You always do.

Anthony

ON THE COUNTER IS A CHARCUTERIE BOARD, LAID OUT with cheeses, meats, and a variety of other goodies that I threw together quickly. "Wow," Leo says quietly. "You didn't have to do all this."

I glance up and catch sight of Leopold wearing my clothes. His blond hair is damp and tousled. Attraction, mixed with a profound desire to care for him, completely floods my senses. The urge to envelop him in my arms and provide for him in every way consumes me entirely.

"It's the Italian in me. I can't cook just a little bit," I chuckle, trying to lighten the mood. "Before we eat, let me take care of your wrist."

I lead him to the table where the open First Aid kit waits. Leo sits on the upholstered dining chair.

"May I see your arm?" He tentatively extends it. Blood slowly seeps from the slice on his wrist. "This is going to sting," I say a second before I wipe it with an alcohol prep pad. Leo hisses and bounces his leg. "I'm sorry." I blow on it like my mom did for me when I was a child. "The boxcutter was pretty rusty. Is your tetanus shot up to date?"

"It is. Before I left California, Ramiro made sure I was able to see a doctor," he explains.

"We need to talk about this."

"I know," he says without looking up.

Working in the culinary field, I have plenty of first-aid experience. I put two butterfly strips on the wound to keep it closed and then cover it with gauze. "Let's make our plates," I suggest, closing the plastic case and sliding it back into the cupboard. "Would you like a drink?"

"No," Leo says too quickly.

I pull two cold plastic bottles out of the fridge. "It's only water."

"I'm sorry." He wrings his fingers.

"You don't need to apologize." We make our plates and sit across from one another at the table.

We begin eating in an awkward silence. I'm unsure what questions to ask and don't want to pressure him, but we do need to have an honest conversation.

"I guess you want to know why I did this?" Leo asks.

"I'd like to understand," I say softly, my gaze steady as I lock eyes with him, silently urging him to open up.

"My life has been one fuck up after another," Leo says and forces a laugh tinged with heaviness. "Do you want the long version or the cliff notes?"

"Whatever you're willing to tell me," I answer, trying to convey patience.

Leo's voice falters as he describes the day his parents caught him with another boy, the anguish of that experience palpable in his words. The next day, they packed him up and sent him off to conversion therapy. My jaw clenches as he recounts the abuse he suffered at the hands of his therapist—not that the piece of shit deserves that title.

"When the police told me they couldn't prosecute, I couldn't handle it and took off. That's when I met Krew," he explains.

As Leo bares his soul, I realize his story is far more devastating than I ever imagined. Tears spill from his eyes as he reveals the torment inflicted upon him by the man he thought he loved. Suddenly, his apprehension about coming home with me becomes painfully clear.

"New York was supposed to be my fresh start. I tried so hard to make things work, and I did everything right," he sobs. "And then, in a matter of a few hours, it was all gone. I had nothing. I was alone." Leo presses the heels of his hands under his eyes, trying to stop the tears.

"The voices in my head. Everything everyone's ever said about me. It got so loud, you know? When I reached into my pocket and felt the boxcutter, it was like a promise of the pain finally ending. I just cut." He looks up at me, his blue eyes shimmering with tears. "And then you showed up."

It takes me a few seconds to get my thoughts and emotions under control. Part of me wants to gather up everyone who ever hurt him and do worse to them. The more rational part of me realizes it wouldn't change anything. The only thing that matters now is ensuring Leopold's okay from today on. "And how do you feel now?"

"Numb." He shrugs. "Part of me wishes you didn't stop me. That I'm better off dead."

My heart sinks. "I know what it's like to feel hopeless. After Kam died, my world was black. We were on the phone when the tower collapsed on him. Just like that, he was gone. I didn't see a reason to keep living for a long time," I explain. "If it wasn't for my friends and their tough love, I don't know if I'd be here today. They helped me realize my life wasn't over. I had a purpose to be alive even if I couldn't see it at the time."

"There's one of the many differences between you and me," Leo says. "You had people around you who cared. I have no one."

"You have me." Leo's beautiful blue eyes meet mine. "I'm not a therapist. I don't know all the right things to say or do, but I'm going to ask you to do something for me. Will you hear me out?"

"Okay," he says hesitantly.

"I want you to give me thirty days."

"What do you mean?"

"I need your word that you won't do anything to harm yourself for the next thirty days. I'll find you a therapist, someone trustworthy," I add. "Who can guide you through this darkness. We'll get you a job, and I'll introduce you to all my friends." I reach out and touch his hand, feeling that undeniable spark of attraction, the same magnetic pull I felt the first time we met. "Let me be the one to show you that your story isn't over. That there's so much love waiting for you on the other side of this pain."

Leo bites his bottom lip as he considers what I've proposed. "I don't want to bring all my shit to your doorstep. You don't deserve to have to deal with it."

"You didn't *bring* anything. I asked you to be here." I give his hand a gentle squeeze. "Please, Leo. I know thirty days seems like a long time right now. We'll take it one day at a time. I promise you won't be alone."

He closes his eyes for a brief minute and sighs. "Okay. I promise."

"Thank you." I release the breath I was holding. "First things first. Do you know the number for your landlords?"

"I do." Leo relays it to me.

"What they did is illegal. Star, one of the owners of Fire and Ice, is also an attorney. I'll text her. We'll get your things back and the money they took."

"You don't—"

"I know," I interrupt. "I don't have to. Anything I do is because I want to."

"Thank you," Leo says quietly.

I'm in so far over my head right now, but there's no way I can walk away from Leopold. I'll fight with everything in me to make sure he comes out of this. He has to. I refuse to accept anything less.

Anthony

When I finally get Leopold settled in his room, it's after four am. It takes all my willpower not to stay and watch over him while he sleeps. Instead, I settle for leaving my door open in case he needs me. Although I'm mentally exhausted, my body is wired. My eyes refuse to close. Instead of fighting an unwilling body, I put my time to good use.

First, I text Star.

Me: I'm sure you're still sleeping. When you get up, please text me.

Several minutes later my phone vibrates with an incoming call.

"Hello?"

"Is everything alright?" Star asks.

"No." With the knowledge that she's one of two people I know I can confide in, I tell her what's happened with Leopold over the past twenty-four hours. Starting with the theft of cash from his room and the death of his boss. "The landlords took the last of his money and locked him out of the apartment without warning. He only had the clothes on his back."

"What's their number? I don't care that it's Christmas Eve. Come morning, they'll be getting a call from his attorney."

"Thank you," I say, grateful to have such good friends.

"At the risk of overstepping," Star adds. "Leo's going to need a therapist. You know that, right?"

Star's co-owned Fire and Ice for close to twenty years. During that time, she's encountered all kinds of situations. Over the years, she's compiled a list with numerous resources.

"Can you point me in the right direction?"

"I'll text you a few names."

After we hang up, I text Owen.

Me: Dinner is at six tomorrow.

Owen: You're up early.

Me: I haven't gone to sleep.

Owen: What's wrong?

Me: After I left the party, I ran into Leo.

Owen: Oh? That sounds exciting.

Once I realized Leopold was doing the food deliveries for Fire and Ice, I made it a point to be there every week. The three of us would sit down and have lunch together. I was desperate to spend whatever time I could with him. At first, I played it off as a coincidence, but Owen quickly saw through my story. I haven't said anything, but I'm sure he knows I'm interested in Leopold.

Me: It's not like that. I found him at the park—cutting his wrist.

Owen: What the fuck? How bad is it?

Me: A few minutes later and he wouldn't be here. Thankfully, it isn't too deep. I was able to take care of it. He's here with me.

Owen: What do you need? What can I do?

Me: Help me give him a reason to live.

Owen: I'll do everything I can. Leo has all of us by his side now.

Me: Thank you.

For the next few hours, I scour the internet for every resource I can find on helping someone suffering from depression or who's suicidal. Most of what I read suggests he should be inpatient, where professionals can counsel him and administer medication, but I'll be damned if I'm going to trust a stranger to care for him. Leopold's scared and vulnerable. He needs to be with someone who cares about him.

While I'm engrossed in reading, a text from Star arrives, containing a list of therapists for Leo. Before sharing the names with him, I take a moment to check each one's reviews. I'm oblivious to the time passing until sunlight streams into my room, breaking my concentration.

It's only when I reluctantly tear myself away from my reading that I notice the time glaring back at me – 8 am. I've completely lost track of the hours. I take a quick shower and pull the blankets up on my bed. On my way to the kitchen, I pause outside Leo's room. He appears serene and at peace, curled on his side, his hands cradling his cheek as he sleeps. With a soft smile, I leave him to rest while I go to the kitchen and start cooking.

The last two pieces of French Toast sizzle on the griddle as footsteps approach from behind. Glancing over my shoulder, I find Leopold rubbing his eyes. His blond hair tousled from sleep.

I feel an overwhelming urge to close the gap between us and press a soft kiss on his lips. Suppressing the impulse, I opt for a friendly greeting. "Good morning. How did you sleep?"

"Better than I have in a long time," he says with a yawn.

I flip the toast before it burns. "I'm glad to hear that."

"That smells delicious," he says as he steps closer. "Can I help with anything?"

"Would you mind getting plates and silverware?"

"Sure thing," he replies, and I guide him to the appropriate cupboards and drawers. Leo takes charge of setting the table while I pull the bacon out of the oven.

"Star called Phil and Maureen bright and early this morning."

"She did?" he asks, his forehead wrinkled in worry.

"After she identified herself as your attorney, they informed her about the mistaken lockout," I remark with a roll of my eyes. "They provided her with a code so you can access the apartment to gather your belongings," I explain as I place the food in the center of the table and take a seat.

"You're kidding?"

"We can go over after breakfast if you want."

"It's Christmas Eve." Leo pushes his food around on his plate. "I'm sure you have better things to do."

"I wouldn't be anywhere else but by your side," I assert warmly. "They'll be returning your two-hundred and fifty dollars as well," I add. "You can pick it up after the holiday."

"She didn't have to do this. I don't deserve any of it," Leo says, his eyes filling with tears.

"That's where you're wrong. You deserve this and so much more," I say tenderly. "You're not alone anymore."

"I don't know what to say."

Tears spill over his lower lids, and I ache to wipe them away.

"You don't need to say anything."

The expressions of disbelief etched on Leo's ex-roommates' faces as he and I entered the room are unforgettable. I'm grateful Leo remained unaware of the whispered snide comments they made while he retrieved his personal belongings.

While I wait, I make a pre-planned phone call to Star.

"It's me."

"You got into the apartment without issue?" she asks.

"We did." It's showtime. "Have the authorities been contacted?"

"They most certainly have," she says. "I spoke to someone I know in the department."

"Yes, I understand."

"There's not much they can do, but he's going to send someone out to question the roommates."

"The NYPD will be coming to the apartment to look for evidence of a robbery?" I repeat what she told me.

"If we get lucky, they'll just confess, and Leo will get his money back. At the very least, he'll put the fear of God into them for the next person," she chuckles.

"Yes, ma'am." I glance at the three young men. Their previous chatter is now silent. All attention is on me. "I have faith that they'll uncover evidence of whoever stole Leopold's money."

"You two good there?" she asks.

"Thank you for representing Leopold on such short notice, Ms. Winslow."

"I'll see you tomorrow."

The room has gone deadly silent. When Leo reenters, he casts a quizzical glance between the guys and me. Hurrying over, I take one of the bags from him. "Your attorney called while you were in there."

"She did?"

"A report has been filed," I say, turning my attention to the stunned boys. "An officer will be stopping by to question you about who may have had access to the apartment," I continue firmly. "I trust you'll fully cooperate with the NYPD's investigation."

"Investigation into what?" the dark-haired one asks.

"The stolen money from Leopold's room."

"What would we know about it?" he asks with a cocky attitude.

"That's for the NYPD to figure out." I turn my attention back to Leopold. "Are you ready to go?" He nods. I open the door, allowing Leo to exit first. "Merry Christmas, gentlemen."

It's mid-afternoon when we arrive back to my apartment. While Leopold finishes putting the few items of clothing he owns into the dresser, I sit on the edge of his bed. "I know you lost your job." He stops and eyes me warily. "Don't feel obligated to say yes if you don't want to work in a restaurant, but I'd like to offer you employment as a busser."

He returns to folding a pair of pants before he replies nervously, "I didn't graduate high school."

How did he slip through so many cracks? My heart aches for this man. "Do you have a GED?"

"No."

"Do you want to get your GED?"

"Yes," he says without hesitation. "I started studying for it when I was at Safe Haven. When I moved here, I wanted to but didn't know where to start." He turns to face me. "Phil and Maureen weren't anything like Ramiro, and without a computer or cellphone, I was at a bit of a disadvantage."

"The community center where I take art classes offers GED prep courses on weeknights. We can get you signed up after the new year if you'd like," I offer.

"I'd like that very much."

"If you're interested, you can start work this week. If not, we'll find a job you'd prefer."

"I don't know much about working in a restaurant, but I'd like to give it a try," he says, the corner of his mouth turning up with a small smile.

"It can get pretty fast-paced on a busy night, but overall, it's not a difficult job. I'm sure you'll do just fine."

"I don't know why you're taking a chance on me," Leo says, his blue eyes that hold so much innocence for someone who's lived through hell lock on mine.

Every fiber of my being yearns to hold him tightly and confess that my heart was his from the moment he stepped over the threshold at *Italiano Desiderio*. I want to tell him that he's mine now, and I'll never allow anyone to hurt him again. Just as I'm on the brink of confessing feelings I have no right to have, my cell rings, sparing us both from a conversation Leopold may not be ready for.

"Hello?"

"Where's Leo?" Ramiro asks, his tone almost frantic.

"He's right here. Why?"

"I've been trying to call him for the past two hours. When he didn't pick up." He pauses. "Let me talk to him?"

I hold the phone out. "It's Ramiro."

Leo brings it to his ear. "Hello?"

"You had me worried sick." Ramiro's voice rises, anxiety evident in his tone. "Where have you been?"

"We went to my old apartment to get my things," Leo explains.

Standing up, I make my way to the window, offering them a semblance of privacy.

"I'm not used to having one. I didn't even think about bringing it." Leo goes quiet. "Why are you on the phone with me when your wife is in labor?" He pauses again. "Please don't worry about me. I'm in a safe place." Leo stops again. "I'll keep my phone on me, I promise. Let me know when the baby's here."

Leopold

With everything that's gone on today, I almost forgot it was Christmas Eve. Tony lets me know he's hosting his annual Christmas dinner party tomorrow.

"I don't know much about cooking," I admit.

"I'll teach you everything you need to know," he says, and my stomach gets butterflies.

We spend the rest of the afternoon and evening baking cookies and prepping all kinds of fancy foods for tomorrow's dinner. Being beside Tony in his kitchen feels natural. Somehow, we don't get in each other's way. Instead, our movements are in sync as if we've done this every day for years.

Several times, his arm brushes against mine. The contact sends electricity coursing through my body. It's exciting and alarming. This man stumbled upon me last night while I was trying to take my own life. He not only saved me but opened his home to me. I don't know what my future, let alone tomorrow, holds. I'm safe with Tony, but I can't be stupid and screw this up.

"Have you heard anything from Ramiro?" Tony asks as he loads the last of the dishes into the dishwasher.

"Nothing yet." I pick up my iPhone triple checking that my

ringer is turned up. I don't want to miss any texts or calls. "Is it normal for it to take this long?"

"Kam's sister was in labor for three days before Calliope was born," he says.

"My mother's labors were fast. A few hours at most." I feel a pang of loss thinking about my family, especially today.

"How many siblings do you have?" Tony asks as he wipes his hands on a dish towel.

"I have two younger sisters. Arianna's twenty and London will be turning eighteen on New Year's Day."

"Do you keep in touch with them?"

"Arianna and I never got along," I explain. "London and I were always close. She gave me her cell phone number and a gift card to help me get out of Walking in the Light, but I haven't ever reached out to her."

"Why not?" he asks with genuine curiosity.

"My father. I don't trust him. I didn't want to risk him turning on London."

"Despite everything you've been through, you're always thinking about others," Tony says. "You're a good man, Leopold."

I shrug. "I don't think so."

"Look at me," he says with a quiet authority, and I lift my eyes to meet his. "Negativity is often louder than positivity. I understand that. But don't you go believing any of that. You, Leopold," Tony says, taking a step closer to me. "Are a good man."

For the briefest of moments, we stand close, our gazes locked with each other. I almost think he's going to lean in and kiss me, but then he takes a step back, and I realize what a ridiculous thought that is.

Why would a man like him be interested in a loser like you? He's just pitying you.

I force a yawn. "I'm pretty tired. Do you mind if I turn in?"

"You don't have to ask."

"I didn't want to ditch you if you still needed me."

"You were a huge help today," Tony says with a smile.

"I had a good time. Thank you for being so patient with me," I say quietly. "Goodnight, Tony." I turn and start walking out of the kitchen.

"Leopold." I stop and turn around. "Merry Christmas."

"Merry Christmas," I smile.

I reach into my wallet and pull out the piece of paper with my sister's phone number on it. I haven't allowed myself to think about London in a long time. Even though five years separated us, she and I were always close. She could always brighten any day. I swore I'd never reach out to her, but my resolve wavers. I pull out my phone and start typing in her number until I come to my senses.

"Don't be selfish, Leo," I say aloud. "You can't risk London getting hurt because you're feeling sorry for yourself."

I tear up the paper and flush it down the toilet, ensuring I won't do anything stupid in the midst of another weak moment.

Last night, Tony left my bedroom door open. I was grateful for that. It made me feel less trapped and alone. Tonight, I do the same thing. Then, I crawl beneath the covers and fall into a dream-filled sleep of a man with soft brown eyes that hold a quiet strength.

The sounds of Christmas music playing in the other room wake me. I stretch my arms above my head before sitting up. Swinging my legs over the side of the bed, I stand and pull up the blankets.

When I get out to the living room, I find a Christmas tree with twinkling lights and wrapped gifts under it. Tony's in the kitchen, standing over a large pot on the stove. I watch him move around the kitchen with practiced ease, enjoying the way his muscles flex as he reaches into his upper cabinets.

"Good morning," I say when he turns around and sees me watching him.

"Merry Christmas." He smiles brightly.

"You should've woke me up so I could've been out here helping you." I make a note to set an alarm to ensure I don't oversleep every day.

"I don't mind," he says. "Have a seat. We'll eat and then open gifts."

I freeze. "I didn't get you anything."

"It's nothing big," he says as he sets several plates in the center of the table. "The espresso will be ready in a minute."

"Did you stay up all night decorating?" I ask, motioning to the tree that wasn't there yesterday.

"I haven't put up a tree in a few years." He sets a small cup of coffee in front of me and another by his plate. "I decided it was time to take it out."

"I'm glad you did."

"Help yourself."

"It looks so pretty. I hate to mess it up."

"Don't be silly," Tony says, sliding the plate with the halved pears over to me. "Food is made to be enjoyed."

I've gone hungry more often than not over the past two years. Once I started deliveries, Tony always had something ready for me to eat at his restaurant and at Fire and Ice. I began to look forward to those days partially for the food but more so because I got to spend time with Tony.

"You're going to spoil me," I say, only half-joking.

"I fully intend on doing just that."

Anthony

LEOPOLD'S ALWAYS GENUINELY HAPPY WITH ANY FOOD I make him. It's the kind of joy that only someone who's been deprived of food, something I consider a human right, can exhibit.

"How do I eat this?"

"May I?" Leo nods and passes me his plate. He watches as I make a bed of ricotta and lay two pieces of the poached pears on top. "I didn't know if you were allergic to nuts, so I kept them separate."

"I'm not."

"Good. The candied walnuts are my favorite part," I sprinkle some over the pears and top it with a drizzle of honey. "I hope you like it," I say as I set his plate in front of him.

Watching Leo carefully load his fork with a bit of everything, I can't help but be captivated by the fluid motion of his lips as he savors the flavors. His tongue darts out to capture a stray drop of honey from his lip. For a fleeting moment, my thoughts veer into more sensual territory, imagining his lips wrapped around my cock. Thankfully, the table obstructs the view, and Leo doesn't notice. I avert my eyes, forcing myself to focus on my own plate.

"This is incredible, Tony," he gushes. "I've never tasted anything like it."

"It's not very hard to make. I can teach you if you'd like."

"I'd like that very much." Leo's smile lights up his face.

While we enjoy a leisurely meal, Leo begins to inquire about this evening's party. Apprehension is palpable in his tone. I offer reassurance, promising to stay by his side throughout the evening and suggesting we can slip away to take a break if it gets too much.

After we finish eating, Leo insists on loading the dishwasher. That frees me up to get started on the tomato sauce for tonight's meal.

With the sauce simmering lightly, I ask, "Are you ready for your present?"

"I wish you didn't get me anything. I have nothing to give you."

"I didn't do it to make you feel bad or because I expect something in return," I explain. "It's something small that I thought about yesterday."

"You didn't leave the house, though."

"I asked Owen to grab it for me," I say as I walk into the living room. Leo sits on the sofa with his legs pulled up under him while I get his gift from under the tree. I pass him the package wrapped in shiny silver paper and topped with a red bow, and then I sit beside him.

Leo bites his lower lip as he carefully unwraps the gift. He folds the paper and sets it on the sofa beside him with meticulous care. With a sense of awe, he lifts the lid of the white box, revealing the soft brown leather journal resting inside.

"Embrace the storm, for within its fury lies the promise of a rainbow," Leo reads the inscription, his voice carrying a mix of contemplation and hope.

"I wasn't sure if you preferred to draw or write, so I made sure it had both unlined and lined paper," I explain. "I wanted to give you a safe place to express your thoughts and feelings."

Leo's voice trembles as he confesses, "I don't know what to

say." He meets my gaze with wide baby-blue eyes that mirror the wonder in his voice.

"I hope you like it."

"It's the most thoughtful gift anyone's ever given me. I love it." Leo surprises me by wrapping his arms around me and resting his head against my chest. Without hesitating, I return the embrace, feeling a sense of warmth and connection. "I'm sorry," he whispers, pulling away and flushing pink. "I shouldn't have done that."

"Don't apologize." I smile warmly. "I liked that you did."

My words hang in the air until his phone rings, breaking the spell we're under.

It's Ramiro," he murmurs.

"You should answer it."

With a look of regret, he swipes the screen, connects the call, and puts it on speaker. "Is she here?"

"The baby was born early this morning. But it's not a she," Ramiro says.

"What do you mean?"

"The ultrasound was wrong. It's a boy," he says excitedly. "I have a son."

"Oh my gosh." Leo brings his hand to his mouth. "You and Jacinta must be so happy."

"It's the best Christmas surprise we could've ever asked for."

"Congratulations. How's your wife feeling?" I ask.

"She's tired but doing well. Thank you for asking."

"Tell me everything," Leo says excitedly.

"He's tiny. Five pounds and sixteen inches with a head full of dark curly hair," Ramiro gushes.

"What's his name?"

"We'd planned to name our daughter after our mothers. Instead, we decided to name our son after our fathers, Tiburan Alfonso Vega."

I leave Leo to talk with Ramiro while I return to the kitchen to assemble the lasagna. Yesterday, Leo and I made homemade noodles, which have sat out to dry all night. I have a few layers put together when Leo comes to stand beside me.

"I'm sorry I took so long. Ramiro couldn't stop talking about the baby."

"You don't need to keep apologizing," I say patiently. "This is your home to come and go as you please."

Leo studies me before asking, "Can I help?"

"Sure."

While he washes up, I stir the sauce.

"Here's what you do," I explain, showing him the order for the noodles, sauce, and cheese, then stepping aside to let him take over. As he works, he occasionally shakes his head, struggling to keep his hair out of his eyes. "Do you have anything to tie your hair back?"

"No." He blows out a frustrated breath.

"I'm sure I have something around here."

Opening a large drawer filled with miscellaneous odds and ends that have no other home, I rummage around until I find what I need. Approaching Leo from behind, I comb my fingers through his silky, soft hair. Leo tenses from the unexpected touch, and I realize my mistake. Leaning in, I murmur softly, "I'm just pulling your hair back." His tension melts away instantly, and I gather his hair and tie it back with a rubber band. "It's a bit messy, but it should keep it out of your face."

"Am I doing this right?" he asks, his brow furrowed in uncertainty.

"You're doing great," I reassure him, offering him an approving smile that he reciprocates with one of his own.

When he finishes, I cover the tray with aluminum and slide it into the oven.

"That's the last of the big things. We can take a little bit to relax before Owen and Astrid get here," I say as I wipe down the counter. "He always comes early."

Broaching the subject of therapy with Leo is daunting, to say the least. While I'm cognizant of the trauma he's endured at the hands of his previous therapist, I have to believe there are trust-worthy individuals who could provide him with the support he deserves. Despite my apprehension, I'm acutely aware that delaying seeking help from a trained professional will only prolong his suffering.

"There's something I want to talk to you about."

Leo wrings his fingers, a nervous habit I've noticed. "That sounds serious."

I join him where he's sitting at the kitchen island. "First, I need to be completely transparent with you," I say, my voice steady. "Star and Owen are aware of the situation," I continue, choosing my words carefully. "You have my word that your confidence will be respected. It won't go any further than them."

"I'm sure they think I'm a huge screw-up," Leo says, looking at his hands in his lap.

"No, they don't." Leo knows how I lost Kam, but we've never talked about my own struggles with suicidal thoughts. If I'm going to be able to connect with him, I need to be transparent and tell him everything. "After Kam died, I put up walls to keep everyone at arm's length. I tried to convince everyone I was fine. All the while, I was slowly withering away inside." I shift in my seat. Talking about the night of the attack on my restaurant still affects me—I'm a work in progress. "My carefully constructed façade fell apart when I was the victim of a hate crime."

"A hate crime?" Leo asks, shocked.

I recount the details of that awful night. The names I was called. "Being compared to one of the terrorists whose actions stole the person I loved broke me. I ignored what I thought was a heart attack."

"Why would you do that? What if it had been something serious?"

"I couldn't see a way out of the suffocating grief I'd been struggling to hide. I wanted to die."

"What happened?" Leo asks quietly.

"Owen found me and practically dragged my ass to the emergency room. After a battery of tests, they decided I was having anxiety attacks," I say, motioning with my hands for dramatic effect. "He pinned me down and had a serious heart-to-heart talk with me, pointing out the fact that I hadn't processed my loss and suggesting I go to therapy," I continue. "As upset as I was that night, I'm thankful for his persistence despite my difficult demeanor that night."

"I refuse to go to a treatment center," Leo says and stands. "I need to get out of here."

I place my hand on his arm, a silent plea in my touch, "Please stay and hear me out," I implore softly. He hesitates for another moment before sinking back into his seat. "I want to make something clear—I would *never* suggest you go inpatient," I assure him. "This is your home for as long as you want it to be. But I do believe seeing a therapist is crucial to your recovery," I pause, choosing my next words carefully.

"You've had experiences that no one should ever have to bear. A compassionate and trustworthy therapist will help you find the peace and healing you deserve," I pause again, letting my words sink in. "I need you to know you're not alone in this. I'll be with you every step of the way."

"How do you know if they're safe?" he asks.

"Star gave me the names of therapists she knows personally. I trust her judgment implicitly."

"I don't have insurance," he replies quickly. "I can't afford a therapist."

"I give my employees insurance on day one." My part-timers don't usually get insurance, but Leopold doesn't need to know that he's the exception.

"I don't know," he hesitates.

"You promised me thirty days," I remind him firmly. "While I won't use that to control you, attending *outpatient* therapy is nonnegotiable. I hope you'll come to realize it's in your best interest. That this world is a brighter, better place because you're in it."

Leopold

"You've done so much for me already. You can't keep doing—"

"I can and will," Tony interrupts. "We'll get all the paperwork taken care of tomorrow. Will you agree to go to therapy?"

The answer to his question should be easy. In today's society, going to therapy is more normalized than ever, but for me, it's synonymous with abuse—trauma.

You're being set up again. He only wants to use you. Hurt you.

The doorbell rings, startling me.

"It's okay." Anthony reaches out and touches my arm. "It's just Owen and Astrid." He walks away to answer the door. "Merry Christmas."

"Merry Christmas." Owen, who's wearing a Santa hat, chirps. "You put up a tree?" he asks, shocked.

"Don't act so surprised. It is Christmas, isn't it?" Tony turns his attention to the dark-haired woman and kisses her cheek, "Merry Christmas." Then, motioning toward me says, "Astrid, this is my friend, Leo."

"It's a pleasure to meet you," she says.

"You as well."

"It's good to see you again," Owen greets me, giving me a hug.

"I'm not sure what you did to get that Scrooge to decorate, but thank you."

"I don't think it had anything to do with me."

"It had everything to do with you," he says quietly.

Tony's the epitome of the perfect host. Within minutes of his guests' arrival, he's already serving coffee and an extravagant lunch spread, including a wreath-shaped antipasto salad, clam and mozzarella dip, mouthwatering stuffed mushrooms, and arancini.

"Everything's perfect as always," Astrid compliments him.

"I can't take all the credit. Leopold was a huge help," he humbly remarks, a smile playing on his lips when he looks at me.

Tony's gaze is filled with warmth and kindness, sending a gentle flutter through my heart as our eyes meet.

"I really didn't do much," I say, averting my eyes.

"Do you like to cook?" Owen asks.

"I think so," I respond with a shrug. "But I can't make very many things."

These people are accomplished and confident. I can't help feeling inadequate in their presence.

"You're already better than me," Astrid says kindly. "Sir has been trying to teach me how to cook since we met, but all I can manage to make without burning are scrambled eggs and grilled cheese."

"Tony's a pro. He'll have you cooking like a five-star chef in no time," Owen reassures, offering a supporting smile.

While Tony and Owen discuss the club, Astrid shifts her attention to me. "How did you and Tony meet?"

"At his restaurant. I was delivering food," I reply nervously.

"He's quite taken with you," she says quietly. "I haven't seen him look at anyone like he does you in a long time."

"Oh no. We're not." My words come out rushed. "I'm just staying here for a little while."

"I'm sorry. I didn't mean to assume," Astrid apologizes.

"It's okay," I say, eager to shift the conversation away from me. "How long have you and Owen been together?"

"I've been his submissive for four years. It's only the past few months that we've started exploring our feelings outside of our dynamic," she says dreamily.

"I don't know what all of that means, but it sounds good," I admit with a chuckle.

"It is." She looks at Owen admiringly before saying, "You should come to the club sometime. I bet you'd love it."

Sensing my unease, Tony gracefully shifts the conversation to Astrid's job as a high school science teacher. Her enthusiasm for teaching shines through as she animatedly discusses her students.

With him deep in conversation, I didn't realize he was paying attention to our discussion, but I'm grateful and offer a relieved smile. It's not the first time he's come to my rescue, and I'm starting to realize it's one of his many talents.

As the afternoon shifts into evening, the house fills with a small gathering of Tony's friends. We indulge in yet another exquisite meal, surrounded by friendly and easy-to-talk-to individuals. Despite the knowledge that Owen and Star know my situation, they treat me with the same warmth and kindness. I find myself relaxing and enjoying the party.

Tony's sitting on his sofa talking with Star's submissive, Corbin, and a few others. Uncertain if it's appropriate for me to join, I approach hesitantly. Tony catches my eye and motions for me to join him.

"Are you enjoying yourself?" Tony speaks softly to me.

"I am," I reply, finding comfort in our private exchange.

"I'm pleased to hear that." His voice carries a hint of something more profound.

With the laughter and chatter of the gathering swirl around us, Tony's question affords us a moment of intimacy, allowing our connection to deepen amidst the whirlwind of activity.

As the night winds down and the last guest departs, I feel a twinge of regret. Despite my initial hesitations, I found myself relaxing and enjoying their company.

"You look exhausted," Tony remarks. "Why don't you turn in."

"But there are still dishes."

"I'll take care of them."

"Are you sure?" I ask, not wanting to ditch him with a mess.

"I'm positive," he reassures me. "Sleep well."

"You too." He responds before turning to load the dishwasher.

"Tony?" I call, and he pauses, turning to face me. "Would you stay with me? At least for the first session?" I ask nervously, feeling the weight of my request hanging in the air.

"Of course," he replies without hesitation.

As I make my way down the hall to my bedroom, an unfamiliar emotion begins to stir within me—a feeling I haven't experienced in a very long time—hope.

Leopold

WORKING IN A RESTAURANT ISN'T ANYTHING LIKE I'D imagined. When Tony warned me that things could get busy, I thought I understood, but I hadn't fully grasped the reality until now. It's a constant battle keeping up with clearing tables, fetching drinks, and doing whatever else is necessary to help the other team members.

Surprisingly, though, I find myself enjoying the challenge. There's a certain thrill in the hustle and bustle of the dining area, a satisfaction in knowing that I'm contributing to the smooth operation of Tony's business. I never would've guessed that I'd enjoy working in a restaurant. Still, there's a sense of accomplishment that comes with each successfully cleared table and satisfied customer.

In addition to supporting me at work, Tony also followed through on getting me set up with health insurance and a therapist. Now, as we sit in the luxurious waiting room, awaiting my first therapy appointment, I can't help but feel overwhelmed with gratitude. It's a new chapter in my life, one that wouldn't have been possible without Tony's unwavering support. As I glance at him, a sense of peace washes over me, knowing I'm not alone in this journey toward healing and self-discovery.

Don't get used to it. He's not going to stick around. He'll leave you like everyone has.

"Leopold?" a red-headed woman snaps me out of my thoughts when she steps out of her office and calls my name.

"That's me," I say as I stand.

"I'm Sarah," she introduces herself. "Come on in."

I look back at Tony, who rises to his feet, a determined expression on his face.

"You can wait out here," she says kindly.

"No." My feet freeze in place. "He needs to come with me."

"Okay. We can do that," Sarah assures me, her kind smile easing my nerves a little bit.

When I don't move, Tony places his hand on my lower back, a silent show of his unwavering support. "I'm right here with you."

I step inside the office, Tony and Sarah following close behind. When Sarah moves to close the door, a surge of panic washes over me. "Is it possible to leave the door open?" I ask nervously. "I don't mean to be a pain."

"Asking a question is never a problem," she reassures me with a comforting smile. "I'll always do my best to accommodate your requests."

Tony and I sit on a beige microsuede sofa, our legs brushing against each other. Looking around her office, I mentally note the differences between Sarah's office and David's.

This office is bright and welcoming. Sunlight shines through the large window behind Sarah's desk. One side of the room contains bookshelves. The other, where we are, is a sitting area with a couch and two chairs. There are no other doors, something that puts me at ease.

"Do you prefer Leopold or Leo," Sarah asks as she picks up a notebook and pen from her desk.

"You can call me Leo."

Sarah sits in one of the chairs across from us. "May I ask who you've brought with you today, Leo?"

"This is my friend, Tony."

"It's a pleasure to meet you," she greets him.

"You as well," he replies politely.

"Can you tell me a little about you, Leo?"

"What do you want to know?" I shrug, uncertain what to say.

"Let's start with why you've come today?"

"Right before Christmas, I tried to kill myself," I confess.

"How did you do it?"

"I tried to slit my wrist." I look down at my arm and run my finger over the lightly colored scar. "Tony was the one who stopped me."

"Before we continue, I have to ask. Are you still thinking about hurting yourself?"

"Sometimes I wish I'd been successful," I say, refusing to look at Tony. I don't want to see what I know will be a hurt expression. "I still hear the same thoughts I did that night."

Sarah jots something down on the paper before asking, "Are you willing to share any of those thoughts with me?"

"Things like I'm a screw-up. I'm not good enough. That I'm better off dead." I look up. "Stuff the people in my past told me all the time."

"I'm sorry you were subject to that kind of cruelty," she responds empathetically.

You deserved everything you got. She probably thinks the same thing. Because it's true. You're a loser.

"Thank you," I whisper, feeling a lump form in my throat.

Sarah nods, her expression filled with compassion. "Understandably, those words would linger, but they don't define you."

"I want to move past them," I say quietly.

"We'll work on that together," Sarah's voice is steady and reassuring. "You're not alone in this journey."

Sarah begins by asking about my family history, a topic that's full of tangled emotions and buried memories. A knot tightens in my stomach as I reluctantly talk about my upbringing, tiptoeing around certain painful truths. With each question, I find myself grappling with conflicting emotions, torn between the desire to be honest and the fear of exposing too much.

When the conversation shifts towards my history with therapy, a wave of nausea washes over me. Sarah notices right away and changes the direction of our conversation.

"You're doing great," She encourages with a kind smile. "Before we finish up, I'd like us to develop a safety plan."

"What's it for?" I ask.

"It's a personalized tool you can rely on if your anxiety becomes overwhelming. It'll help empower you by offering support and strategies to help you maneuver rough patches and hopefully prevent another crisis."

"Okay," I answer hesitantly.

"Who do you consider your support system?"

I look at the man sitting next to me. "Tony."

She writes his name down. "Who else?"

"That's everyone."

Sarah looks up at me. "There's no one else?" I shake my head.

"What about Ramiro?" Tony asks.

"I guess so, but he's in California."

"He can still be a support," She adds.

Tony also suggests I add Star and Owen.

We discuss potential triggers, but other than closed doors, I don't know any. Sarah lets me know there are blank lines that Tony and I can fill in if something comes up. Next, we make a list of coping strategies including listening to music, meditation, and writing in my new journal. The last section contains Sarah's office number and an after-hours emergency number where I can reach her.

"Don't hesitate to call or text me during the week," she offers.

Despite my apprehensions, I sense that Sarah is genuinely invested in helping me unravel the complexities of my story and guiding me toward a path of healing.

Leopold

JANUARY 23

I've had three sessions with Sarah. She's very nice, and she lets Tony come into my sessions with me. When I told her I had a rough past, I don't think she was anticipating how rough—and we only got through my first few weeks at Walking in the Light. She did her best to school her features, but I saw the subtle way she crossed and uncrossed her legs and how, at times, she struggled to maintain eye contact. That's when I decided to be more cautious with what I tell her. I don't want to scar her for life, or worse, she asks me to not make my next appointment.

It'll be fine. I can get by without confessing my darkest secrets.

And then there's Tony. Occasionally, I think I've seen him watching me, only to look away quickly. Several times, he's brushed up against me, and I've gotten hard. Thankfully, Tony didn't notice. I don't want to embarrass myself in front of him.

That man is everything. Every dream I never dared to dream. Every wish I never dared to wish.

If only I could be deserving of him.

Anthony

OWEN: WHY DON'T YOU COME DOWN TO THE CLUB
tonight? It's been too long since we've seen you. I am.

Owen: Then get your ass down here.

Me: I'm home with Leo. I can't.

Owen: You can't stop living your life. At some point, he's
going to have to be alone.

Me: Not yet.

Owen: This is getting to be unhealthy for you.

Me: I have to go.

I turn my ringer off and slide my phone into my pocket.
Owen means well, but he doesn't understand. He has no idea
what I went through during those first few weeks. I'm the one
who was with Leopold when he'd wake terrified from nightmares.
It was me who held him and rocked him until he settled. I saw
each time he startled at a loud noise or stiffened when I reached
out and touched him.

I've seen him smile more. I fall for him a little more each time
I see his lips turn up and his eyes sparkle. But even though everything appears to be going well, I'm still terrified to leave him
alone. Leopold promised me thirty days, but we're past that, and I

feel as though we're living on borrowed time. I refuse to let my guard down. I cannot lose him.

When I opened *Italiano Desiderio* and stressed the importance of teamwork and precision with my staff, I didn't realize how much I'd come to rely on it one day. Since Leopold came to live with me, I've been putting in fewer hours at the restaurant to be with him. Knowing my restaurant is being run properly in my absence is one less thing I have to worry about.

Leopold has kept his word and attends therapy every week. I still go with him, but now I'm able to stay in the waiting room as long as Sarah leaves the door open. I'm not an expert, but I think he's making progress. He's also enrolled in GED prep classes at the community center. While I go to art class, he goes to study. He's an intelligent man, and I have no doubt he'll excel and pass the exam without issues.

"Dinner's almost ready," I say when Leo walks into the kitchen.

"What did you make tonight?"

"It's only a frozen pizza."

Leo's eyes open wide, and he takes a step back.

"What's wrong?"

"I—"

I reach out to take his hand, but he jerks it away. "Leo, talk to me."

Without warning, he turns and runs down the hall, slamming his bedroom door.

"Leo," I call and knock on the door. "What's going on?" There's no reply, so I knock again. "Please talk to me."

I don't know what happened, but this doesn't feel right. I try the handle, but it's locked. The hairs on the back of my neck stand on end. Hurrying into my room, I grab the master key.

"Leopold. Please open the door," I call one last time. He still doesn't respond. Ordinarily, I'd never unlock the door and enter his private space, but this is different. What if he's harming himself? "I'm coming in," I warn. My hands shake as I slide the key into the lock. Not knowing what I'll find, my hand trembles as I open the door.

I find Leo sitting on the floor on the far side of the room. His legs are pulled up to his chest, his arms wrapped tight around them. Silent tears are streaming down his face.

"Hey," I say quietly as I lower to my knees. "What's wrong?" I reach out, placing my hand on his knee. He flinches from my touch, pulling his legs in tighter. His eyes are open, but he looks far away. "I'm not going to hurt you." I use my thumbs to wipe away his tears. "Please talk to me."

A few long seconds pass before his eyes focus, and I know he finally sees me.

"Tony?"

"I'm right here." Reaching out, I tuck some loose hairs behind his ear. Leo leans into my hand, and I cup his face. "I won't let anything happen. You're safe." He closes his eyes as I stroke his cheek with my thumb.

"I'm sorry," he says, lifting his head.

"What happened?"

"The pizza. You never make frozen pizza," he says, his voice cracking.

"It's not something I do often, but every now and then, I give in to the desire for something not homemade." I shift from my knees to sit against the wall beside him.

"The night Krew brought me home, he made a frozen pizza," Leo confesses.

My stomach sinks as the weight of Leopold's anguish settles over me. "I had no idea," I admit, my voice laced with remorse. Opening my arms, I silently offer him the shelter of my embrace. Leo accepts without hesitation, settling onto my lap as though seeking refuge from the storm raging within.

Holding him tightly against me, I offer silent reassurance through the warmth of my touch. "I'm so sorry," I murmur quietly, my lips brushing against the soft strands of his hair in a tender kiss. It's a move that feels natural, a gesture born from a deep-seated need to provide him with comfort and reassurance.

"But you like it," he says quietly.

"I like you more." He shifts on my lap to meet my gaze. "It's something that bothers you, so I'll never buy it again."

"You like me?" he questions, his eyes searching mine for confirmation.

"Yes, Leo," I say, my voice low. "I like you very much."

He lifts his face, and our lips meet tentatively as if testing the waters of forbidden desire. The kiss is soft, almost innocent, but with each passing moment, it deepens into something more profound. As our tongues entwine, a surge of longing courses through me, setting every nerve ablaze with desire. Unable to resist the magnetic pull between us, my hand instinctively finds its way to his hair, fingers tangling in the soft strands as I deepen the kiss. Leo responds eagerly, a soft groan escaping his lips.

But as quickly as the passion ignites, a wave of reality crashes over me, dousing the flames of desire with a harsh dose of truth. With a sharp intake of breath, I pull away, my chest heaving with the weight of realization. "We can't do this," I whisper, my words heavy with regret.

Leo's expression crumbles, his eyes filled with hurt as he pulls away, putting distance between us as if to shield himself from the pain of rejection. "I get it," he mumbles.

"I don't think you do."

"You're letting me stay here, and you're being nice because you feel bad for me." His voice trembles with raw vulnerability, and I can see the pain etched in the depths of his cerulean eyes. "When you said you liked me, you didn't mean like *that*."

"I'm attracted to you," I confess, my voice faltering under the weight of his accusation. "I have been since the first day you walked into my restaurant all bundled up." A fond smile tugs at my lips as I recall the memory of that moment.

"Then, why did you stop?" His question hangs heavy in the

air, laden with uncertainty and longing, echoing the ache in my own heart.

"You just had a panic attack and locked yourself in your room," I clarify gently, hoping to convey the sincerity of my words. "As much as I wanted to keep going, it wouldn't be right." Despite my explanation, I can see the doubt lingering in his eyes, his uncertainty palpable. "If... No, when—" I correct myself, realizing the weight of my words. "When we take our relationship to the next level, I want to be sure it's for the right reasons."

"You want to be with me?" His voice trembles with a mixture of hope and disbelief, uncertainty coloring his every word.

The tension between us crackles in the air. The unspoken attraction that I've been trying so hard to conceal is now laid bare before us.

"Yes, Leo," I answer, my voice steady despite the tumult of emotions swirling within me. "I very much want to be with you."

Leopold

FEBRUARY 2

I kissed him. I had a meltdown over a frozen pizza, and then I kissed him. What was I thinking? Sure, he's gorgeous, and he's always kind to me, but why did I assume it was because he felt anything other than pity for me? I mean, why would a man like Anthony want to be with someone like me? I was devastated when he pushed me away, certain I just ruined everything. But then he said it. At first, I wasn't sure if I heard correctly. But then he said 'when' not 'if' we take our relationship to the next level, and I felt the evidence of his attraction between his legs.

What happens now? I'm not exactly an authority on healthy relationships.

I wish I could talk to Ramiro about this. But after what happened with Krew and then Phil and Maureen, he's become even more protective—almost suffocating. He's begged me to come back to California despite any threats Krew may or may not still pose. But my answer is always no.

Ramiro was already familiar with Tony's name. I told him I met him when I was doing deliveries and that we'd sometimes talk and have lunch. I left out that it was every time and that some of those times were at Fire and Ice. I also left out that I'm attracted to

Tony. Ramiro was already distrusting of everyone. I didn't want Tony to become an argument between us.

Tony's unlike any man I've ever met. He's genuine and kind. Over the past month, he's proven that he has no ulterior motives for opening his home to me. When I told him I never graduated high school, he helped me enroll in GED prep courses. In a few weeks, I'll be taking my test. He's also given me employment. Unlike Krew's 'job' offer, this one is legitimate. I get paid more than a fair wage with health insurance benefits that have made it possible to see Sarah regularly.

Therapy. I have a love-hate relationship with it. Sarah, my therapist, is very nice. She allowed me to bring Tony into my sessions until I felt comfortable being in the room alone with her. Then, we took baby steps until I could be in her office with the door shut and Tony in the waiting room.

Talking about my memories and feelings isn't comfortable, though. As nice as Sarah is, I don't trust her enough to open up fully. To tell her the darkest, most depraved things that I lived through. No one knows the worst of what happened, and no one ever will.

Leopold

"LEOPOLD," TONY CALLS FROM THE HALLWAY AS HE walks into the house from work.

Tony's gradually grown more comfortable with the idea of leaving me alone. I'm glad to have earned his trust, but I can't deny how much I miss him when he's not with me.

"What is it?" I ask as I hurry from my room. "Is everything okay?"

He holds up a large white envelope, waving it slowly. "Your scores came."

My GED exam was several weeks ago. I knew the results would come in the mail, and until now, I couldn't wait for them. Now that they're here, I'm hesitant to open them. "What if I failed?" I wrap my hands around my waist, trying to calm the queasiness in my stomach. "I don't think I can open it."

"You've been waiting for them for weeks," Tony encourages, holding the envelope to me.

"I can't." I shake my head. "Will you open it?"

"Are you sure?" he asks, and I nod.

Carefully, Tony slides his finger under the seam, opening the envelope. He pulls out a sheet of white paper, studying it intently.

Slowly, a subtle shift in his demeanor hints at his disappointment as he reads.

"It's bad, isn't it?" I mumble, a knot of dread forming in my stomach. "I failed. I knew it."

Tony's laughter fills the room. "You didn't fail, not even close."

"I didn't?" I ask in disbelief.

"You scored 175 on Reading through Language Arts. 150 on Mathematical Reasoning. That was your lowest score, by the way," Tony adds. "190 on Social Studies and 165 on Science for a cumulative score of 675." He reaches into the envelope and pulls out another paper. "Congratulations, Leopold. You've earned your New York State High School Equivalency Diploma."

My hands tremble as I take the diploma and read aloud, "Be it known that Leopold Wagner, having satisfactorily completed the requirements prescribed by the Commonwealth of Education, is thereby entitled to this High School Equivalency Diploma." I turn to Tony, whose eyes gleam with pride. "Is this even real?"

"Yes, it is," he murmurs, his voice low and velvety, sending shivers down my spine.

"I did it. I finally have my diploma," I say proudly. The sheer satisfaction I experience while clutching this piece of paper is beyond words.

"I'm incredibly proud of you, Leopold," Tony says warmly, opening his arms. I step into his embrace. "Let's go out and celebrate tonight."

"I'd like that," I whisper, resting my head against his chest as he holds me tight. Since that first kiss, we've become more accustomed to these tender gestures. "I wouldn't have been able to do any of this without you." I lift my head to meet his gaze.

"That's not true." He gently runs his knuckles down my face. "You did this all on your own." He leans down, pressing his lips to mine.

Tony's touch is both tender and insistent as he trails his tongue along my lower lip. Yielding to his advances, I grant him access, and our mouths merge in a heated exchange. With one hand firmly grasping the back of my neck, he guides me closer while the other traces down my spine to my ass, melding our bodies together. I feel the heat of his desire pressing against me, matching my own arousal, and I can't help but moan into his mouth.

His cell rings, but Tony makes no move to answer it. Instead, his mouth descends to my neck, where he expertly nips and sucks, igniting a trail of tingling sensations.

His phone buzzes incessantly. "Shit," he says, pulling away and leaving me breathless. "Hello?" he answers, his voice gruff. "There's no one else?" he asks, pausing to listen to whoever's on the other end. "Leo and I are planning to go celebrate tonight." Another pause. "He got his diploma today," Tony says, smiling.

He switches the phone to speaker mode and extends it towards me. "Congratulations," Owen's voice booms with excitement from the other end.

"Thank you. I can hardly believe it." I look at the paper I'm still holding and reread it to make sure the words don't magically change.

"You put in the hard work. You deserve every bit of it," Owen praises me before directing his attention back to Tony. "I hate to impose, especially on such an important evening, but I'm really in a bind."

"Just a moment," Tony says, muting the phone. "Star was supposed to manage the club tonight, but she's down with a terrible migraine. Owen asked me to step in since he's out of town, but I explained we have plans."

"It's okay. He needs your help," I answer.

"I'm more concerned with letting you down."

I hesitate, chewing my lower lip briefly before suggesting, "I could go with you."

"To Fire and Ice?" Tony asks, surprised.

I've been intrigued by the club since I was doing deliveries there. But other than casual comments, they never shared much about it with me. Despite living with Tony for over six months, he's not gone to Fire and Ice at all. I've done some reading and am eager to see for myself what this lifestyle he's a part of entails.

"Yes," I answer and nod slowly.

"Are you sure?"

"I'd like to learn more about what you like."

Tony's eyes linger on me with a mixture of admiration and affection before speaking softly, "You never cease to amaze me, Leopold." He unmutes the phone. "We'll be there."

Anthony

LEO CATCHES ME OFF GUARD AS HE EXPRESSES AN interest in going to Fire and Ice and learning more about BDSM. For a moment, I'm at a loss for words. I can only take in the sight of this man I just fell more in love with. "You never cease to amaze me, Leopold." I finally say before taking the phone off mute. "We'll be there."

I haven't been this nervous to go to the club since my first days in the lifestyle.

Being raised in Manhattan meant that from a young age, I was surrounded by diverse cultures and communities. My parents, who I believe recognized my homosexuality before I did, celebrated my individuality and encouraged me to explore my interests and pursue my dreams—which included my passion for cooking.

During my time in culinary school, I became interested in one of my classmates, Oliver. He shared my passion for experimenting both in the kitchen and in life. Our chemistry was explosive. We'd barely made it out of school and into his apartment before we were ripping each other's clothes off and fucking all night long.

One night, he invited me to go to a new club he heard about through another friend. Intrigued by the promise of adventure, I accepted the invitation, unaware of the journey it would set me on.

Nestled discreetly in the heart of New York City's eclectic underground, The Velvet Sanctuary catered to those seeking an escape from the ordinary. A haven of indulgence and exploration, this exclusive BDSM club offered a refuge where fantasies came to life in a realm of opulent decadence.

Stepping through the unassuming entrance, I found myself transported into a world of sensuality and intrigue. The ambiance is rich with the scent of exotic incense and the soft murmur of whispered desires. Plush velvet drapes adorned the walls, giving the space an intimate, inviting glow.

In the main lounge area, guests gathered in clusters, their laughter and conversation mingling with the sultry strains of ambient music and the sensual moans of couples having sex. Plush couches and low tables offered comfortable seating, while discreet alcoves provided privacy for more intimate encounters.

Venturing further into The Velvet Sanctuary, I discovered a labyrinth of luxurious bondage chambers, dimly lit dungeons where leather-clad Dominants reigned supreme, and decadent sensory deprivation rooms. The club boasted diverse play spaces where guests were free to unleash their imagination and indulge their darkest desires. For me, it felt like I was home.

Oliver liked to take charge in the bedroom, and, at the time, I was open to trying almost anything, so I assumed the role of submissive. I surrendered to the exquisite agony of pleasure and pain. With each binding restraint and whispered command, I felt myself slipping deeper into the throes of ecstasy, my senses ablaze with the heady rush of adrenaline and desire.

However, as our relationship progressed, my dominant nature began to assert itself. Despite my initial attraction to submission, I found myself yearning for control and authority. At first, the transition was subtle. Small gestures and hints of dominance crept into our interactions, igniting a spark of excitement and anticipation between us. But as our connection deepened, so did my hunger for power and control. The more I thought about it, the more I realized that submission alone could never satisfy the depths of my cravings.

Oliver confessed his intrigue with the idea of witnessing my Dominance in action. It wasn't a request born out of jealousy or insecurity but rather a genuine curiosity and desire to explore the boundaries of our connection. With his encouragement, I embraced my Dominant nature. Knowing that Oliver was watching heightened the intensity of the experience.

But we were young and didn't have a clue how to manage a dynamic. We never vetted one another or adhered to any list of limits. Communication wasn't high on our list of strengths.

For Oliver, the thrill of watching soon gave way to a sense of unease and discomfort. What had once been an exciting exploration of our desires now felt like a constant reminder of his insecurities and vulnerabilities. As he struggled to reconcile his conflicting emotions, resentment and jealousy began to fester. What had once brought us together now served as a catalyst for our downfall. In the end, our shared exploration into my Dominant side proved to be our undoing.

My journey into submission left an indelible mark on my understanding of the BDSM lifestyle. Through the exploration of my desires, I discovered my true calling as a Dominant. I sought out a new club with a strict code of conduct that prioritized consent, communication, and respect.

That's how I found Fire and Ice. The club has become more than a simple venue to push the boundaries of pleasure and liberation. It's a community—a family where individuals from all walks of life come together to explore their sexuality, forge deep connections, and celebrate the beauty of human desire.

Could Leopold be exactly who I've been waiting for? With everything in me, I hope Leopold feels like this place could be his home, too. A place where we could explore our desires together.

"Are you sure you're okay that I came with you?" he asks nervously.

"Of course," I say, looking up from the computer screen. "I'm sorry if you think I'm ignoring you. I'm not. I don't want to screw anything up."

"Is there anything I can do to help?"

"Just be your charming self." I smile. "And maybe unlock the doors."

"I can do that." Leo steps out from behind the desk.

As he strides across the carpet, I can't help but notice the changes in Leo's physique. Thanks to regular visits to the gym in my apartment building, he's become more than just handsome—he's mouthwateringly gorgeous. The image of him, all rippling muscles and raw masculinity fills my mind, igniting a fire of primal longing. I've stroked myself to orgasm more times than I care to admit, thinking about him.

The taste of Leopold's lips lingers on mine, a potent reminder of the desire that simmers between us. Owen's call prevented us from crossing a line that I'm not sure we're ready to navigate. I want nothing more than to be with Leopold, to explore the depths of our connection, but I can't ignore that it's only been six months since his suicide attempt. He's just beginning to put his life back together—to learn who he is and what he wants. Starting a relationship now feels like tempting fate. I don't want to complicate his recovery by beginning a relationship that may or may not fit the person Leopold grows to be.

"Are you okay?" Leo asks, getting my attention.

"What do you mean?"

"You look a million miles away," he says as he perches on the stool beside me.

"I've just got a lot on my mind," I reply, turning toward him. "We need to talk about what almost happened at home."

"You regret it—"

"Tony, it's so good to see you," Lacey, one of the club's regulars, says as she walks in, and once again, we're interrupted.

"I haven't seen you in forever. How are you?"

"I'm doing well," she smiles and glances between Leo and me.

"Leopold, I'd like to introduce you to Lacey. She's one of our regular Domme's."

"It's very nice to meet you," Leo says politely.

"You as well." She looks at me. "It's nice to finally see you with a new sub."

"Leopold's not my sub," I clarify, hoping to nip any misunderstandings in the bud. "He's just curious about Fire and Ice."

"I see."

"How's the baby?" I ask while I finish checking her in.

"He's perfect." Lacey beams.

"Lacey and her husband just had their first child," I explain. "Where are Caleb and Shawn?"

"Shawn had to work late, and Caleb is waiting for the sitter to get to our house."

Leo's forehead is scrunched as he tries to figure out the dynamic. "Caleb and Shawn are Lacey's submissives." He nods in understanding.

"How did you end up at the desk?" she asks.

"Star's home sick, and Owen's out of town," I reply. "I'm filling in for them."

"How is Leopold going to experience the club from out here?" She taps her long red nails on the counter.

"I haven't worked out the details yet."

"If Leopold consents. I'll gladly escort him this evening so he gets a proper introduction," Lacey suggests.

"What do you think?"

Leo's gaze meets mine, his big blue eyes wide with concern. "Is that okay with you?" he asks, his voice carrying a hint of uncertainty.

"Excuse me for one second," Lacey says, holding up her phone. "It's Caleb."

After Lacey steps away, Leo says, "If you'd rather I stay with you, I will."

"You came to see what the club's like, and that can't happen if you're out here all night." Leo looks between Lacey and me, and I answer his unspoken question. "I've known her for many years. She's trustworthy," I say, trying to ease his nervousness. "If you'd like to join her inside, you're more than welcome."

"What about the conversation we need to have?" Leo's voice is tinged with apprehension.

"We'll continue it at home." I lower my voice. I assure him, my voice softening. "But know this, Leo—I have no regrets about what happened."

"Are you sure?" Leo's doubt is evident.

It pains me that Leo continues to question his worth. "I'm positive."

"Am I going to have a third man on my arm tonight?" Lacey asks.

"Yes, ma'am," Leo says politely.

"Such good manners." Lacey leans closer to me and whispers, "If you don't scoop him up, I just might." She winks at Leo, and he laughs softly.

Turning my attention back to Leopold, I begin to explain the rules. "We have a color-coded system to identify everyone in the club," I explain and point out the sign on the wall.

Listed are the colors of the rainbow and what each color signifies.

White- Vanilla, very new, wishes to take it slow.

White with polka dots- Looking to play with multiple partners.

Silver with Bells- Into pet play/ role-play bottom.

Grey- Bondage, top, rope play, latex fetish.
Blue- Mentor, safe person, willing to instruct.
Dark Purple- Likes spanking.
Light Purple- Likes Wax play.
Red- Do not approach directly. If interested, go directly to sponsoring Dominant only.
Red with stripe- Do not approach. Just watching and learning.
Pink- Females only.
Orange- Monogamous, Not likely to play.
Brown- Interested in role-play.
Yellow- Watersports. Likes urine-play.
Green- Wants to play. Open-minded.

"You'll get this one tonight." I secure a red with white stripe bracelet to his left wrist. "Other than Lacey and her subs, no one will approach you."

"Okay," Leo says, his grip tightening on my hand. His body is tense with apprehension.

Sensing his discomfort, I lower my voice. "If you're uncomfortable, you don't have to do this. We can come back another night."

"You said you trust her, right?" Leo's voice trembles slightly.

"I do," I respond, offering him a reassuring smile.

"And I can come back out any time I want?"

"Of course."

Leo takes a deep breath, visibly collecting himself. "Then, I'll be okay," he says, his voice steadier as he steps around the counter.

"Are you ready?" Lacey asks.

"I am," he states, his smile warm and reassuring as he shoots me a quick glance.

"Don't worry. I'll return you to Tony in one piece."

As Leopold steps into Fire and Ice, immersing himself in the world of BDSM, I can't help but feel a pang of jealousy that I'm not experiencing it with him.

My thoughts keep returning to Leopold, wondering what he's

thinking and feeling. I can't shake the feeling that I should be in there with him—that we should be exploring this together, but the busy night keeps me tied to the desk.

Leopold

"WHERE WOULD YOU LIKE TO EXPLORE FIRST, LEO?"
Lacey asks.

I look around the large space, already feeling overwhelmed and uncertain about where to go or what to ask about. Part of me wants to run back out to the safety of Tony. The other part knows that if I'm going to be a part of Tony's life, I need to stay and see what this BDSM stuff is all about.

Lacey's touch startles me, causing me to jump slightly. "I'm sorry," she says quickly, retracting her hand. "It can be a lot your first time here."

"Yeah, it is," I reply.

"Let's start at the beginning," she suggests. "What do you know about the lifestyle?"

"I know there's kink and stuff."

She watches me expectantly, waiting for a response. When I don't say anything more, she nods understandingly. "How about we go grab a table and sit and chat?" The petite woman moves gracefully across the concrete floor, exuding confidence with each step. I trail behind her, feeling a twinge of inadequacy in her presence. Lacey chooses a table in the café and gestures for me to sit opposite her. "Would you like something to eat?"

"No, thank you." I'm too nervous to eat.

With a soft clink, the server places two glasses of ice water in front of us, and I waste no time taking a refreshing sip, grateful for the relief it brings to my dry throat. Around us, the room slowly starts to come alive as people of all kinds filter in. Couples, both same-sex and opposite-sex, move through the crowd with ease.

There are those adorned in elaborate fetish gear, their outfits a testament to their commitment to the lifestyle. Others opt for a more casual look, blending seamlessly into the diverse crowd. It's a melting pot of desires and orientations. A place where everyone is free to express themselves authentically without fear of judgment.

"How did you and Tony meet?" Lacey asks.

"At work." I fidget my fingers on the table in front of me.

"You seem really nervous." She glances at my hands, and I still them. "There's no reason to be. I don't bite. Well, I do," Lacey chuckles. "But I won't bite you."

"I'm sorry. This is all very new to me," I confess.

"We were all new at one point." She smiles warmly. "What has Tony told you so far?"

"Nothing."

"Wait a minute," she says, surprised. "You two are together, but you haven't discussed the lifestyle at all?"

"Oh, we're not together," I say quickly. "We're just—"

Lacey holds up her hand, stopping me. "It's okay. You don't have to explain it. There's no judgment for whatever is or isn't going on. Let's go back to the very beginning," she says, then takes a sip of her water. "BDSM stands for bondage and discipline, dominance and submission, sadism and masochism."

"That's quite a mouthful."

"It is," she acknowledges, her tone gentle yet confident. "There are many different roles one may fit into. A Dominant, submissive, or switch are probably the three most common."

"What's Tony?" I ask quietly.

"Tony's a Dominant," Lacey says matter-of-factly. "He's also a master of body art with wax." Two men walk over to our table, Lacey smiles at them. "Leo, I'd like you to meet Shawn." She motions to the taller of two men. "And Caleb. This is Leo, he's a friend of Anthony." After we exchange greetings, they join us at the table. "Leo's not currently in the lifestyle," she explains. "But he's curious. We were going over some basics."

I remain quiet as I observe their interactions. The care they show for one another is evident, but what strikes me most is the respect Lacey affords each of the men. Despite her Dominant role, they still have a voice in their dynamic. It's not what I imagined a BDSM relationship to be or what I experienced in my toxic relationship with Krew. "I'm confused," I admit. "I thought they didn't get a say in anything."

"What do you mean?" Lacey asks.

"You're their Dominant, right?"

"I am," she confirms with a nod.

"But you ask their opinions, and you listen to them?"

"This lifestyle is built on three tenants. Safe, sane, and consensual. Nothing happens between us that we all haven't consented to," she explains. "Consent is the most important part of this lifestyle."

Consent has been something missing in my life. With my father, it was a silent decree— an unspoken rule. His wishes superseded my own. David abused his role by using manipulative tactics that coerced compliance and broke every sacred boundary between therapist and patient. Consent became a weapon Krew wielded against me in moments of vulnerability.

Their disregard for my boundaries left me feeling powerless and voiceless. As a result, I was robbed of healthy interactions and loving relationships. I withered away into near nothingness, a shell of the person I once was.

I was broken and alone.

"The bondage demonstration is beginning," Lacey announces, pulling me from my thoughts. "Let's go get some good seats."

Anthony

"You've been quiet since we left the club. Is everything okay?" I ask.

"Yeah. It was a long night, and I'm tired," Leo answers but doesn't look up. "I'm going to head to bed."

"Leo." I reach out and touch his arm, but he flinches away. "I was hoping we could talk about us."

"Us?" he asks, taken aback.

"I don't think it's just me that feels things shifting. At least, I hope it isn't just me."

Leo forces a smile on his face, but I know him too well and see through his façade. "Do you think we can talk about this tomorrow?"

"Are you okay?" I ask concerned.

"I'm just tired."

Something feels off, and I don't like it. "Leo," I call, and he stops. "The lifestyle, if it's not something you're interested in, that's okay. I'll walk away from it right now to be with you."

"Good night, Tony."

Leo disappears into his room closing his door with a soft thud, shutting me out. I ache to follow him, but I don't want to push. Too wired for sleep, I turn to my sketch pad and pencils, losing myself in the soothing rhythm of drawing until my eyes are heavy and my body's ready to settle in for the night. The tranquility of the night is abruptly shattered by a loud crash echoing from Leo's room.

Abandoning my art supplies, I rush down the hall and knock on his door. "Are you okay?" My question is met with silence. "Leopold, answer me," I demand, my worry mounting as I hear his muffled voice from inside. I try the handle, but it's locked. "Unlock the door," I plead, my fist hammering against the unforgiving wood.

A sense of déjà vu washes over me as I recall the frozen pizza incident from months ago. He's come so far since then. I never anticipated a setback like this.

Grabbing the key from my dresser drawer, I unlock his door and push it open.

"Get away from me," Leo yells, holding his bedside lamp in front of him like a weapon. His eyes are wide, and his pupils are dilated, but it's as if he's looking through me rather than at me.

"Leopold," I say softly, my hands held up in front of me. "What's going on?"

He waves the lamp around wildly. "Stay back," he yells and lunges forward.

I take a step back. "I'm not going to hurt you." I lower my voice. "But I need you to tell me what's happening."

"You know exactly what's happening," he snarls, his breaths coming fast and heavy. "This is all because of you." My heart sinks. Going to Fire and Ice was too much, and now he thinks I'm going to hurt him. "I liked you and wanted to be with you. You. Not all these other people." He looks around the room, and it's as if he's seeing people who aren't here.

"It's only me and you, Leopold," I say, taking a cautious step forward.

"Don't come near me." Leo lunges again, swinging the lamp like a bat. "They'll be here soon. They always come."

"Who's going to be here?" I ask, trying to understand. Trying to find any opening to bring Leopold back to the present.

"I don't know who they are. They're *your* friends." He gasps for air. "I don't like them."

"You know *our* friends. They—"

"No, I don't," he yells. "You bring them all in here, and you let them hurt me." He stabs his finger in my direction. "I've begged you to stop, but you don't. You don't help me." Leo's voice cracks. "You laugh and make them do more. Then, you hurt me, too," he says as tears pour down his face. "I didn't *consent* to any of this, Krew."

My breath catches. "Leopold, It's me. Tony." I manage to choke out, my heart racing.

"Get out," he screams and lunges at me again. "Or I'll hurt you."

"I'm leaving," I say and slowly back up.

I'm barely through the door when he slams it, the sound echoing in the hallway as the lock clicks into place. On the other side, Leo's voice rises in a frenzy, lost in his own world. My hands tremble violently as I dial the emergency number Sarah gave us at his first appointment.

"Hello?" The voice on the line is groggy as if roused from sleep.

"It's Tony Genovese," I say, managing to compose myself somewhat. "I'm sorry to call in the middle of the night, but I didn't know what else to do."

"Tell me what's happening?"

Describing the unsettling encounter, I struggle to articulate the details. "He thinks I'm Krew," I admit, a mixture of confusion and concern coloring my tone.

"It sounds like he's having a flashback," she says in a clinical tone.

"It's happened before, but not like this." I run my hands through my hair nervously. "He's yelling and breaking things. Leopold doesn't know who I am."

"You're going to have to call 911 and have him brought to the emergency room for a psychiatric evaluation," she states matter-of-factly.

"There's no other option?" I ask, desperation evident in my voice.

"I'm afraid not," she replies with a somber tone.

I pace back and forth, each step heavy with nervous energy as I struggle to decide what to do. Behind the door, Leo's voice wavers with fear, his pleas growing increasingly desperate. I don't know how much more of this I can take.

"Tony," Sarah says softly, her voice gentle and understanding. "I know this is hard, but you have to think about what's best for Leo right now."

"What the hell else do you think I'm doing?" I snap, my frustration bubbling over. "All I'm thinking of, all I ever do, is what's best for Leopold."

"I'm not the enemy here," Sarah replies calmly.

"I'm sorry," I apologize. "I didn't mean to yell at you."

"It's okay. I understand."

"I'll call for an ambulance," I concede, my resolve crumbling.

"You're doing the right thing, Tony," she reassures me.

"I hope you're right," I admit, uncertainty clouding my words.

As soon as we hang up, I dial 911. The dispatcher takes all the information and assures me an ambulance is coming.

My hand slides into my pocket, and my fingers run over the smooth metal of the boxcutter in its protective sheath. My irrational fear tells me I can't leave it in the house because Leopold could find it. What if seeing it triggers those thoughts and feelings to return? What if he uses it to hurt himself? And I don't think throwing it away is the right thing to do with it. So, I carry it with me. Letting go of the boxcutter, I take the key out.

"Leopold," I say with a hint of urgency as I unlock the door. He continues muttering to himself as I cautiously enter the room. He whirls around to face me, the lamp now broken at his feet.

"How about you let me get you out of here? Let me take you away from Krew," I offer, taking a chance by using his delusion to help me.

"Where are you going to take me?" he asks, desperation evident in his voice.

I falter, unsure of how to respond. Fear grips me, knowing that the wrong words could trigger another outburst. "Where would you like to go?" I ask tentatively.

He stops to consider my question. "Will you bring me to Donnie and Lindsay? They'll keep me safe," he says, his voice small and scared.

"We can go there, yes. There are some people in uniform," I say cautiously, opting not to use the word *friend* so I don't trigger him. "They'll help us get to them safely, okay?"

"How are they going to do that?" he asks, suspicion evident in his voice.

"They have an ambulance. We'll go in that, so we trick him," I explain, trying to keep my voice steady while my heart silently breaks. "Does that sound okay to you?"

"Why should I trust you?"

"Because I love you, Leopold," I respond earnestly, hoping wherever he is that he recognizes the truth in my words. "I promised you I'd keep you safe."

"Do you know Ramiro?" he asks, his eyes narrowing.

"I do."

"You are a good guy, then," he concedes, a glimmer of trust returning.

"Yes, Leo. I am," I say, extending my hand to him. "Will you come with me and let me help you?"

He hesitates for a moment before tentatively threading his fingers through mine. "I think I like you," he murmurs softly.

"I'm glad to hear that," I respond with a warm smile, brushing a strand of hair away from his face. The doorbell rings, and I glance toward it. "That's them."

"I'm scared," Leo admits, his voice barely above a whisper. "Krew's going to try to find me."

"Keep holding onto me. I won't leave you. I promise," I assure him as we answer the door together, his hand clutching mine tightly.

"We got a call for an emergency," the female EMT says.

"Yes, please come in." Leo and I step aside, letting the pair in.

"Is this Mr. Wagner?" she asks.

"It is," I reply. "I explained that we're going to use your ambulance to keep us hidden so we can get Leopold to safety," I say, hoping the EMTs go alone with my narrative.

"Mr. Wagner, can you tell us what's going on?" the male EMT asks, disregarding me.

"I don't know you," Leo says, stepping behind me. "I'm not telling you anything."

"We're medical technicians—"

"I know them, Leopold," I interrupt, narrowing my eyes at the man. "They're going to keep us safe while we go to Donnie and Lindsay." I turn my attention to the pair. "Isn't that right?"

"Yes, that's right," the female replies, finally catching on. "My name's Kate, and this is Vince. What's yours?"

"Leo."

"It's nice to meet you, Leo." She smiles brightly. "How about you come with me and my partner?"

"My friend needs to come too."

Kate's gaze shifts to me, her expression questioning.

"I promised I'd stay with him," I explain quietly, hoping she'll understand.

"Okay," she relents after a moment, her tone softening. "We can do that."

The EMTs follow us into the elevator, where Leo tucks himself into the corner shielded by my body. Everyone's silent as we ride to the lobby and walk out the front door to the waiting ambulance.

Kate opens the back of the vehicle, and we help Leo inside.

"Okay, Leo, how about you sit down right here," Kate suggests, pointing to the gurney. Leo hesitantly perches on the edge. "Can you slide back so we can buckle you in?"

Leo's eyes fly open. "You tricked me," he accuses, his voice trembling with betrayal.

"It's okay, Leopold," I reassure him, reaching out to touch his shoulder.

"No, it isn't," he retorts, pulling away from my touch. "Get away from me."

"You need to relax," Vince intervenes, attempting to guide Leo back with a gentle touch on his shoulder.

"Don't touch me." Leo pushes him away.

"Can't he just sit there?" I ask, hoping for some sort of a compromise.

"It's against policy. He needs to be buckled in," Kate explains. "Leo, can you please sit back so we can secure you safely?"

"No. I won't let you hurt me again," Leo shouts, his voice filled with anguish and fear.

"You're going to need to relax, Mr. Wagner, or we'll be forced to medicate you to make you calm down," Vince says sternly.

"You lied," Leo shouts, his voice cracking with emotion. "I need to get out of here." He shoves Kate aside. His movements are frantic as he tries to escape.

"Leopold, please," I implore, reaching out for his arm. He whirls around with alarming speed, his fist connecting with my face in a swift, unexpected blow. I reel backward, colliding with the hard metal bench.

"That's enough, Mr. Wagner," Vince states firmly, moving to restrain Leo. Despite his resistance, Vince manages to overpower him, securing him onto the gurney with tight buckles around his arms, legs, and chest.

My heart shatters as I witness the distressing scene playing out before me. Leo's face contorts with agony as he struggles against the restraints, lost in his delusion.

"Please help me," Leo begs desperately, tears streaming down his face. "You promised you'd keep me safe."

"You are safe, Leopold," I assure him, my voice trembling with sorrow and regret.

Movement catches my attention from the corner of my eye, and Leo's gaze follows suit. Kate finishes filling a syringe.

"I don't want that. Don't drug me." Leo's guttural cries fill the space as he fights against the restraints.

"Please, Leopold, listen to me," I beg. "You're only making it harder." I turn to Kate. My expression is desperate. "Please don't do this. He'll calm down. Won't you, Leopold?"

"No." He thrashes back and forth. "I won't let them do this."

Kate nods to Vince, who holds Leopold tight as she approaches with the syringe. "I'm sorry, Leo," she says a second before she pierces his arm with a needle. "This will help you relax."

"What is that? What did you give him?" I ask, panicked.

"It's a sedative. It'll help him relax," Kate explains, her tone compassionate.

"Why did you do that?" My voice wavers as tears blur my vision.

"He's too combative to transport safely," she responds matter-of-factly, handing me an ice pack. "Put this on. Your eye's already starting to bruise."

I accept the ice pack and set it next to me. "I don't care about me."

"Please don't hurt me," Leo sobs, his voice quivering. "I promise I'll be good," he repeats softly, his words a desperate plea.

"Everything's going to be okay," I whisper, tenderly caressing his tear-stained face. "I'm right here. I'm not leaving you."

"Don't let them hurt me," he murmurs as his eyes close.

Vince and Kate work in tandem, their movements focused and determined as they start an IV. Once it's in place, Vince takes his place behind the wheel, his demeanor calm yet urgent as he steers us through the maze of city streets toward the hospital.

Each moment feels like an eternity, my mind swirling with doubts and fears about the consequences of my actions. Silently, I question whether I've made the right decision, agonizing over the possibility that bringing Leopold to the hospital might exacerbate his distress. That instead of bringing us closer, I've driven him further away.

Anthony

Vince and Kate unload a drugged and sleeping Leo. I follow them through the ambulance bay doors into the New York Presbyterian Hospital Irving Medical Center, where we're placed in a small sterile room.

"Good luck with everything," Kate says before she and Vince leave us with a nurse.

"My name's Patty," the woman says. "We got most of Mr. Wagner's information from the EMTs. Can you tell me a little bit more about what happened tonight?"

My voice is shaky as I recount the events of the evening. The terror Leo relived and how he didn't recognize me. "His therapist suggested bringing him here to get him stabilized. Everything was going okay until they tried to strap him in," I explain.

"Is that when he became violent?" she asks, motioning to my swollen eye.

"He didn't mean to do this," I whisper, my voice strained with emotion as I glance at the man lying on the bed beside me, his face peaceful in slumber. Tears prick at the corners of my eyes, but I force myself to hold them back. "Leopold wouldn't intentionally hurt anyone."

"I'm sure that's true," she replies softly, her eyes reflecting understanding and compassion. "But sometimes, during a mental health crisis, people can behave in ways that are out of character."

The weight of her words hangs heavy in the air, a stark reminder of the unpredictable nature of mental illness. I feel a knot tighten in my chest as I grapple with the realization that, despite his gentle nature, Leopold's struggles have led us to this harrowing moment.

"He's not a violent person," I insist, the words a fervent plea for understanding. "He's just... lost right now, and I don't know how to help him."

Her expression softens with empathy as she meets my gaze, offering silent reassurance.

"What happens from here?" I ask.

"One of our crisis specialists will be in shortly to talk to you and eventually to Mr. Wagner when he wakes up," she explains, her voice professional and composed. "Then, they'll consult with one of our staff psychiatrists to determine the best course of treatment." Her words come out rehearsed and lacking any emotion. "Most likely, they're going to recommend a stay in our in-patient facility to get him stabilized and on medication."

"No. He doesn't need to be admitted," I insist.

"Let's leave that up to the professionals," she says, a tight smile on her face. "For now, just relax. I'll put in an order so someone can look at your eye, too."

When the nurse leaves the room, I dim the lights so Leo can rest peacefully. My hope is when he wakes, he'll be cognizant of his surroundings. Then, we can go home and try to forget this awful night ever happened.

Although it's the middle of the night, I pull out my phone to text Ramiro. He'll want to know what's going on.

Me: I'm at the emergency room with Leopold. He had a flashback and was completely disoriented. His therapist suggested I bring him in for an evaluation. I don't know anything yet, but I knew you'd want to be made aware.

Not expecting an immediate response from him, I carefully stow my phone away and press the ice pack against my swollen eye. The swelling feels like it's closing it shut, and the relentless pounding in my head isn't doing me any favors.

My phone suddenly starts ringing, shattering the silence of the hospital room. I quickly retrieve it from my pocket, swiping to answer before the noise disturbs Leo's rest.

"Hello?" I answer in a hushed tone, jumping to my feet. Dizziness washes over me, and I stagger, reaching out to grab onto Leo's bed for balance.

"What's happened?" Ramiro asks.

I check to be sure Leo's still asleep before walking out to the hallway and closing the door behind me. "I'm not positive on what triggered it," I hesitate. "Well, I have an idea."

"Go on."

"Leopold and I have been growing closer, romantically," I disclose, adding context to my statement. "We went to a club tonight."

"What kind of club?" Ramiro inquires, his curiosity piqued.

"A BDSM club."

"What the hell were you thinking?" Ramiro's voice explodes with anger. "I knew letting Leo stay with you was a mistake. I shouldn't have accepted no for an answer."

"You're not Leopold's father. He doesn't require your approval for his living arrangements," I state, my anger simmering beneath the surface.

"Leo's been drugged and raped. And you bring him to a seedy BDSM club? What kind of monster are you?" Ramiro's accusation slices through the air.

I clench my teeth, fighting the urge to lash out. "I'm not a monster. I don't know what you think the club is, but whatever you're assuming is wrong." I pause, taking a deep breath to regain composure. "We can pick up this conversation another time. The only thing I care about right now is ensuring Leopold's okay."

"Excuse me. Are you Mr. Genovese?" a woman in a white doctor's coat asks.

"Hold on." I drop the phone from my ear. "I am."

"I'm Dr. Thompson," she introduces herself. "I'd like to take a look at your eye."

"Sure. One second." Bringing the phone back to my ear, I say, "I'm going to have to call you back. The doctor's here to examine me."

"You? What for?"

He's going to lose his shit again. "Leo and I had an altercation on the way to the hospital."

"An altercation?"

"He hit me," I explain, my voice strained. "The doctor's waiting for me. I'll explain it to you later."

"Don't you hang—"

I disconnect without letting him finish.

"I apologize for making you wait."

"It's not a problem," she says kindly. "If you'll follow me, we'll go to an exam room."

"What about Leopold?"

"He'll be sleeping for a while still," she explains. "The staff will keep an eye on him while you're gone."

"Can I look in on him first?"

"Of course," she smiles kindly.

I crack the door and look into the darkened room. Leo's silhouette is visible, curled up on his side, sound asleep. Another wave of dizziness washes over me, and I instinctively reach out, grasping the doorframe for support.

"Are you dizzy?" Dr. Thompson asks, concern lacing her words.

"I'm fine," I say and close the door softly. "Is this going to take long? I don't want Leopold to wake up and find me not there."

"I understand. I'll be as brief as possible," Dr. Thompson reassures as she leads me through a maze of hallways before we come to an empty exam room. She opens the door, and the lights automatically turn on, illuminating the space. "Have a seat on the bed," she instructs.

Reluctantly, I rest my weight on the edge of the bed, understanding that the less I resist, the sooner we'll finish, and I can return to Leopold.

Leopold

STRANGE SOUNDS AND UNFAMILIAR SCENTS SWIRL around me. My eyelids are heavy and remain stubbornly closed. Snippets of conversation filter through each one, tugging at the fringes of my awareness.

"His partner described a dissociative event at their apartment earlier this evening," a male voice says.

"I heard they were at some kind of sex club," a female voice says.

"Crazy, right?" another voice, deeper and gruffer, responds. "I can't believe someone would drag their mentally unstable partner into shit like that."

"What kind of freaks are they?" the female voice asks.

"Some people are into all kinds of kinky stuff," the male voice says.

"Should we be gossiping about this?" a quieter voice questions.

"We're not gossiping. We're just discussing," the first voice retorts defensively. "It's not like he can hear us."

"I know, right." They share a laugh. "Dr. Morgan already read the chart. He's recommending an inpatient stay. We have to wait for his partner to get back and sign the papers for an involuntary admission."

My heart pounds. Tony promised he'd never send me to an inpatient facility. He lied.

What did you expect? Lies. Everything is lies. He was waiting for his turn to control you.

"He's going to be a little while. Dr. Thompson ordered a CT," the female says, "I guess he got hit pretty hard on his way here."

"Come on," a deep voice says. "I have to message Dr. Morgan and let him know this guy's still out cold."

I wait until I hear the door click closed before forcing my eyes to open. Tony's hurt? He got hit. I try to force myself to remember what happened.

When we got home from the club, I felt off. Snippets of the evening replay in my mind. The cross. The ropes. The blindfold. The whips. While the submissive's skin turned red with welts and he cried in pain, memories of the atrocities I endured at Krew's hands paralyzed me with fear.

I assumed I'd be okay once we left the club, but then Tony wanted to talk about the kiss, and I couldn't focus. All I could think was that Tony would like to do those things with me—to me and that I couldn't do it. After that, there's nothing until I woke up here.

A heaviness settles in my chest as I confront the truth—Tony lied. He's going to admit me to a psychiatric hospital. How could he do this?

What did you expect? You're a screw-up. You'll never deserve someone good like him.

The last time I was inpatient—no, I can't go through that again. Grabbing the IV, I pull it from my arm and press the palm of my other hand over it until the bleeding stops. In my other pocket is my cellphone. It's my connection to everyone I know, but it's also a way to be traced.

Thankfully, I still have my shoes. It wouldn't be the first time I've gone without, but it's not a pleasant experience. Stuffing cash into my pocket, I toss my wallet onto the bed. Then, I pull my cellphone out of my pocket. I wrestle with conflicting emotions on what to do with it, finally settling on placing it beside my wallet. Walking out of this room means leaving Tony and the life we've started to build together behind. I'll be alone again, but I don't have another choice.

Turning the handle, I crack the door open and peek out into the quiet hallway. I take a tentative step out and scan my surroundings. To the left is a nurse's station, so I go to the right, hoping it will lead to an exit. With my hands stuffed into my pockets, I keep my gaze low, hoping to avoid attracting unwanted attention. But it's taking too long and feels like I'm walking in circles. I can't find a way out.

"Excuse me," I say to someone in scrubs walking my way. "I've got myself all turned around in here. Which way is the exit?"

"Down the hall, make a left and another left."

"Thanks," I mumble and hurry down the hall until I'm pushing the door open and stepping onto the unfamiliar side street.

For a brief moment, I have second thoughts and consider going back inside and running into Tony's arms. But then, a bitter realization crashes over me. It's his fault that I'm here. He always promised he'd never leave me, but when I woke up, I was alone.

Of course, you're alone. Nobody wants you. Nobody loves you. You're always going to be alone.

With tears dripping down my face, I start walking away from the hospital and into the anonymity of the city.

Anthony

"Your CT is clear," Dr. Thompson says. "You might still have a mild concussion, so I'd like you to take it easy for a few days." A knock on the door interrupts her instructions, and she calls, "Come in."

"I'm sorry for interrupting," Patty says as she enters the room. "Is Mr. Wagner with you?"

"No, he's in his room sleeping," Dr. Thompson answers.

"May I speak to you in the hall, doctor?"

"Whatever you have to say about Leopold, you'll say in front of me."

Patty looks between me and the doctor before explaining, "I went in to check his vitals, and he was gone."

"What do you mean he was gone?" My heart rate increases, exacerbating my headache. I jump up from the bed, my movements fueled by panic. Thankfully, the pill Dr. Thompson gave me for the dizziness appears to be working. "How could a patient just disappear?"

"Perhaps he got up to use the restroom?" the doctor suggests.

"He pulled his IV out," Patty explains, her brow furrowed. "And he left his cell phone and wallet on the bed."

"Excuse me, I have to go find him," I say, already hurrying toward the door.

"Mr. Genovese, I haven't discharged you yet," Dr. Thompson calls after me.

"I don't care. I have to find Leo." I look to the nurse. "Can you help me get back to his room?"

"Take him to Mr. Wagner's room. I'll alert security," Dr. Thompson directs.

"Please don't do that. He's going to be scared—" I protest, but the doctor cuts me off.

"It's protocol, Mr. Genovese," she states firmly.

"Do what you need to do," I concede, turning back to Patty. "We're wasting time here. I have to go find him."

Security felt it was better for me to wait in Leo's room if he wandered off and found his way back. Meanwhile, they're scouring the halls of the hospital. I'm going stir-crazy sitting in an empty room, knowing he's not coming back. He's not here. I can't feel him—he's gone.

An hour later, my concerns are validated as Nurse Patty enters the room, followed closely by a doctor.

"Mr. Genovese, I'm Dr. Morgan, one of the staff psychiatrists," he introduces himself, offering his hand. "I was assigned to Mr. Wagner's case when he arrived."

"Were you able to locate him?" I ask, although I already know what his answer will be.

"When we couldn't find him in the hospital, we had security pull the footage from the exits. Mr. Wagner was seen exiting onto 168th St. almost two hours ago," Dr. Morgan confirms."You're telling me you have cameras, and you just thought of checking them?" I'm livid. "How could he walk out of here without being noticed?"

"It was an oversight, and our staff will be educated on patient safety," Dr. Morgan replies calmly.

"Have the police been called?"

"They have not. Since Mr. Wagner hadn't been evaluated or

admitted, he was within his rights to leave."

"You're kidding me, right?" I scoff, gripping my head in an attempt to soothe the throbbing headache assaulting my temples. "When we arrived, everyone was in a panic, insisting Leo was dangerous and needed to be admitted. And now that he's disappeared, suddenly his safety doesn't matter?"

"I understand your frustration, Mr. Genovese, but—"

"Enough," I cut in sharply, holding up a hand to silence the doctor. "I don't want to hear any more excuses. Bringing Leopold here was a mistake. I have to go find him." I brush past the doctor and nurse and hurry to the exit.

Outside, the sun's gentle rays are just beginning to peek over the horizon, painting the sky with hues of rose and gold and offering a glimmer of hope in the stillness of the morning. I find myself standing alone in the middle of the sidewalk, praying Leopold is out here waiting for me. But after I scan the area, my greatest fear is realized. He's not here.

Gripping his wallet and cell phone tightly—the only remnants of him I have left—I begin walking the maze of the city's streets, searching for any sign of him but finding nothing.

My head throbs and the vision in my right eye is blurry from the swelling. The doctor said I have a mild concussion and need to rest. But how can I rest when Leo's out here, alone and vulnerable? Is he lost in a world of delusions, running from shadows in his past? Or did he wake up thinking I not only betrayed him but also abandoned him?

"Leopold, where are you?" I ask quietly. "Please come back to me."

I walked the streets until exhaustion made my steps nearly impossible, and I returned to an empty apartment. I sink onto the couch and drop my head back. I'll only close my eyes for a minute, enough time to regroup and come up with a plan.

I don't know how long I've been asleep when my phone rings, startling me. "Hello?" I answer quickly, hoping it's news about Leopold.

"I've been waiting all night for an update," Ramiro says, frustration lacing his words.

I groan inwardly. "He's gone."

"What the hell does that mean?" Ramiro demands.

I explain the situation calmly. "I don't even know where to start looking," I confess. "He could be anywhere."

"I'm getting a plane ticket and coming out there," Ramiro says. "And when I find him, he's coming home with me."

"You're more than welcome to come out and help me search, but Leopold's not going anywhere. *This* is his home," I insist.

"We'll discuss that after we find him." Ramiro doesn't back down.

I soften my tone, knowing Ramiro cares about Leo too. "Let me know when you'll be arriving. You're welcome to stay at my place."

Anthony

"It was a mistake to bring him to the club," I say as I sink onto the couch in the office. "What the hell was I thinking?"

"You can't blame yourself," Sarah says calmly. "When someone's living with PTSD, triggers can appear from seemingly nowhere."

"Except this wasn't from nowhere. There was a bondage scene. Leo's terrified of being restrained. I should've known." I bring my hand to my chest. "It's my job to anticipate these things."

"No, Tony. It isn't your job." Sarah pins me with her stare. "Leo's lucky to have you as a support person, but that's where your role ends."

I can't believe what I'm hearing. What kind of therapist is this?

"I know what you're thinking. You feel responsible for Leo's well-being." Sarah shifts forward in her seat and places her hand on my arm. "It's not an uncommon belief, but it's also incorrect." I raise my eyes to meet her. "By providing Leo with the necessary resources, you've offered him a pathway to healing," Sarah explains, her voice steady. "But ultimately, Leo is the one who must take the steps forward. No matter how deeply you care for him, *you* can't fix him."

"Leopold's gotten his life together. He has a steady job, and he's earned his GED," I explain, even though Sarah is aware of his accomplishment. "He comes to therapy every week. He's putting in the work," I insist.

"Showing up for his appointments is one thing. But opening up and being honest with me is another."

"What are you implying?"

"I could lose my license for having this conversation with you." Sarah takes a deep breath. She's clearly at odds with how to proceed. "Leo's holding back. He's allowed me glimpses into his past, but when we get too close to the truth, he puts up walls to keep me out. Then, he tries to assure me he's coping and doing fine."

Fine. There's that word. The same one I used to keep those who cared about me at arm's length. I thought if I told them I was *fine,* they'd believe it and not worry about me. How could I be so blind to not see that Leo's been doing the same thing?

"I feared something like this might happen," Sarah adds, sitting back in her chair. "But Leo didn't want to hear it. Unfortunately, my hands were tied."

"So, what now?" I ask, my voice betraying my uncertainty.

"First, we have to find him. Then, we have to hope he's at a place where he's ready to actually accept the help we're offering," Sarah responds, her words laced with concern.

"I refuse to have him admitted anywhere," I state firmly, my resolve unyielding.

"Tony." Sarah begins to argue, but I cut her off.

"It's not up for discussion. If you're going to try to go down that path, we're done talking," I assert, unwilling to budge.

"For now, I'll go along with it. But, when we find him, if I think he's in danger, I'll sign the admission papers myself," Sarah concedes, her voice steady.

After leaving her office, I make my way to Fire and Ice. When

Owen heard what happened, he cut his trip short and came straight back. He and Star are meeting me there so we can come up with a plan to find Leo.

Instead of taking the subway, like I usually would, I walk, my eyes scanning the streets, hoping to spot Leo. Before going into the club, I take a detour to Hudson River Park. Fate brought us together once before. Perhaps she'll be on my side, and I'll find him there again.

The park is alive with the buzz of summer. Families are enjoying picnics. Dogs chase frisbees with their owners, and children laugh and play. But there's no sign of Leopold. With a sense of defeat settling over me, I reluctantly turn back toward the club.

"Tony." Star rushes over to me and wraps me in a comforting hug. "How are you holding up?"

"I have to find him," I say, my voice hollow with numbness.

"We will," she assures me, pulling away slightly. "What happened to your eye?"

I skirt around the truth, unwilling to cast Leo in a negative light. "It's nothing," I try to brush it off.

"It's not nothing. Who did this to you?" Star presses, her worry evident.

"It was an accident. It happened in the ambulance on the way to the hospital," I fabricate, protecting Leo's dignity.

""Leo hit you?" Her question is barely audible, filled with shock.

"They were trying to buckle him in. He didn't know what was going on. He thought they were trying to restrain him and hurt him." Tears pool in my eyes, but I force them away. I can't fall apart right now. "Leopold was scared. He didn't mean to hurt me."

"We know that," Owen says, joining Star by my side. "I made some lunch. We'll discuss a plan while we eat."

Despite my lack of appetite, I force myself to join them at the table. For the next few hours, we pore over maps and schedules, dividing Manhattan into segments we'll scour daily. It feels like searching for a needle in a haystack, an immense challenge. But the thought of Leopold out there alone fuels my determination. I won't rest until Leo is safely back in my arms.

Leopold

THE HUNDRED DOLLARS I HAD WITH ME IS LONG GONE. I should've kept my phone and sold it at a pawn shop. If I took my ATM card, I could've emptied my account and destroyed the card. Why didn't I think this through a little more?

Because you're a stupid fool. A loser who never gets anything right.

"I did get it right," I say aloud, drawing the attention of passersby.

I stop in the middle of the sidewalk, and the person behind me slams into me.

"What the hell is wrong with you, freak?" the man says as he pushes me out of the way.

What am I doing out here? I duck into the next alleyway and crawl behind a row of dumpsters. Being out in the middle of the day is a recipe for disaster. Krew or one of his minions will find me and drag me back to his house. They'll torture me until they kill me. I have to stay hidden until it's safe—after dark.

The stench of rotting trash jerks me awake. What the hell am I doing here? I crawl out from behind a rusty blue dumpster and brush my hands over my clothes. I'm not exactly clean, but I don't want to be covered in garbage.

Why was I sleeping amongst trash? This isn't the first time something like this has happened. I suspect I'm losing gaps of time, but I don't know why.

I think I'm losing my mind.

A door swings open, and a man wearing a white chef's jacket steps out. The man doesn't see me standing there as he hoists two large bags into the dumpster before returning inside, the door slamming closed behind him.

My stomach growls, and not for the first time, I climb up the side of the dumpster and tear into a bag. It's disgusting, but I don't care. I'm desperate to put something in my belly.

Tonight's a good night. I find a half-eaten burger and some fries—they're still warm. I shove the fries into my mouth before taking a big bite of the meat.

After finishing the sandwich, I start walking around looking for money dropped by one of the many tourists in Times Square. The lie I tell myself is that it's not stealing if I find it on the ground. And like most nights, it doesn't take long before I spot a wadded-up bill lying by the curb.

Trying not to be obvious, I stoop down to tie my shoelace and quickly swipe the cash. I hit the jackpot tonight. It's a ten-dollar bill. After shoving it into my pocket, I hurry away. I don't stop for several blocks until I find a street vendor where I buy a bottle of water. Tonight's a good night. I won't go hungry or thirsty.

Anthony

IN THE WAKE OF LEO'S DISAPPEARANCE, TIME SEEMS TO have lost all meaning. Days bleed into nights and nights into days as I navigate a world consumed by uncertainty. Work has become a distant concern, and sleep is a luxury I barely afford myself. Instead, I wander the streets, my eyes scanning every face and corner for any trace of him. But despite the overwhelming sense of despair threatening to engulf me, I refuse to give up hope.

Ramiro wanted to be here sooner, but Jacinta's mother had a medical emergency, and he was unable to leave California immediately. His plane touched down about an hour ago. He's in an Uber on his way to my apartment. I expect him here any minute.

While I wait, I keep my mind occupied with making dinner. I've hardly been able to eat since Leo disappeared, but I assume Ramiro will be hungry after his flight.

The sound of the doorbell jerks me from my thoughts. The strained dynamic between us leaves me unsure what to expect. Frankly, I don't have the energy to fight.

I pull the door open to reveal Ramiro, clad in jeans and a dark blue T-shirt, a backpack slung over his shoulder. "Come on in," I murmur, stepping aside to let him enter my apartment. "I hope you're hungry. I made dinner," I say, attempting to ease the palpable tension that hangs heavy in the air.

"Dinner sounds great. Thank you," he replies politely.

"Let me show you to your room first so you can put your stuff down," I offer, leading Ramiro down the hallway. "Here we are." I gesture, opening the door to reveal the cozy space. "There's an attached bathroom. Take your time. I'll be in the kitchen."

While Ramiro settles into his room, I ready the table and put the finishing touches on the food.

"Whatever you've made smells good," Ramiro says as he walks over to the table.

"It's eggplant parmesan," I reply. "What can I get you to drink?"

"I'll have whatever you're having."

"Red wine."

"Perfect," he says, sitting at the table while I pour the wine and serve the food.

Dinner unfolds in uncomfortable silence, punctuated only by the clinking of utensils against plates. Each attempt at conversation feels forced, as if we're both grasping at straws to fill the silence. I find myself counting down the minutes until the ordeal is over.

Relief washes over me when Ramiro finally excuses himself and goes to bed early. The quiet of the apartment settles around me, but I can't sleep yet. Instead, I quietly slip out to roam the city streets, praying for a miracle.

As the next afternoon unfolds, my apartment gradually fills with the presence of familiar faces. Owen and Astrid are the first to arrive. "When's the last time you slept?" Owen asks, concern lacing his voice.

"Last night."

"For how long?"

"I don't know." I shrug. "An hour or two, I guess."

"You have to start taking care of yourself. If you end up in the hospital, how will that help Leo?"

I sink onto the couch. "I'll sleep soundly after Leopold is home."

The doorbell rings again, and I go to stand, but Owen puts his hand on my arm, stopping me. "Astrid, please answer it." Owen directs his sub.

"Yes, Sir," she responds and dutifully goes to the door.

"Where's Ramiro?" Owen asks quietly.

"He's in his room. His wife called." I turn toward Star and Corbin, who are entering the room. "Thanks for coming."

"We brought coffee and donuts," Star says, holding up the donut shop bags.

"You didn't have to do that."

The sound of footsteps grows closer.

"You must be Ramiro," Owen says, stepping toward him and offering his hand. "I'm Owen."

"Good to meet you."

"This is my girlfriend, Astrid." The doorbell rings again.

"Excuse me, please," Astrid says as she goes to answer the door.

"This is Star and Corbin," Owen introduces the pair.

"It's a pleasure to meet you all," Ramiro says politely.

Astrid returns with Emmanuel, Pastor Andrea, and Kelly.

I push to my feet as Andrea and Kelly take turns giving me a hug. "Thank you both for coming."

"We're glad to be here."

"This is Ramiro, a friend of Leopold's from California." I motion to the ladies. "This is Pastor Andrea and her girlfriend, Kelly. They run the grief support group I attend."

"It's nice to meet you both."

After getting everyone acquainted, we gather at the table to brainstorm additional strategies to expand the search for Leo.

"Does he have anywhere he likes to hang out?" Ramiro asks.

"Outside of work? Not really." Ramiro raises his eyebrow in disapproval. "He spends a lot of time in the gym downstairs," I explain. "The doormen know to let him in and to call me right away if he happens to show up."

"Who are his friends?" he asks.

"He spends the majority of his time with me." Ramiro narrows his eyes but doesn't continue his line of questioning.

"Drea and I have connections at homeless shelters and soup kitchens. We've shared Leo's picture and your phone number," Kelly says.

"I can't thank you enough."

"We love Leo. Getting him home safe is all the thanks we need," Andrea adds.

"After Sept 11, people put posters up all over the city. Maybe we can do that too?" Astrid offers, her suggestion sincere.

All eyes turn to me.

The vivid memory of the city awash with missing person posters in the aftermath of that fateful day remains seared into my mind. Each one was a poignant reminder of the agony endured by those left behind, a testament to their unwavering hope and determination. At that time, I stood on the periphery. Kameron wasn't among the missing. He was already gone. But today, as I grapple with the agony of uncertainty, I understand the anguish of those desperate souls. Now, I'm among those who cling to hope, desperately searching for a missing loved one.

"That's a great idea, Astrid," I say, sincerity in my voice. "Thank you."

"We can use the church's printer," Andrea offers. "Kelly and I will start on those when we leave here."

"I'll stop by tomorrow if it's okay. I'll distribute them to our volunteers so we can cover the city faster."

"Corbin will call the hospitals again to see if anyone matching his description shows up," Star offers.

"I'm going out again tonight. Leopold has to be out there somewhere," I murmur, my tone filled with desperation.

"I'll go with you," Ramiro adds, and I offer a grateful smile.

After my guests leave, I get my shoes and two bottles of water. Handing one to Ramiro, I say, "Then, let's get moving." I turn and start to walk away.

"Wait," Ramiro says, grabbing my arm. "I want to apologize for how I reacted when you told me Leo was missing. I was out of line," he says, and I see the pain on his face. "I'm protective of Leo, especially after what he went through with Krew."

"He told me everything," I assure him.

"But you weren't there. You didn't see the condition Leo was in." A haunted look shadows his features. "Krew force-fed him drugs and allowed him to be raped repeatedly. We had to watch him go through withdrawal for weeks. There were some days I wasn't convinced he was going to make it," he adds, his voice trembling with emotion. "New York was his fresh start. He was doing so good here. I don't understand what happened?"

"What did he tell you about the night I found him?" I ask, my hand going to the metal in my pocket.

"You were there. You know what he said."

"He never told you anything else?" I ask.

"When I asked, Leo said things were better, and he didn't want to talk about it anymore."

Although I shouldn't be, I'm surprised by Ramiro's answer. I assumed that because they were close, Leo would've told him the whole story. There's no easy way to say it, so I take a direct approach. "When I found Leopold that night, he was in the process of committing suicide."

"Leo would never." Ramiro scoffs, his disbelief evident.

"Everyone has their breaking point, and Leopold was at his," I whisper.

The reality of my words begins to take root. Ramiro asks, "What did he do?"

"He tried slitting his wrist with this." I pull the boxcutter from my pocket. "I've carried it with me ever since that night to remind me just how close I came to losing him. If I was a minute later, it might've been too late."

"You should've taken him to a hospital. He needed the help of professionals with experience treating someone in his condition," Ramiro states.

"The last place Leopold needed to be was in a facility. That's how we ended up in this situation." I take a deep breath, trying to quell the anger threatening to spill over. "When I brought Leo home, I made him promise me thirty days. One month to prove to him why he needed to keep living."

Ramiro listens intently as I bring him up to speed on the events of the past six months. I detail all the progress Leo has made on his journey towards wellness, as well as all of the things Sarah pointed out. Things I'd stupidly been blind to.

"You care about him, don't you?" Ramiro asks.

"I love him," I admit, my voice trembling with emotion. "But I'm so scared."

"We're going to find him, Tony," Ramiro promises, his tone brimming with determination.

The thought of Leopold out there, lost and alone, is almost too much to bear.

Leopold has to be okay.

I'm clinging to the hope that he'll return home—to me, where he belongs.

Leopold

Leaving the hospital that day may be the biggest mistake of my life. Hearing those hospital workers talk about having me admitted for treatment terrified me. The thought that Tony was willing to sign the papers to do that shook me to my core. But as I replay those conversations in my mind, I question what exactly I heard. Did Tony ever agree to sign the papers? Or was I jumping to conclusions?

Why was I at the hospital in the first place? They said Tony was getting a CAT scan. Did I do something to hurt him? Is that why Tony wasn't there when I woke up? I have so many questions that will forever remain unanswered because I walked away from him.

Living on the streets and often waking up in places I don't remember is a constant reminder that something terrible is happening to me. It reinforces the thought that Tony brought me to the hospital because he was concerned about me.

Don't be naïve. He was having you committed. He thinks you're crazy.

"Shut up." I grab the sides of my head and yell, trying to silence the repetitive thoughts in my head.

Deep down in my heart, I don't believe Tony would've

betrayed me. If only I'd waited for him to come back, I could've asked him. He's never lied to me, and there was no reason to think he would've started then.

I've seen him—Tony. He was walking down the street, unknowingly heading straight toward me. He briefly glanced down at his phone, giving me a split-second to duck down an alley. I couldn't bring myself to face him, not after what I had done. But it didn't stop the ache in my chest as I watched him walk past where I hid in the shadows.

He'll eventually move on and forget about me. I'll be left to live with the knowledge that my mistakes cost me the only person who ever truly cared about me.

I'm lost. Torn between the desire to move forward and the fear of facing the consequences of my choices.

How do I find my way back from this?

More importantly, do I have the will to try?

Anthony

RAMIRO STAYED FOR TWO WEEKS. HE WOKE EARLY every day to comb through the streets, hang posters, and go from one homeless shelter to another, hoping to find him or at least get information about any sightings. At the end of each day, he returned home empty-handed. Eventually, he had to return to California. In the time he was here, we were able to come to a tentative truce. But without Leopold, none of that matters.

The thought of facing another day without my love often feels unbearable. It's only through the unwavering support of my friends that I have the strength to continue. While one group of people plastered the city with posters, Andrea and Kelly mobilized their contacts in the city's homeless community. I was sure it would only be a few days before we found him, but as each day came and went with nothing, a sense of futility crept in.

Six weeks have passed since Leopold slipped out of the hospital, leaving me to navigate life without him. My days blur together as I walk the streets chasing fleeting glimpses that might be him. Instead, each sighting turns out to be a cruel tease that feels like a fresh wound slicing through my heart. Truth be told, I don't even know if Leopold is still in New York City. He could be anywhere by now.

After enduring the heartache of losing Kameron, I begged the universe to bring me someone to love. Someone who would be my forever. That's when I met Leopold. The thought that he's gone forever is too agonizing for me to comprehend.

What began as casual conversations and shared meals with a man I knew was going hungry most days gradually blossomed into friendship. Somewhere along the way, I fell in love with him. If I'm honest, it was the very first time he walked into my restaurant, his blue eyes peeking out from behind his scarf. In that instant, my heart fell for him, and in the blink of an eye, he vanished, leaving behind an aching emptiness. Now, I'm left grappling with the sheer magnitude of his disappearance, unsure of how to navigate this new reality where he no longer exists by my side.

"The last table just cleared out, Chef," Raina says, popping her head into my office.

"Thanks," I mumble, my head in my hands as I struggle to comprehend the words on the paper I've been trying to read for the past twenty minutes.

"Please don't give up," she says as she steps further into the room.

My head jerks up. "What?"

"On finding Leo," she states, her voice laced with conviction. "I have a feeling he's closer than you think."

Her comment catches me off guard, and I'm unsure how to respond.

"I'm sorry if I overstepped," she adds, sensing my hesitation.

"Not at all," I respond, managing a faint smile. "I appreciate your support."

"The front is cleaned up and ready for tomorrow," she informs me, changing the subject. "Is it okay if I head out?"

"Absolutely," I reply. "Take care on your way home."

As the night wears on, my staff filters out, each confirming their tasks are completed and their areas ready for tomorrow's opening. It's well past 2 am when I finally conquer the stubborn order form I've been struggling with all night, faxing it to the supplier so they receive it first thing in the morning. Before I leave, I do a quick sweep of the restaurant, ensuring everything's in order before shutting the lights off and locking up.

With a heavy heart and exhaustion deep in my bones, I transition to the next part of my night. The city pulses with life around me as my footsteps echo against the pavement. My heart is heavy as I scour the shadows and peer down deserted alleyways with the hope of even the faintest glimpse of him.

My search comes to an abrupt halt as Owen appears in my path. "What are you doing here?" I question, surprised by his sudden appearance.

"Looking for you," Owen replies, his tone urgent. "Star's been trying to call you for the past two hours."

I pull my phone from my pocket and check the screen, my stomach dropping at the sight of forty missed calls. "I must've muted it accidentally."

"Leo's at the club," Owen states matter-of-factly.

"What?" The intensity of my reaction mirrors the rapid pounding of my heart as Owen's revelation sinks in.

"Star and I were both at the club tonight. She stepped out to get some fresh air," he explains, his voice steady. "She went over to the river walk, and he was there, sitting on a bench."

"Are you serious?" I ask, a surge of hope rising within me.

"I wouldn't joke about this."

"Leopold's with Star?" I ask, my voice trembling with emotion.

"He's not in great shape," Owen explains, concern etched in his voice. "He's dehydrated and thin, but he's there and safe."

I'm afraid to believe what Owen's saying. Terrified I'll find this is yet another dream where I wake up to an empty house.

"Why aren't you moving?" Owen asks, sensing my hesitation.

"I don't want to get there, and this not be real," I confess, my voice barely above a whisper.

"I was there when she brought him to the club," Owen adds.

"You saw him?" I ask, desperate for confirmation.

"When we couldn't get ahold of you, Leo got nervous. I told him I'd come get you," Owen explains, his grip firm on my arm. "Let's go. He's waiting for you."

For the first time since Leopold disappeared, a glimmer of hope pierces through the darkness. Leopold's at Fire and Ice.

He's safe.

Leopold

THE GENTLE RHYTHM OF THE WATER AGAINST THE concrete wall lulls me into a trance-like state. I'm sitting on the bench, the same one I sat on with Tony the night he saved me. Exhaustion, both mental and physical, overwhelms my senses. Hunger gnaws at my stomach while loneliness threatens to consume me. Coming here was supposed to bring me closer to him, even if only for a few minutes. My eyelids are heavy. I pull my legs up tight against me and drop my head onto my knees. "I'll just close my eyes for a minute."

"Leo? Is that you?" a familiar woman's voice causes me to stir. I lift my head and blink a few times until her face comes into focus.

"Oh my God." She throws her arms around my neck, not caring about my grimy appearance. "It's really you." Pulling back slightly, she places her hands on my shoulders. "Let me get a good look at you."

I drop my head, ashamed of my disheveled state.

"Are you okay? Where have you been?" Star rapid-fires before pausing to take a breath. "I'm sorry," she slows down, lowering her voice. "I shouldn't be bombarding you with so many questions."

"It's fine," I say quietly.

"Let's start with one at a time." Star sits next to me. "Are you okay?"

"I don't know," I admit feeling lost.

"We've been searching everywhere for you. Where have you been?" Star's concern is palpable.

"You've been looking for me?" I ask, genuinely surprised.

"Of course we have," Star reassures me. "Tony's been beside himself since you disappeared. He's going to be so relieved to know you're safe."

"I doubt that."

"What do you mean?" Star's concern deepens, her eyes searching mine for answers.

"He brought me to the hospital," I explain, my voice wavering slightly. "They said he was going to have me admitted."

"Who told you that?"

"I overheard some people talking. They thought I was asleep," I admit, chancing a glance up. "I couldn't let them make me stay."

"Oh, honey," she murmurs, cupping my cheek. "Tony wasn't going to let them do that. He took you to the hospital because... We don't need to worry about that right now. All that matters is you're here now. Will you come back to the club with me so we can call Tony?"

"The club?" Uncertainty creeps over me.

"Yes," she says hesitantly. "If you'd like, we'll use the back entrance and go straight to my office."

"Are you sure Tony's going to want to see me?" I ask, my anxiety mounting.

"I'm positive," she assures me, rising to her feet and offering her hand. "Will you come with me?"

If I say yes and Tony refuses to see me, I'll be devastated. I don't know if I could survive that. But if I don't go with her, if I choose to walk away, this is it. I won't get another chance.

Tony's everything to me. I love him. My hand trembles as I consider reaching out to take hers, but at the last moment, I hesitate.

"Please, Leo," her voice cracks. "Come with me."

"I don't want to touch you. I'm filthy," I protest, feeling unworthy.

"That doesn't matter to me," she insists, her hand still outstretched.

Should I trust her?

Don't do it. You're dirty. Damaged. You're nothing.

I hate that voice—the one that always creeps up and makes me doubt everything.

She's using you. Tony doesn't want you. She'll make a fool out of you.

Deciding to ignore my negative thoughts, I push to my feet and place my hand in hers. She gives it a reassuring squeeze.

"Thank you for trusting me, Leo." Star keeps her word and brings me in through the back. "I'm going to text Owen and ask him to come back here, okay?"

"Are you sure he's going to want to see me?" Insecurity plagues me again, and I wonder if I've made the wrong choice by coming here.

"I guarantee he wants to see you."

"Okay," I say, even though I'm still uncertain.

Star texts back and forth. The longer the conversation goes on, the more I lose hope that he's coming. Suddenly, the door to her office swings open.

"Holy shit," Owen says, his hands flying to his mouth. "Where did he come from?"

"I found him on a bench by the river," Star explains, relief evident in her tone.

"We've been looking for you everywhere," Owen says as he takes me in from head to toe. "When's the last time you ate?" he asks, concerned, and I shrug. "Did you call Tony?" He turns to Star.

"I've been trying," she replies, frustrated. "But it keeps going to voicemail."

"I'm sure he'll call back soon," Owen says, turning his attention back to me. "Are you hungry? I'll get you something to eat. Is there anything special you want?"

"Whatever is fine," I reply, grateful for whatever he gets me.

"I'll be back in a few minutes."

Star checks her phone again before shaking her head.

"It's not like Tony to not answer his phone," I say, worry bubbling inside me. "Maybe he doesn't want to see me?" I ask as the negative voice gets louder.

He tried to get rid of you. He wants nothing to do with you.

"I assure you he wants to see you. He's searched day and night for you," she adds. Her phone buzzes, and she grabs it quickly. Her face falls. "Corbin needs me at the desk. Will you be okay alone here for a few minutes?"

"Yeah."

She walks over to the door and pauses with her hand on the knob. "Promise you won't leave?"

"I promise."

She studies me momentarily before nodding and leaving me alone in her office.

I look around, knowing the only way out is through the door. I'm certain Star has someone watching to be sure I don't disappear again. I don't like feeling trapped in small spaces. Standing up, I begin to pace back and forth.

A stack of papers on the filing cabinet catches my attention. Reaching out I take one off the top. "It's me," I mumble. The heading on the page reads: HAVE YOU SEEN THIS MAN? Underneath is a recent picture of me—one Tony took in the garden of his restaurant when we were having dinner together. The bottom of the page has Tony's contact information, asking anyone with any information on me to call him.

"I told you he was looking for you," Star says softly.

"I didn't hear the door," I say as I spin around to face her with the paper still in my hand.

"It's okay," she offers a reassuring smile.

"He was really looking for me?" I ask, swallowing over the lump in my throat.

"Since the day you disappeared," she replies. "He's never given up on finding you."

The door opens again. This time, it's Owen carrying a plate with a steaming burger and fries. Two bottles of water are tucked under his arm. "I'm assuming you haven't eaten in a while," Owen remarks as he sets the food on Star's desk.

"It's been a few days," I reply.

He motions for me to sit. "Go slow so you don't get sick, okay?"

"Mhm," I mumble with my mouth full. My eyes close instinctively, relishing the delicious taste of the freshly cooked food made just for me.

"Any luck reaching Tony?" Owen inquires, his voice filled with concern.

"No," Star replies, frustrated. "It keeps going to voicemail, and my texts are unread."

"I know he's working at the restaurant tonight. I'm sure he's busy," Owen remarks with a sigh. "Let's give him a little more time."

Over the course of the next hour, Owen pops in and out of the office, juggling the responsibilities of running the club and checking on me. "Anything?" Owen asks.

"Nothing," Star responds with a weary shake of her head, her disappointment evident.

"We've waited long enough. I'm going to the restaurant to get him," Owen states before disappearing a final time.

Leopold

STAR'S PHONE DINGS WITH AN INCOMING ALERT. SHE looks at the screen, her face lighting up before she turns it to me.

Owen: We're on the way. Tell Leo Tony can't wait to see him.

I'm relieved he's coming, but another wave of nerves washes over me. "Tony's going to want to know what happened," I say, my voice tinged with apprehension.

"Yes, he'll probably have some questions," Star replies calmly.

"You weren't here, but I came to the club with Tony earlier that night," I explain.

"Did something happen while you were here?" she inquires gently.

"No. Lacey, Shawn, and Caleb were great. I really liked them, but..." My voice trails off.

"You're safe to tell me anything," Star encourages.

"There was a scene where the Dominant tied up his submissive. He was gagged and blindfolded." Squeezing my eyes shut, I try to block out the unwelcome memories. "It brought up a lot of memories. Things that were done to me."

"I'm deeply sorry that you were silenced by so many people. Their actions were cruel and unjust—they were wrong. You didn't deserve to be hurt like that," Star says softly, her voice laced with empathy.

"It was my fault," I whisper, unable to shake the shame and guilt from my past.

"No, Leo. It wasn't. Please look at me," Star says, her voice gentle yet firm. I lift my head, meeting her gaze. "You need to understand that being raped was not your fault," she insists.

"But—" I attempt to protest, my words catching in my throat.

"Let me make this clear," she says. "There's nothing you did or could ever do that would give anyone the right to touch you in any way without your consent." Her tone is unwavering. "But it's important to recognize the distinction between what happened to you and what you witnessed at the club," she says.

"That Dominant and submissive discussed their scene ahead of time. They established rules and boundaries. In addition, the protocol at Fire and Ice requires all public scenes to be written out and submitted to Owen or me as an added security measure," she explains patiently. "Chase, the submissive you saw that night, enjoys bondage. Everything that was done to him was consensual."

"Lacey talked to me about how important consent is in BDSM."

"It's arguably the most important part of this lifestyle," Star agrees. "Nothing happens in a responsible Dominant/submissive relationship—whether it's for one night at the club or a more permanent relationship, that isn't fully agreed to by both parties. There's no room for coercion or not respecting boundaries, and safewords are always respected."

"I like Tony," I confess, my voice barely above a whisper. "As more than a friend."

"I know," Star responds, her smile warm.

"But I can't be with him," I admit, my voice tinged with regret.

"Why not?" Star inquires gently.

"As much as I'm comforted by everything you explained," I say, my heart pounds just talking about it. "I can't get hit or be blindfolded."

"Oh, Leo honey," Star responds, her tone tender and reassuring. "None of that would stop Tony from being with you. If you and he were to be in a relationship and if BDSM was part of it, you'd discuss what things are acceptable and what are not. Tony would never ask you to do anything you were uncomfortable with or that would trigger you."

"Really?" I ask, surprised.

"Yes," Star replies, her tone filled with conviction. "Communication is a big part of this lifestyle. Don't ever be afraid to tell Tony what you're thinking or feeling," she continues, her voice gentle but firm. "He needs to know what you want or don't want. Tony will never force or hurt you."

There's a knock on the door a second before it opens. "Leopold," Tony says, his voice thick with desperation as he takes long strides across the room to reach me. I scramble to my feet, my heart pounding with anticipation, and meet him halfway. With a sense of urgency, he pulls me into his arms, enclosing me in his strong embrace.

"I didn't know how to find you," he murmurs, his voice trembling with relief as he presses a tender kiss to the side of my head, his touch a comforting reassurance. "I was so scared."

Star and Owen make a discrete exit, leaving Tony and me alone.

"I'm sorry," I sob, tears streaming down my face. "I'm so sorry."

His hold on me tightens. "You have nothing to apologize for, Leopold," Tony says, his voice cracking. "God, I'm so happy you're back." Taking me by the shoulders, he holds me away from him as he scans my body. "Are you okay? You're not hurt, are you?"

"No," I shake my head, meeting his tear-filled gaze. "You're crying?"

"I thought I'd lost you forever. I didn't know how I could go on without you," Tony confesses, his voice choked with emotion. "Why did you leave?"

"There were people in the room who said you were going to sign papers to have me admitted," I confess. "They didn't know I was awake."

"The doctor wanted me to sign the papers, but I refused. I made a promise to you, and I won't break that."

"They said I hit you?" I swallow over a lump in my throat.

"Do you remember what happened at home? Why we were at the hospital?" Tony asks cautiously.

"No." I shake my head slowly.

"You were having a flashback of some kind. You thought I was Krew and that I was going to hurt you. I couldn't get through to you. When I called Sarah, she directed me to bring you to the emergency room for an evaluation," he explains, his tone gentle but firm. "When we got in the ambulance, they tried to restrain you to the gurney. I begged them not to, but they didn't listen. You got scared. You didn't know what was happening, and you hit me."

"Oh my God," I utter as my legs give way, and I collapse to the floor. Tony sinks down beside me.

"It's okay, Leopold," he whispers, comforting me. "It's over now."

"It's not. I think I might have had more flashbacks while I was gone," I admit, fear tainting my voice.

"What do you mean?" he asks, his brow furrowing with concern.

"I kept waking up in alleys and behind dumpsters, but I didn't know how I got there," I explain and cling to him. "I'm scared, Tony. What's wrong with me?"

"I don't know, but we're going to figure this out," he murmurs as he kisses the top of my head. "Just promise you won't leave me again," he pleads, his voice filled with desperation.

"I won't leave you. I promise." Drawing a shaky breath, I say, "I want to be with you as your submissive."

Anthony

My eyes open wide. Leopold wants to be my submissive. "You don't have to say that because you're afraid."

"That's not why," he insists. "I knew it before this, but I got scared after seeing the scene at the club and I thought I had to let you do those things to me. But Star explained that's not how it works."

"No, it isn't. You never have to do anything you don't want to do," I reassure him, my heart swelling with affection.

"Will you let me submit to you?" he asks again, his gaze fixed on me.

Leo's blue eyes shimmer with unshed tears. I can't lie and say I've never thought about having him as my submissive. I've done more than think about it, but this isn't the right time. "No," I say with a heavy heart. "Not like this."

"You don't want me." Leo tries to pull away, his voice trembling with insecurity.

"Stop," I plead, gently holding his hands. "I want you, Leopold. I've wanted you for so long, but this isn't the right way. You need to learn more about the lifestyle, and we need to figure out why you're having flashbacks—how to help you heal."

"I need to tell Sarah the truth. I've been keeping so much

from her," he admits, his voice laced with vulnerability. "I was afraid she'd say I was too damaged and needed to be in a hospital and that you wouldn't want me anymore."

"There's nothing that could change my mind about you," I murmur softly, my voice carrying the weight of my emotions. "I love you, Leopold."

"You love me?" he asks in disbelief.

"Yes." I lean in and brush my lips against his. "I love everything about you."

"No one's ever loved me," he whispers, his expression pained.

"You'll never have to feel that way again, Leopold," I promise, gently brushing his hair behind his ear.

"I love you, Tony," he confesses, his gaze searching mine with a mixture of longing and fear. "I don't want to screw this up like I do with everything. I'm so scared."

"Lean on me. Allow me to be strong for you. Let me love you." My words carry a depth of sincerity as I offer him the reassurance he seeks.

Leopold

AUGUST 15

My session with Sarah last week was one of the scariest things I've ever had to do. Even though I've been seeing her every week for months, I never really let my guard down. I kept her an arm's length away. In my attempt to skate by, I only allowed her limited access to my thoughts and fears.

I held back so much—the most important details, not realizing I was only hurting myself. It all came to the surface the night I had a flashback that dissociated me from the current reality.

Sarah allowed me to invite Tony into my sessions while I told them both everything. For real, this time. Then, when I was ready, Tony recounted the full story of what happened that night. I was horrified and embarrassed at my behavior—even though I couldn't remember it.

It was difficult for me to accept that although I did those things, it also wasn't me. Had I not been in a dissociative state, I would never have become violent with anyone.

Then, Sarah suggested something that almost made me quit therapy for good. She proposed seeing a psychiatrist and trying medication for my anxiety and PTSD. At first, I resisted. After being involuntarily addicted to whatever illicit substances Krew fed me, the last thing I wanted was to be drugged. In my mind, I envisioned becoming a groggy mess of a person whose life was once again ruled by the unwanted effects of medication.

Sarah made the case that a reputable doctor would give me the least amount of medication possible to control the symptoms. She challenged me to try approaching the medication discussion with an open mind. She assured me that Dr. Chen wouldn't force me to take something I wasn't comfortable with.

Tony came with me to my first appointment. It was a two-hour intensive, during which Dr. Chen started by taking my entire medical and psychological history. We had a very straightforward conversation about the forced drug use I experienced and subsequent addiction. He was sympathetic and understanding regarding my fear of becoming addicted to drugs again.

Dr. Chen took the time to educate me about the various classes of prescriptions and then proposed what he felt would be an appropriate medication plan for me. Even though Sarah assured me the doctor wouldn't try to coerce me into anything, I was still nervous. What if Dr. Chen insisted I give him an answer right then? But he didn't. When I asked if I could think about the proposed medication, he gave me not only the paper script but also several printouts full of information. And he told me to call him if I had any further questions.

After taking some time to talk more with Tony and think about it further, I decided to give the low-dose anti-anxiety medication a try. It's only been a few weeks, but I already feel some relief from the persistent negative thoughts and feelings of foreboding that have always dictated my life.

I wasn't sure what would happen between Tony and me after I asked to be his submissive, and he turned me down. At first, I was not only hurt but embarrassed. But once I was able to stop and not just listen to him but really hear him, his explanation made more sense. I was in no condition to make an important decision, and he would've been irresponsible in allowing it to happen. But that didn't stop the feelings we now know we share.

He loves me, and I love him.

We're more openly affectionate with one another. However, Tony will not allow our physical relationship to go any further than kissing, especially while we're still getting to know each other on a deeper level and while I'm learning more about the BDSM lifestyle.

Star has agreed to be my mentor. She's teaching me all the basics of the lifestyle. What it means to be a submissive in a healthy relationship. I'm learning important lessons about communication and how it's essential, especially in a Dom/sub relationship where one person is surrendering so much power to another and where the couple is often participating in activities that could be dangerous.

We talk about consent all the time. Something I didn't realize is that consent is equally essential for the Dominant as well as the submissive. Many people in the lifestyle debate who holds the power, the Dominant or the submissive. The way I understand it, neither role is able to be fulfilled without the other.

The Dominant must prove themself worthy of the trust the submissive is gifting them with. Likewise, the submissive has the responsibility of being open and honest with the Dominant about their experience, past traumas, limits—everything really. It reminds me of a circle. There's no beginning or end. There's no Dominant without submission and no submissive without domination. I don't think one is more powerful than the other.

I've been going to Fire and Ice with Tony more often. With the lessons Star's been teaching me, I'm better able to understand what I'm witnessing. Seeing a person on their knees willingly giving themselves to another brings tears to my eyes. The look of pure devotion on the Dominant's face, whether they're doing a one-time scene or in a committed dynamic, is incredible. Seeing two individuals wholly trusting one another is breathtaking. I want that so badly with Tony, but I don't want to push.

Thankfully, Sarah's a kink-friendly therapist, and I'm able to freely discuss this new part of my life with her as well. We've included Tony in many of my sessions because he wants to learn how best to support me. We're talking about known triggers and plan-

ning for the unknown ones that are certain to creep up when we're least expecting them. She's given him tools to help ground me and hopefully keep me from dissociating again.

I'm not without responsibility for this. Being open and communicating my thoughts and feelings is the first line of defense. When I keep those things to myself under the guise that I'm 'fine,' is when I run into trouble. Part of my therapy goals are to be accountable for my internal thoughts and to be willing to reach out to someone I trust so they don't build up. It's not always easy, but it does work.

Together, Tony, Sarah, and I have decided it would be safer and in my best interest to not make any decisions regarding a Dom/sub dynamic until I'm stable on my medication for longer and a bit farther into my therapy. It's not an answer I'm thrilled with—something I've openly communicated to both of them, but it's one I understand and accept.

Most importantly, I'm having good days—more good than bad. The negative thoughts that were so loud are still there. I've learned a lot of people have them. I'm also learning that I have power over them, not the other way around. Thoughts cannot harm me. It's okay to have them and then to let them float away.

I am not a loser.

I am not damaged beyond repair.

I am deserving of love.

Leopold

DECEMBER 23

I've been seeing Dr. Chen for several months, and I think it's safe to say that his treatment plan is working. I haven't felt this good in well, ever. In the beginning, I'd leave my appointments feeling exhausted from information overload. Naps were almost non-negotiable.

Once I understood the quirky doctor better, that went away. He's a brilliant man who cares deeply for his patients. Now, I find myself looking forward to our conversations.

It's been one year since I hit rock bottom. One year since Tony stumbled on me attempting suicide. I want to say every day has been perfect, but that would be a lie. Some days, my path seemed effortless. Others, it felt like an unattainable uphill climb.

One of the hurdles I've dealt with was feeling like a coward for trying to end my life. What kind of person thinks it would be better to be dead than to confront their problems head-on? It's taken a lot of therapy to be able to not only say but also accept as truth that I was not a coward that night.

I was a man who was depressed and alone. I couldn't see a way out. Those thoughts and feelings were nothing to be ashamed of. The *fact that I put the blade to my wrist and cut doesn't make me any less of a person—doesn't make me unworthy.*

I've worked hard with Sarah on being completely honest and vulnerable, even when I would rather say I was fine and move on to something easier.

Sarah has proven herself to be trustworthy and has given me the tools I need to take ownership of my life and my story. I no longer allow others to choose my narrative. That's mine and mine alone. It feels good to finally take control over my life and to believe I am good enough.

Star and I have continued to meet, and I've learned so much about the BDSM lifestyle. Tony has assured me that he'd walk away from BDSM if it wasn't what I wanted. It's been a part of his life for so long, and I know how important it is to him. I would never ask him to give that up for me. I decided that if I couldn't see myself in the lifestyle, I'd walk away from Tony.

One of the most important things I've worked on with Star and Sarah is learning more about healthy submission and what it would mean to submit to a Dominant. They were both concerned with my mental and emotional health, not because they feared Tony would ever take advantage of me. It's more about being responsible and safe, ensuring I'm well and strong so I'm making the best decisions for me. I don't want to offer my submission to Tony if I'm going to crack under the pressure and end up hurting both him and me.

My biggest concern is still being strong enough within myself to recognize what my wants and especially needs are and not be afraid to voice them. Without that, it would have put Tony at a disadvantage, always trying to guess if my needs were being met. If what we were doing was hurting me. The results could be disastrous for us both.

Star has ensured I have a solid understanding of the lifestyle and what my role would be if I were a submissive. She's helped me develop a detailed list of what I'm okay with and what are limits— soft and hard. We've had very frank discussions after scenes at the club I was unfamiliar with or made me uncomfortable. She and I dissected every action and word in the scenes, trying to ensure my limit list was as accurate as possible.

Which brings me to today. I'm not entirely sure how Tony is going to respond. I hope he's going to accept what I offer him.

Anthony

I'VE BEEN ON EDGE ALL WEEK, BRACING MYSELF FOR today. One year ago tonight, I found Leopold in the park, ready to end it all. In the year that followed, I witnessed his struggles and came dangerously close to losing him again. Since then, I've had the privilege of watching him flourish and soar. Despite that, the anticipation of tonight and the memories it holds still weighs heavily on me. I suggested we stay home tonight, but Leopold insisted he wanted to join me at the annual Christmas Eve Eve Party at Fire and Ice.

Our connection has only deepened as Leopold has healed. The love we confessed to one another that night in Star's office has blossomed with each new day. There have been countless nights when I've said goodnight to him outside his bedroom door, only to struggle with returning to my own room alone. It's been the ultimate test of my self-control and resolve.

We both want more, but I don't know when the right time is to take the next step. My biggest concern, the thing that holds me back, is the fear of causing Leopold any pain. Owen insists that I'll know when it's right. I'm trusting him on that.

"Are you ready?" Leo asks from my doorway.

As I turn around to respond, I'm momentarily rendered

speechless by the sight before me. Leopold stands leaning against my doorway, his arms casually crossed over his chest. He's dressed in dark trousers paired with a navy blue dress shirt, the top buttons left undone, hinting at the sculpted chest and abdomen beneath.

It's evident that Leopold's been diligently hitting the gym downstairs daily. He's regained a few pounds and added substantial muscle. My hand instinctively moves to cover my mouth in awe. "You're... wow," I manage to utter, making my way across the room with determined steps, my eyes never leaving his mesmerizing form.

"You don't look so bad yourself." His lips quirk up in a smile.

The age gap between Leopold and me has been an ongoing source of insecurity. With nearly fifteen years between us, I couldn't help but question if he'd ever see me as anything more than a friend despite being attracted to him from the moment we met.

"You're positively edible," I say, licking my bottom lip.

His eyes roam up and down my body, pausing at the bulge in my pants. "It wouldn't hurt if we were fashionably late to the party," he murmurs, his voice low and deep.

It would be so easy to give in to the allure of his proposal. The thought of undressing him and worshipping his body like I've dreamt of so many times sends a shiver down my spine. "I'd love to," I confess softly, pressing my lips to his before reluctantly pulling back. "But they're expecting us. Let's go."

The club's already full. Holiday music plays through the speakers when Leo and I arrive.

"Glad you two could join us," Star says, hugging us both.

Astrid, who's talking with Shawn and Caleb, waves from

across the room. "Do you mind if I go say hello?" Leo asks, glancing at me for approval.

"You don't need my permission," I reply, giving him a reassuring smile.

"I won't be long," Leo assures before heading off to greet his friends.

As I watch Leo gracefully weave through the crowd, my heart swells with pride. A sense of admiration washes over me, seeing him interact effortlessly with everyone around him.

"When are you going to do something about that?" Star's voice cuts through my thoughts, drawing my attention.

"What do you mean?" I ask, raising an eyebrow in confusion.

"If you don't ask that boy to submit to you, someone else might beat you to it." I whip my head around to look at her. "Ah, that got your attention," Star says, her voice laced with amusement.

"Why would you say something like that?" I ask, feeling a pang of unease. It's not just the thought of someone else vying for his attention, though that certainly nags at me. It's the fear of losing him again, of him slipping away from me once more.

"Just look at him." She gestures discreetly. "He's not only stunning to look at, but his personality shines brighter than any star. Everyone in this room adores him—and I mean everyone," she emphasizes.

My muscles tense from a surge of jealousy. "Who was asking about him?"

"Not answering that."

"You can't dangle that in front of me and then not tell me who," I argue, casting a glance around the club, trying to spot any telltale signs.

"I can, and I did." She touches my arm, pulling me back into the conversation. "He's strong and ready to take the next step."

"I don't know," I reply, feeling a familiar sense of uncertainty.

"Excuse me, Mistress," Corbin says, interrupting us. "Master Owen sent me to get you. He needs your assistance."

"Thank you," she responds, dismissing him. "Think about what I said." With that, she turns and walks away.

Choosing to remain on the periphery, I take a moment to quietly observe Leopold. Star's words ring true—there's an undeniable strength exuding from him, and it's apparent he's garnered quite the following within the club. Surrounded by a supportive network of friends, he's thrived, shedding his inhibitions and embracing his true self.

"Tony?" A familiar voice calls my name. I turn my head and am shocked to see Trevor. "It's been a while," he says with a hint of nostalgia.

After our scene, we kept in touch for a while, but it seemed like overnight, he disappeared. "It has," I reply, trying to process his unexpected appearance.

"I apologize for losing touch," Trevor says, a hint of remorse in his voice. "Paisley and I were moving around a lot, and my phone went missing. I lost all my contacts, including yours, and I didn't have your last name to try to find you."

"No worries," I assure him, offering a forgiving smile. "Life happens."

"But I want you to understand," he insists earnestly. "You've been on my mind since that night."

"It's really okay. You don't owe me any explanations," I insist.

"Paisley and I are living in Manhattan now."

"Permanently?" I ask, surprised by his revelation.

"Yes," Trevor confirms, nodding. "The company I work for offered me a management position. It meant no more traveling. With Paisley being old enough to enroll in school, it was time to settle down, so I took it."

"That sounds like a wonderful opportunity," I reply, offering him a warm smile.

"They gave me the choice of three locations, and I chose New York City," he confesses.

"It's a fantastic place for families," I remark, reflecting on my upbringing in the city.

"It is, but there's more," Trevor adds, his hand resting on my bicep. "You were a factor in my decision."

"Me?" I ask, taken aback by his admission.

"Before we lost touch, I felt like we were building on the connection we had that night," Trevor explains, his eyes searching mine for a reaction.

My mind drifts back. The atmosphere between us was undeniably charged with sensuality, catching me off guard with its intensity. Trevor and I kept in touch for quite a while, but my feelings toward him had always remained platonic. When we first crossed paths, it was too soon after I lost Kam, and I wasn't ready for anything beyond friendship. I didn't realize Trevor was experiencing something entirely different.

I don't want to cause him any pain, but my heart belongs to someone across the room—to Leopold, the man I'm in love with.

Leopold

Fire and Ice is so much more than just a BDSM club. It's a community of individuals from all walks of life who've come together not only to indulge in sensual delights but also to support each other. Within these walls, I've found my tribe. The people who accept me just as I am—faults and all. It's what I've been longing for my whole life. Finally, at almost twenty-three years old, I'm healthy and whole in a way I never imagined.

While conversation continues around me, I take a moment to center myself. I've known for some time now that I was ready. Not wanting to force anything, I didn't plan how or when to do it. But as I was getting dressed earlier, I knew this was it. If all goes well, tonight will mark a significant milestone in my relationship with Tony. Despite the butterflies in my stomach, everything feels perfectly aligned. It's time.

"If you guys will excuse me, there's something I have to do," I state, excitement beginning to build.

"Does it have anything to do with your handsome man?" Astrid teases.

"Possibly," I tease back, unable to hide my grin.

"When are you and Tony going to stop dancing around each other and finally become a couple?" Shawn asks.

"Hopefully tonight," I reply, my gaze darting around the room until I find Tony in the corner, engaged in conversation with a stranger. Our eyes meet briefly, sending a jolt of electricity through me before he returns to his discussion.

"Good luck," Shawn says. "We're all rooting for you."

My gaze remains fixed on Tony and the handsome stranger, whose hand rests casually on Tony's arm. They seem comfortable with each other, a familiarity that sends a pang of jealousy and hurt simmering just beneath the surface. "Who's that?" I finally manage to voice my question, unable to mask the hint of concern.

The trio exchanges worried glances before Caleb answers cautiously, "That's Trevor."

"Trevor?" I repeat, glancing back at them over my shoulder. "Is he another Dominant?" I ask, puzzled by the lack of mention of Trevor in my conversations with Tony, yet they clearly share a connection.

"He's a submissive. Trevor and Tony have a history together," Astrid says casually. "Trevor has a *thing* for Tony."

"Oh," I reply quietly, processing the new information.

"Really, Astrid?" Caleb shoots her an annoyed look before turning to me. "It was a long time ago," Caleb assures me, though his attempt to help falls somewhat flat in the face of my growing discomfort. "I'm sure it's nothing," he adds.

"Yeah. I'm sure you're right. I have to go," I say quietly, my voice fading as I move away.

Watching Trevor lean into Tony twists my emotions painfully. My heart begins to fracture as I hurry toward the heavy wood doors that mark the exit to the club.

"Is everything okay, Leo?" Corbin, who's sitting at the desk, asks.

"I'm not feeling well," I reply, not bothering to stop as I push open the doors and step outside into the biting cold of the winter air.

Anthony

"THIS IS SOMETHING I'VE THOUGHT ABOUT, HECK dreamed about for so long now. Wow. I can't believe I'm finally doing this," Trevor admits, his words rushing out in a jumble. "I know you weren't ready for anything more when we first met, but I'm hoping that maybe now... you might consider exploring what's between us."

"Trevor," I say softly, trying to process his sudden confession.

"I probably just broke all kinds of protocol," he continues, his hand anxiously reaching for the back of his neck. "I really screwed this up."

"It's okay, really," I reassure him, trying to ease his nerves. "You're a great guy—"

"I read things between us wrong, didn't I?" he interrupts.

"The scene we did together was an important night for me. One I'll always remember. It was the first time I scened with anyone after losing my partner," I explain. "I enjoyed getting to know you after, but as a friend."

"Oh no," Trevor murmurs softly, his expression falling. "I must look like a complete idiot."

"Not at all," I try to reassure him, hoping to ease the weight of his embarrassment.

"I asked around and was told you were still single. A part of me hoped that you were as affected as I was that night and that you were waiting for me to come back," he confesses, shaking his head in disbelief. "Now that I say that out loud, it sounds ridiculous."

"I don't think it's ridiculous," I offer, feeling compelled to provide an explanation. "I met someone a year ago. It was complicated for a long time, but we're finally ready to make a more serious commitment." Trevor's disappointment is palpable. ""You're a great guy, Trevor. Any Dominant here would be lucky to earn your submission," I add, hoping to comfort him.

"Whoever he is... He's a very lucky man," Trevor says sadly before walking away.

I feel guilty for hurting him, but I genuinely didn't realize he felt that way, especially after he stopped contacting me. I assumed he understood I wasn't interested in pursuing anything further and had moved on. Fortunately, there are plenty of experienced Dominants in the club who I'm sure will be more than interested in Trevor.

But right now, I have something else I need to do. I glance around, searching for Leo, but he's nowhere to be seen. I'm sure someone in the group will be able to point me in the right direction, though.

"Do you know which way Leopold went?" I inquire asking the group of his friends.

"I'm not sure," Shawn responds cautiously, uncertainty lacing his words. "He seemed a bit upset, and then he just left."

"What was he was upset about?" I probe further.

"He saw you talking with Trevor," Astrid adds.

"Sir Genovese," Corbin calls as he rushes across the room toward me.

"What is it?" I ask sensing the urgency in his voice.

"It's Leo," he says, catching his breath.

"What about Leopold?" I demand, a knot forming in my stomach.

"He left about a half hour ago," he confesses, and a wave of dread rushes over me.

"Left?" I repeat, my heart sinking.

"Yes, sir. He seemed in a hurry," Corbin explains, his voice filled with regret. "I didn't know. Didn't think to come get you."

"Did he say where he was going?" I press, trying to mask the panic rising within me.

"He just said he wasn't feeling well," Corbin replies, his expression apologetic.

"No. Oh God, please, no," I whisper frantically as I push the glass door open and rush outside. Memories of last year surge back with brutal force.

Snow falls softly around me as I sprint down the sidewalk toward the river park, my breaths coming in ragged gasps. This cannot happen. I will not lose him.

Leopold

SNOW GENTLY BLANKETS THE PARK BENCH WHERE I SIT, overlooking the Hudson River. I ran out so fast that I forgot my coat at the club, but even though I was shivering, I couldn't bring myself back for it.

Confusion clouds my thoughts as I replay the scene with Tony and Trevor in my mind. Our conversations about what I was learning with Star about the dynamics of dominance and submission had seemed to draw us closer, but seeing the way Trevor touched Tony shattered that illusion. Finding out they had a past together was more than I could bear.

Perhaps it's my own boundaries that are the problem. It's the only thing that makes any sense right now. I know Kameron enjoyed bondage. Maybe being free to restrain or blindfold his submissive are things Tony needs in a future dynamic.

Could I compromise on that? Change me to be what Tony needs? The thought twists my stomach with uncertainty because deep down, I know it's not possible. If this is what's going to stand between Tony and me being together, it hurts. It hurts so bad, but it's the painful truth I'll have to accept. Maybe in another life—

"Leopold," Tony's voice breaks through my thoughts as he hurries toward me. "What are you doing out here?"

"I needed some air," I reply, my voice barely audible.

"You're not even wearing a coat. You'll catch a cold," he scolds gently, worry etched on his face.

I don't feel the cold. Perhaps I'm too numb from the hurt and disappointment. "I'm okay. You should go back and enjoy the party," I insist, trying to push him away.

"Why did you leave?" Tony asks as he sits next to me.

This is the moment of truth where all the self-work I've done over the past year is put to the test. It would be so easy to revert to old habits—deflect and shut down. I know that path always leads to isolation. So, I choose to do something terrifying, hoping it will lead to a different result.

"I saw you talking with Trevor," I admit quietly, bracing myself for his reaction. "Astrid told me about you two."

"And what exactly did she tell you?" His tone is edged with frustration.

"That you have a history together," I confess, my voice barely above a whisper. "And that Trevor's interested in you."

"It's true, we have scened before—once," Tony acknowledges, his tone calm but resolute. "And yes, he expressed an interest in me. I made it clear to him that there could be nothing between us. What you saw was me respectfully declining his advances."

"Oh," I murmur, feeling a knot form in my stomach as I wring my hands in my lap.

"Do you really think I would betray you like that?" Tony's voice carries a hint of hurt.

I shrug, unable to meet his gaze. "We aren't anything official. You don't owe anything to me."

"I came looking for you to change that. Look at me, Leopold," Tony's voice holds a quiet intensity, urging me to meet his gaze. With a hesitant breath, I lift my eyes to his, seeing a depth of emotion I hadn't expected. "You've breathed life back into me.

Made me feel things I never thought I would again. It's been my own fear holding me back for too long."

Tony rises to his feet, his movements deliberate as he retrieves something from his pocket. With a solemn expression, he extends his hand, revealing an object that sends a shiver down my spine. "The boxcutter," I whisper, my voice barely audible. "Why?"

"It's been with me for the past year," Tony admits, his voice thick with emotion. "Initially, it was a precaution, a fear that you might stumble upon it and use it to hurt yourself. But over time, it became a symbol of the fragility of life. How close I came to losing you." His voice wavers with emotion. "Then they told me you rushed out," he continues, anguish washing over his features, "I feared the worst. I couldn't get here fast enough."

"I'm sorry," I murmur, my heart heavy with guilt. "Seeing him touch you, and then Astrid's words..."

"She crossed a line," Tony says firmly. "I'll address it with Owen."

"No, please don't—" I begin, but Tony holds up his hand.

"Astrid insinuated there was more to my history with Trevor than there ever was," he explains, his tone resolute. "She was wrong, and Owen will ensure she understands that in whatever way he sees fit."

I nod in understanding.

"This boxcutter has become a crutch for me," Tony continues, his voice softer now. "As long as it's in my pocket, a part of me remains tethered to that night—to the past. It's time for me to return it to you."

With gentle reverence, he passes the shielded blade to me. It's the first time I've seen it and held it in a year. My hand trembles as memories flood back, overwhelming me like a tidal wave. "I remember that night so vividly," I say, looking up at him. "The voices of my past were deafening, but now they're nothing more than a distant memory. This little object seemed to hold so much power over me, but it doesn't anymore. It's nothing because I'm strong."

"Yes, Leopold. You are incredibly strong," Tony affirms quietly.

I walk to the edge of the railing, watching the dark water below. With a steady hand, I release the boxcutter, watching it sink into the depths with a soft splash.

Silently, I turn to face Tony, who's still sitting on the bench, and drop to my knees. The gesture is one of both reverence and vulnerability. Tony's sharp inhale punctuates the quiet air as I place my open palms on my thighs, head bowed in submission. "The day I walked into *Italiano Desiderio* and looked into your eyes, all I saw was kindness," I confess, my words gentle but weighted with emotion.

"I fell for you then, though I never dared to hope that a man like you would ever notice me. Night after night, I dreamt of you, longing to understand what it would mean to be loved by you. Before you, I never truly understood what it meant to be cherished," I admit, my voice trembling with vulnerability.

"You took me in without knowing me, showering me with kindness and equipping me to become a better man—a stronger man," I express, my voice filled with gratitude and sincerity. "Each day, my love for you deepens." Lifting my head, I meet his gaze and know I've found my home. "Last year, in this very spot, you saved me. Now, I kneel before you, flawed but deeply in love. I offer you all that I am—my life and my heart. My submission."

In the heart of the bustling city, where chaos usually reigns, a profound silence descends. No honking horns, no blaring sirens —just the tranquil hush of a world blanketed in snow. It's a silence so complete it's almost tangible.

"Leopold," he breathes my name like a prayer. "I've never felt fear like I did last year when I found you here. The thought of losing you nearly destroyed me. Witnessing your healing and growth has been a profound privilege. "And now, seeing you kneel before me, offering yourself," his voice softens. "Your submission is a precious gift I cherish. I promise to honor and protect it as we navigate this lifestyle together."

"You're accepting?" I ask, a glimmer of hope in my voice.

"I never planned to let another moment pass without binding myself to you," he answers, leaning down to cup my face in his hand. "From now on, I'll be your guide, your mentor—your Dominant. I'll introduce you to pleasures beyond your wildest dreams."

Our lips crash together in a passionate embrace as Tony pulls me closer. I eagerly climb onto his lap, straddling him as our kiss deepens. His fingers tangle in my hair as we lose ourselves in the moment. A low moan escapes my lips as I grind against his erection.

Tony breaks the kiss, his breath coming in ragged gasps. "If we keep this up, we'll end up getting arrested for public indecency," he murmurs, a hint of amusement in his voice. "Do you want to head back to the party?" he asks.

"No." I shake my head slowly. "Will you take me home?" I ask as I crawl off him and then stop. "Wait, what should I call you?"

"How about we stick with Tony for now," he suggests, standing up. "We can figure the rest out later." He takes my hand. "Come on. We'll stop at the club to get your coat, and then we're going straight home."

As we step back into Fire and Ice, Tony leads me straight to the coat room. I'm sliding my arms into the sleeves when Owen appears.

"I've been looking for you everywhere," Owen says, looking between us. "Are you two leaving already?"

"We are," Tony replies firmly.

"It's early even for you," Owen observes, his smile fading. "Is everything alright?"

"It is," Tony reassures him, squeezing my hand.

Owen looks between us. "I wanted to ask you about—"

"Whatever it is will have to wait," Tony says, his grip firm on my hand. "We'll talk tomorrow."

"Goodnight," I call with a grin and give a final wave as I turn to leave. "Happy Christmas Eve Eve."

The subway ride back to our apartment feels agonizingly long. Tony's posture is tense, his silence unsettling. I'm starting to worry that he's having second thoughts, but I don't voice my concerns in public. When we're finally in the safety of the apartment, I finally speak up. "Is everything okay?"

"What do you mean?" Tony's response is guarded.

I crack my knuckles, trying to summon the courage to continue. "You seemed distant on the way home."

"If I didn't," Tony replies in a low, gravelly tone. "I wouldn't have been able to control myself. I've wanted you for so long, Leopold."

Hearing Tony say he wants me is a dream come true, but at the same time, I'm scared. "I don't know how to do this," I admit.

"Our situation is somewhat unique, considering our discussions about your limits for the past few months, even though we weren't officially vetting," he explains. "But if you prefer, we can take a step back and formally vet each other."

"You know everything about me, and I trust you to respect my limits. That's not what I mean," I admit, taking a deep breath. "It's... sex. I've never willingly experienced it before. I'm scared, and I don't know what to do..." I pause, feeling the weight of my fear pressing down on me.

"Thank you for telling me. I know it wasn't easy," Tony replies, his voice gentle as he presses a tender kiss to my lips. "We'll take things at your pace, and we can stop whenever you need to. Let's establish safewords now. Yellow means you're nearing your limit, and red means stop immediately. Your voice will always be heard in everything we do together."

Tears well up in my eyes as Tony's words wash over me. We'd discussed safewords extensively before tonight, and he understands my fear, my past trauma of having my voice silenced. Knowing that's one of his top priorities quiets my fears.

"Are you ready?" he asks softly.

For most of my life, I felt unworthy of love. A failure in every sense of the word. A hopeless screw-up. Last year, Tony found me at my lowest. He could've turned a blind eye and left me to fend for myself. Passed me off as someone else's problem. But he didn't.

Instead of abandoning me, Tony brought me home. He didn't just lend a helping hand. He empowered me with the means to chase my dreams, including ones I hadn't dared to envision. He celebrated my victories with me and held me close when I stumbled and fell. Through it all, Tony has demonstrated what it truly means to love someone unconditionally. Submitting to him feels like the most natural thing in the world.

Nerves still flutter in my belly, but I take comfort in his gentle reassurance. With Tony as my Dominant, I have faith that everything will be okay.

Leopold

THE ONLY TIMES I'VE BEEN IN TONY'S BEDROOM ARE when I put his clean laundry on the bed. But tonight, it's different. Tonight, I'm here with him—as a couple.

"You're trembling," Tony observes, taking my hands in his. "What's your color?"

"Can there be a color before we even start?" I inquire hesitantly.

"Yes, absolutely. Where are you at? Talk to me," he encourages.

"I'm nervous, but I think I'm green," I stammer, unsure of myself. "I don't know what to do. How to touch you," I admit. "Could you teach me how to please you?"

"There'll be plenty of time for that," Tony murmurs, his hand tender against my cheek. I lean into his touch, feeling a sense of comfort. "Tonight is about making this moment special for you." His lips meet mine.

The kiss is gentle, filled with a sense of wonder and excitement. We explore each other's mouths slowly, as if savoring every moment. When we finally pull away, I find myself breathless. "I can't believe this is happening."

"Believe it, Leo," Tony says with a reassuring smile, his eyes reflecting sincerity. "Tonight is real, and it's just the beginning." He runs his fingers through my hair, his touch calming my nerves. " This moment, this connection between us—it's the start of something beautiful," he says as he trails kisses down my neck.

My hand hesitates in mid-air, unsure whether to reach out or withdraw. Tony's slight step back makes me second-guess myself, fearing I've already crossed a boundary. "You're free to touch me," he reassures me, undoing the buttons of his shirt and letting it fall to the floor. " Just as much as you belong to me, I belong to you."

Taking a deep breath to steady my nerves, I run my trembling hands over his chest, marveling at the firmness of his muscles beneath my fingertips. Feeling the warmth of his skin beneath my touch. It's smooth and inviting, and I'm filled with a sudden desire to explore every inch of him. Leaning in, I press a soft kiss to his chest. A quiet moan escapes Tony's lips, and his fingers find their way into my hair, urging me on.

I continue to trail kisses down his torso, tracing the contours of his abs with tender reverence. As I near the waistband of his pants, my fingers instinctively move to undo the button, but Tony's hand stops me before I can proceed. "You don't have to," he whispers, his voice filled with understanding.

"You don't want me to—" I start to say, my fingers hovering over the button of his pants.

"Leopold," he says, his voice breathy. "It's not that I don't want you to. I can't wait to feel your mouth wrapped around my cock, but not tonight," he says with a pained groan. "But I want to make love to you tonight," he says, his gaze meeting mine.

His hands move to my shirt, his touch deliberate as he undoes each button. "We'll take it slow," he murmurs, his voice filled with reassurance. With each button released, he adds, "I'll ensure your body is ready to accept me," he promises, his voice low and intimate as he opens the last button. He slides my shirt off my arms and tosses it to the side.

With practiced ease, he undoes the button of my pants, his touch gentle yet purposeful. "You'll feel every inch of me as I enter you," he repeats softly, his fingers sliding down the zipper as he slowly lowers my pants. "But I won't hurt you." Stepping out of them, I kick them aside, feeling exposed yet liberated in his presence. His touch remains tender as he removes my boxer briefs, leaving me bare before him.

He steps back, studying every curve and contour of my body with a mixture of desire and reverence. At this moment, I realize this isn't just about physical intimacy—it's about trust, connection, and the promise of something deeper.

"You're beautiful," Tony murmurs, his words causing a warmth to spread across my cheeks. I glance away shyly, unable to meet his gaze.

"I hope I don't disappoint," he adds, his tone tinged with vulnerability as he removes his pants and boxers.

Despite the age gap between us, Tony's physique is nothing short of impressive. His dedication to his fitness routine is evident in the way his body is toned and muscular, with a well-defined six-pack drawing my eyes lower to his cock that hangs long and thick.

"You could never," I breathe, my voice barely above a whisper as I take him in. This is the first time I've seen him completely undressed, and I can't help but feel a rush of desire at the sight of him. He's more than perfect—he's everything I've ever wanted.

"Lie down," he says and then opens one of his drawers, taking out lube that he tosses next to me.

Tony climbs onto the bed, straddling my legs. Leaning down, he kisses me tenderly, his tongue exploring my mouth. I reach up and caress his back, noting the muscles contracting in response to my gentle pressure. Pulling him to me, his erection presses against my stomach, and I moan into his mouth.

Breaking the kiss, Tony explores my body with his lips, leaving a trail of kisses along my chest. He gently takes one of my nipples into his mouth, sending waves of pleasure coursing through me. My anticipation grows as Tony moves to the other nipple, grazing it with his teeth and causing me to gasp in delight. "Do you like that?" he asks, his voice husky with desire. "Yes," I reply breathlessly.

A pleased smile graces his lips as he moves lower, leaving a trail of kisses in his wake. "You are going to look amazing with my wax covering you."

Every touch sends a jolt of sensation through me, and I can't help but wiggle slightly as his tongue dances over my navel. When he reaches my thighs, a sense of anticipation fills the air. "Are you ready?" he asks, his gaze fixed on mine.

I've never had a man touch me there. Never had anyone offered me pleasure that didn't come from coercion. Consensual wasn't a part of the narrative—until now. I nod, my voice caught in my throat. I'm aching for Tony to touch me again.

I feel his warm breath on me as his tongue caresses my slit, teasing the head until he slowly takes my length into his mouth. He licks the underside from root to tip before he takes me deeper into his mouth. My back arches off the bed. "Fuck, that feels so good," I moan.

He pulls off and looks at me, "I'm glad you like it." Then he moves his attention to my balls, licking and sucking them before sitting back on his heels.

Lifting my head, I watch him open the lube and squirt some onto his fingers. "What's your color?"

Pausing briefly, I assess my current emotional state. I've never felt pleasure like what Tony's giving me, but at the same time, knowing he's about to touch me triggers a wave of fear through my body. Gritting my teeth and squeezing my eyes shut, I attempt to force the memories of searing pain from unwanted invasions from my mind.

"Leopold, look at me," Tony's voice is firm. I blink, meeting his gaze, and I find nothing but love and concern. "Stay with me," he implores softly. I nod in response. "What's your color?"

"Yellow," I whisper, my voice barely audible. "I want you to keep going even though I'm scared."

"Remember to stay calm and breathe. I'm right here with

you," Tony says soothingly as his finger presses against my entrance. The sensation is overwhelming, but his steady presence grounds me. "You're doing so good, *cuore mio.*" When he's fully inside, he stills and asks, "Color?"

"Green," I say quietly.

"Good boy." Tony's voice carries a note of approval, sending a shiver of excitement through me. "I'm going to start moving."

As his finger moves in and out of me, it banishes the memories of pain and replaces them with pure, unadulterated pleasure. Pre-cum beads at the tip of my cock. With his spare hand, Tony traces a finger along my slit, then brings it to his lips. "You taste divine."

"I'm going to add another finger," Tony says, his touch deliberate and controlled. I feel the pressure as a second finger joins the first, stretching me in a way that's pleasurable but not painful. Once fully inserted, he pauses, allowing me to accommodate the sensation before adding a third.

Then, he begins to move, starting off with slow, deliberate motions as he leans down to tease the tip of my cock with his tongue. Tony gradually increases the rhythm, finger fucking me while he works my body, taking me deeper, sucking harder, and using his tongue with skill.

"Tony," I whimper, my voice barely audible amidst the heat of the moment.

Tony withdraws his fingers, shifting up the bed to kiss me tenderly. His erection presses insistently against my stomach as I taste my essence on his lips. Maintaining our connection, he rolls onto his back, drawing me on top of him.

I press against his chest and sit up, taking his throbbing cock in my trembling hand and stroking it slowly. Leaning down, I lick the tip, swirling my tongue around the head before taking him eagerly into my mouth. He groans appreciatively as I suck, guiding him deeper.

Tony's hand weaves through my hair, but he doesn't force my movements. Meeting his gaze, the satisfaction on his face bolsters my confidence. Shifting my focus, I massage his balls with my free hand, intensifying his pleasure as I continue to suck him.

"Leopold," he whispers, tilting my head back tenderly. "I need to be inside you."

"I don't know what to do," I confess, feeling uncertain.

"Take the lube and rub it on me," he instructs. Squeezing a generous amount onto my palm, I coat his rigid length with the slick substance, my movements hesitant. "Remember, you're the one in control," Tony reassures me.

With his arousal in my grasp, I align it with my entrance. Tony places his hands on my hips, supporting me as I slowly descend onto him. Despite his preparation, the initial penetration burns, and I inhale sharply in discomfort.

"Don't force it," he advises, his touch steadying me.

I take a deep breath, steeling myself for the sensation as I lower myself onto him. The pain is sharp, but I push through it, determined to feel him inside me.

"That's it," he murmurs, his voice laced with encouragement. "Take your time." I proceed cautiously, feeling every inch of him stretching me.

"Fuck, you're so tight," he groans, his words sending a thrill through me.

I pause, allowing my body to adjust to the intrusion. Gradually, the pain gives way to a pleasurable sense of fullness. I begin to move, rocking my hips back and forth, savoring the sensations of every vein and ridge of him rubbing against me. It's a feeling of intense pleasure I've never known.

Leaning forward, I capture his lips in a passionate kiss, our bodies melding together in perfect harmony. Pleasure builds with each thrust, and I feel myself nearing the edge.

Tony senses it, too. "Sit up. I want you to come with me," he urges, his voice hoarse with desire. I comply, resting my hands on his muscular thighs as his hands begin to roam my body.

He reaches up, teasing my nipples before pinching them

gently, sending jolts of electricity through my body. I ride him harder, craving deeper penetration with each thrust.

"Yes, just like that," he encourages, stroking me in time with my movements. Gripping me firmly, he thrusts up into me, his movements becoming more urgent. "You've never looked more beautiful—more powerful than you do right now. Come for me," he commands, and I obey, surrendering to the pleasure as I reach the peak of ecstasy.

As I convulse around him, Tony finds his own release. "Leopold," he whispers my name as he fills me with his cum. My body trembles as another wave of pleasure crashes over me.

He pulls me close, his cock still buried inside me, whispering words of love and reassurance as we bask in the afterglow. "You're perfect, Leopold," he murmurs.

Tears stream down my cheeks, overwhelmed by the intensity of our connection. "I've never felt like this before," I confess. "I love you, Tony."

His touch soothes me as he kisses away my tears. "I love you too, Leopold."

Anthony

I'VE BEEN FORTUNATE THAT MY PAST SEXUAL encounters have always been positive experiences. But the connection Leopold and I shared tonight transcended everything. It was as though our bodies had been waiting for this moment, and our souls found their missing piece.

Leo lays in my arms, his shoulder shaking as he sobs, hopefully purging himself of everything negative from his past. Never again will sex be used as a weapon to hurt him. I brush the hair off his face, whispering words of love and reassurance, promising him a future free from fear. "You're safe." I kiss his forehead.

As he drifts into a peaceful sleep, his breathing steadies against my chest. In the still of the night, I vow to be his rock, his constant companion in a world that once felt so lonely.

***

Leo's lips brush against mine. "Happy Christmas Eve," he says between kisses.

I blink awake, relief flooding me as I realize last night wasn't just a figment of my imagination. "Happy Christmas Eve," I reply, meeting his gaze.

His innocent blue eyes, so full of wonder, search mine. "What's on the agenda for today?" he asks, his voice filled with anticipation.

Tracing circles on his bare chest, I murmur, "As much as I'd love to stay in bed with you all day, we've got a houseful of guests coming tomorrow. That means food prep today."

Leo groans dramatically. "Can't we just skip the whole Christmas thing?"

I laugh, sitting up and pulling him with me. "Nice try, but no. We've got work to do."

His playful expression shifts, a hint of sincerity in his eyes. "Yes, Master," he says, the words slipping out without thought.

I pause, a pang of concern flickering through me. "You don't have to call me that."

He meets my gaze, his expression serious. "I know. But that's why I want to. If you're okay with it."

I nod slowly, needing to understand his reasoning. "Can you explain why 'Master' and not 'Sir' or something else?"

"I understand your concern, given everything with Krew." I nod in acknowledgment. "But to me, that title holds no power when it's forced. With you, it's a choice—a symbol of my trust and love. You are the Master of my heart and soul."

His vulnerability touches me deeply, leaving me in awe of the man beside me. "You never cease to inspire me," I confess, my voice filled with reverence.

"Why?" he asks, genuinely confused.

Taking his hand in mine, I speak from the depths of my heart. "You've been to hell and back, yet you're willingly offering me everything." Pressing a gentle kiss to his forehead, I vow, "I treasure you and will spend every moment proving that to you."

Leo's response is a soft affirmation. "There's nothing left for you to prove. I already know."

With a loving kiss, we solidify our commitment to each other.

"Let's go shower," I suggest, a smile gracing my lips.

Leo trails behind me as we enter the bathroom. While I busy myself gathering towels, he takes charge of adjusting the water to just the right temperature. With everything ready, we step into the spacious walk-in shower together. My body ignites as our tongues explore each other in a passionate kiss.

Leopold's movements catch me off guard as he pulls back and drops to his knees, his lips parting to envelop me. As he takes me into his mouth, his gaze meets mine through the mist of water droplets, intensifying the sensation. Watching him with his lips wrapped around my dick is incredibly erotic, sending shivers of pleasure down my spine. I'm so aroused it's almost painful. I feel every movement as he swallows, his throat working to accommodate more of me.

His technique is exquisite, alternating between sucking and lightly grazing his teeth along my shaft. With a firm grasp at the base of my cock, he licks the bead of pre-cum from the tip, sending a jolt of pleasure through me. "God, you feel incredible," I groan, my voice strained with lust. "Touch yourself. I want to watch you pleasure yourself while you suck me."

With one hand steadying himself on my leg, Leo's other hand finds its way to his own arousal. He strokes himself in time with the movements of his mouth, each stroke pushing us both closer to the edge of pleasure.

"Leo, damn, this is incredible." My fingers tangle in his hair as I thrust into his mouth, gauging his limits. He nods eagerly, and I guide him deeper until I'm hitting the back of his throat. He relaxes, surrendering control to me as I dictate the pace. His hand moves faster around his own cock. His eyes never leave mine, adding to the intensity of the moment.

"I'm close," I warn, feeling the familiar tightness in my groin. "If you want me to stop, raise your hand." His grip on my thigh tightens, a clear signal to continue. As my thrusts grow more urgent, my release approaches with unstoppable force. He moans around my cock, and I reach the peak of ecstasy, my body trembling as I release into his waiting mouth. He swallows eagerly, his hand working furiously on his own arousal until he's coming at my feet.

As the last waves of his orgasm subside, Leo leans back, breathless. "Holy shit," he gasps.

After helping him to his feet, I kiss him deeply, tasting myself on his tongue. "That was—amazing."

"One by one, you're erasing every bad memory," he whispers, his eyes filled with gratitude. "Soon, you'll be all I know."

"That's my goal," I reply, my voice thick with emotion.

Turning him around, I reach for the shower gel, eager to care for him as tenderly as he has for me. After washing each other clean, we wrap towels around ourselves and return to the bedroom to get dressed.

"We should move your clothes in here," I suggest.

Leo's eyes widen in surprise. "You want me to share your room?"

I smile, the warmth of his presence filling me with joy. "I want us to share everything, including this space. I want you in my arms every night as we sleep."

"If this is a dream, I don't ever want to wake up," Leo murmurs.

But this isn't a dream—it's the beginning of something far greater. It's the start of forever.

***

It's as if Leopold and I have completed a journey back to where it all began. Last Christmas, I clung to the fragile promise he made not to harm himself for thirty days—my opportunity to show him his value. Terrified doesn't begin to capture the depth of my emotions. Leopold's life rested in my hands, and I was grossly underqualified for that responsibility.

Watching him tonight, you'd never believe he's the same man whose life hung in the balance just last year. He's radiant, effortlessly working the room, engaging in lively conversation with our Fire and Ice friends. I can't take my eyes off him.

"It's about time," Owen says, a grin spreading across his face.

"What are you talking about?" I ask, pretending I don't know what he's referring to.

"You and Leo." He nods toward Leo across the room. "You two have been dancing around each other since the first day he walked into the club making his delivery."

"He wasn't ready to commit to anything, then. It would've been irresponsible," I explain.

"Maybe not," Owen muses.

"We're together now. That's all that matters."

Leo joins us, looking curious. "What's going on?"

"Just discussing you," I reply with a smile.

Leo looks concerned. "I hope it's nothing bad."

"All good things," Owen reassures him. "I was just telling Tony that it's about time the two of you made things official."

Leopold's face lights up. "I've never been happier."

"I can't wait to see you two scene at the club. It's been too long since we've gotten to experience one of your wax masterpieces," Owen adds.

"It's going to be a while before we do that," I interject.

Leo speaks up, his gaze determined. "I've been thinking. I'd like our first scene to be at the club."

"Are you sure?" I ask, surprised. "I don't want it to be too much for you."

Leo nods, his gaze steady. "I've thought about it. It might be tough, but it'll also mark my progress—that I'm no longer controlled by fear."

Once again, this man has rendered me speechless. The things that were done to him would make most of us cower in fear, yet Leopold is suggesting our first scene as a Dominant and submissive be done at Fire and Ice. What have I done to deserve the trust and love of this man?

"Unless you don't think it's a good idea?" he asks, his eyes searching mine for validation.

"If you feel it will be a positive experience and will continue your healing, then I support it," I reassure him.

"Thank you, Master," Leopold says quietly.

For the rest of the evening, my attention is only half on the conversations around me. The rest is focused entirely on Leopold. Images of him, naked and covered with my wax, dance through my mind. The urge to dismiss our guests so I can fuck him senseless grows with each passing moment.

Leopold

As I chat with Shawn and Caleb, I feel the weight of Tony's stare on me from across the room. His gaze is a palpable force, undressing me with an intensity that leaves me breathless. Despite my attempts to maintain composure, a smile tugs at the corners of my lips, unable to resist the magnetic pull of his attention.

The hours stretch on before the party slowly winds down, each moment feeling like an eternity as we bid farewell to the last of our guests.

As I'm finishing loading the dishwasher, I feel Tony's presence behind me before his lips make contact with my neck, igniting a wave of desire that courses through my body. "I want you to fuck me," he whispers, his voice deep with longing.

"What?" I spin around, shocked, and ask, "Why?"

"I've had the exquisite pleasure of being inside you," Tony murmurs, his breath hot against my ear. "Tonight, I want to feel you inside me."

"I'm not sure I can do that," I confess, my heart racing with uncertainty. "I've never done that before."

"I know," Tony reassures me, pressing a gentle kiss to my lips. "I'll guide you through it."

I've never experienced the sensation of being inside another man, of being the one to bring pleasure in that way.

"If you're uncomfortable, we don't have to," he offers.

"I want to," I reply, the intensity of my desire matching him. "I want us to explore everything together."

Taking my hand, Tony leads me to our bedroom.

"Undress me," he commands, firm yet tender.

"Yes, Master," I respond, eager to fulfill his wishes.

His intense gaze never wavers as I slowly peel off his deep red shirt, revealing the chiseled contours of his chest. My fingertips dance over the taut muscles before I discard it, captivated by the sight before me. Leaning in, I capture his lips as my hands move to the button of his pants. As I push them down, his thick cock springs free.

Tracing a path of kisses down his torso, I revel in the taste of his skin, each caress igniting a spark of desire. Finally reaching his throbbing erection, I take it in my hand, relishing the sensation of his arousal against my skin. Meeting his gaze, I find a hunger burning in his eyes as I take him into my mouth, eliciting a low growl of pleasure.

Tony's hands find their way to my hair, guiding me with gentle pressure as I continue to pleasure him. "Fuck, your mouth feels so good," he says, his voice deep. "You have to stop, or I won't last." His eyes are full of desire as I stand up and remove my clothes. "Lie down," he says softly.

I comply eagerly, my heart racing as Tony crawls on top of me, his body over mine. Pressing his lips to mine, we grind against each other, igniting a firestorm of desire. I lose myself in the intoxicating rhythm of our passion, surrendering to the ecstasy of our shared intimacy.

Without breaking the kiss, Tony rolls us over so I'm poised on top. He reaches into the nightstand drawer, retrieves the lube, and hands it to me with a silent understanding.

"Do you need me to prepare you like you did for me?" I ask, my voice laced with uncertainty.

"Yes," he replies, his tone leaving no room for doubt.

With trembling hands, I apply the slick gel to my fingers before slowly inserting them into his waiting entrance. Tony's soft moans of pleasure urge me on, my own excitement mounting with each movement until I can barely contain myself.

"I want you inside me, now," Tony whispers, his legs parting to welcome me in.

"Fuck," I whisper, taking in the sight of him spread and waiting for me.

I position myself at his entrance, gently pushing inside as I watch his reaction, his eyes fluttering closed in rapture. Tenderly brushing his cheek, I ask, "Are you okay?"

"Yes," he breathes, his voice filled with need. "Feels so good."

With a slow, deliberate motion, I push further, feeling his muscles stretch to accommodate me as I sink all the way in, and a wave of pleasure washes over me. "I've never felt anything... Oh my God," I murmur, my voice breathy. After taking a second to compose myself, I begin to move, the rhythm slow and deliberate.

I reach out to touch him, but he stops me, his voice filled with determination. "No, this is for you. Only you," he insists.

I nod, my desire fueling each thrust as I continue to penetrate him deeply. "You feel incredible." My voice is hoarse from desire. Despite the building pressure of my impending release, I'm determined to make this moment last.

"Fuck me harder, Leopold," Tony demands, his voice laced with a hunger that mirrors my own.

"Yes, Master," I respond eagerly, seizing his hips and increasing the intensity of my movements. "I'm so close," I admit, the tension coiling tightly within me.

"Come inside me," he urges, and I do, releasing myself completely as my climax crashes over me in waves.

Collapsing against him, I struggle to catch my breath as he strokes my back soothingly, grounding me in the aftermath of our passion. "That was incredible," I say, my voice filled with awe.

He smiles, his eyes alight with satisfaction. "Now, it's your turn to please me," he says, his voice a promise of what's to come. "Get on your knees and look back at me."

I watch, transfixed, as he retrieves my cum from between his legs, using it to slick his own cock before positioning himself behind me. With a sharp intake of breath, I feel him enter me, his size stretching me in the most delicious way.

He grabs my hips and starts to move. "You're so big, Master. I feel you everywhere," I moan, the sensation overwhelming yet exhilarating. I'm already growing hard again.

"Fuck your hand while I fuck your ass," he commands, his words sending a thrill through me.

Following his directive, I reach between my legs, stroking myself eagerly.

"Your ass belongs to me," Tony growls, his thrusts growing more urgent with each passing moment.

"Only you, Master," I gasp, my hand moving faster as I feel my climax approaching.

"I'm almost there," he grunts, his movements becoming more frenzied. "Now, Leopold, come with me."

With a final, desperate thrust, he plunges into me, his release flooding me as my own orgasm consumes me, painting the bed in ribbons of cum.

As we collapse together, spent and sated, he whispers, "I love you so much, *cuore mio*."

"I love you, too, Master."

Leopold

DECEMBER 31

Tony was surprised, to say the least, when I suggested I'd like our first scene to be public. Of course, we discussed it at great length after we had the most mind-blowing sex of my life. When Tony asked me to fuck him, I was completely thrown off. In my head, I thought a Dominant always did the penetrating. Looking at that now, I realize how naïve and foolish that assumption was. Regardless of who was physically on top, Tony was every bit in charge.

Being given the privilege to be inside of him is something I'll never forget or take for granted.

It's been over a year since I was at my lowest point imaginable. At times, I still struggle when I look back and realize how desperate I was for the pain to stop and the awful voices in my head to be silenced. That night, as I stood alone in the park, I felt so alone and unworthy. I honestly believed I had no business being alive.

Tony will never know how grateful I am that he happened to walk that way. I genuinely believe something greater was at play that night. Since then, he's not only given me the tools to succeed, but he's also shown me love like I've never experienced.

He knew I wanted to get a tattoo, so for Christmas, one of his presents was a gift certificate to Infinite Ink. I now have two mean-

ingful pieces of art on my body. The first is a semi-colon that's over the scar on my wrist.

Although it seems plain in design, it's a statement that's become widely recognized for its deep meaning. The semi-colon symbolizes the continuation of a story. It's a reminder that I've overcome hardship, abuse, and severe depression, and even though I attempted suicide, I didn't succeed. Instead of trying again, I made a choice to keep living. To say that my life matters and my story isn't over.

The second design I got was a surprise for Tony. When he saw it, he was moved to tears. On my chest, above my heart, is a scene of a tumultuous sea, the ink deep indigo. Waves crash with unrestrained fury. Amid the chaos, an anchor emerges—a symbol of strength and stability. The anchor, intricately detailed with weathered textures and rugged contours, has the name 'Tony' subtly etched in it. It's a reminder that even in the darkest of storms, there's always hope.

For the rest of the week, Tony and I spent countless hours planning every detail of our scene for tonight. I know he's still worried that it'll be too much for me and I can't say that I'm not nervous, but I'm also very much looking forward to it.

My history is filled with being forced to be naked in front of people who wished to use me. To make me feel less than human—a toy for their sick pleasure. Everything we're going to do has been discussed and agreed upon. The only thing I don't know and asked Tony not to tell me are the specifics of the design he'll make on my body.

Tonight is my choice. Tonight, I will reclaim everything that was taken from me.

Leopold

Fire and Ice is busier than I've ever seen it. The energy in here is electric. It's a fitting backdrop for what promises to be a night of empowerment and liberation. Trying to avoid the gnawing anxiety clawing at my insides, I focus on my task at hand, arranging his candles on the table like I practiced all week.

"Are you holding up okay," Tony asks, his voice familiar and reassuring as he approaches from behind.

I lean back into his chest, and he wraps his arms around me. "I'm scared out of my mind."

"We don't have to do this," he reminds me, concern evident in his voice. "It's not too late. We can put this all away and do it at home."

"Is that what you'd prefer?" I ask.

"No matter the setting, you are the only thing that matters to me," Tony replies, his voice deep and velvety. "But if doing our first scene at Fire and Ice is important to you, then our journey begins here. The decision lies with you, *cuore mio*."

The temptation to call it off and retreat to the safety of our apartment is there, but I refuse to take it. "No, I want—need to do this here," I say, looking out at the crowd. "This is about reclaiming my body and sexuality—my power. Showing the world that I refuse to be a victim defined by my past."

Tony's expression softens, a mixture of pride and tenderness in his eyes. "What did I ever do to deserve you," he murmurs, his fingers tracing patterns against my skin.

"You saved me," I whisper back.

Dressed in a black one-piece accentuating her voluptuous curves, Star's heels click as she steps to center stage, and a hush falls over the crowd. The nerves I felt earlier calmed and gave way to a serene calm. Nothing has ever felt more right to me.

After the PTSD episode that shattered the fragile semblance of control I was clinging to and sent me spiraling out of control. I found myself at a crossroads. I could continue on as I was, barely hanging on and hurting those around me, or I could allow myself to be vulnerable and honest in my therapy sessions.

With Tony by my side, I bared my soul and recounted every harrowing detail of the abuse inflicted on me by David and Krew. It was the scariest thing I've ever had to do. I feared Tony would turn his back and walk away when he learned of all the depraved things that were done to me. How could a man as good as him love someone as dirty as me?

The most difficult lesson I had to embrace was to stop judging myself and accept my worth as a person is not defined by the abuse I lived through. I am more than the sum of my traumas. I'm a whole and worthy individual—a proud gay man deserving of love and happiness. Accepting those truths was more challenging than it sounds. It was a revelation that eluded me for far too long, buried beneath layers of guilt and shame. But tonight, as I step out onto the stage alongside my Master, I embrace my truth with unwavering conviction.

"Ladies and gentlemen," Star addresses the audience, her voice carrying across the room with a commanding presence. "Tonight, we have a very special presentation for you. Anthony and Leopold have finally entered into a Dom/sub relationship." Star glances our way with a knowing smile as the room erupts in cheers.

When they quiet, Star continues, "They've chosen to mark the occasion by allowing us to witness their first scene together," she says, followed by more applause. "Many of you are long-standing members of Fire and Ice and know the amazing work Tony does with wax. For those of you who are newer, you're in for a special treat. I'm as excited as all of you, so I'm going to make my exit and allow these two men to take the stage."

Star stops in front of me and takes my hand in hers. "I'm so very proud of you," she says, her voice tinged with emotion. "The strength you're demonstrating tonight is something I don't ever want you to forget."

"Thank you, Mistress," I respond respectfully.

"And you," she says, turning to Tony, her eyes brimming with tears. "I'm so happy that you've found love once again. No one deserves happiness more than you—both of you," she adds, casting a warm glance between us.

Tony leans in to embrace her, his lips brushing against her cheek as he whispers something I can't quite catch in her ear. With a nod of gratitude, she gracefully exits the stage.

The lights dim, and sensual music begins to play.

Tony turns to me. "Take off your robe."

With his words, everything else fades away. This intimate moment is reserved for only Tony and me. Our eyes lock, and in that silent exchange, I feel a surge of connection that transcends words. My eyes are locked with his. Those deep brown eyes and the kindness they've always held when he looked at me. His deep brown eyes, always a source of comfort, now hold a newfound tenderness that fills me with warmth. It's a love born from mutual respect and unwavering support, a love that has carried us through the darkest of times.

"Yes, Master," I whisper as I open my robe, letting the silky fabric flutter to my feet.

"You're perfect," Tony says as his gaze travels down my body. "There's no one else I'd rather share this moment with."

"Are you ready?" he asks, his voice filled with anticipation.

"I've been waiting for this moment my whole life."

Anthony

Star stops in front of Leo and reaches for his hand. "I'm so very proud of you," she says, her voice steady yet laced with emotion. "The strength you're demonstrating tonight is something I don't ever want you to forget."

"Thank you, Mistress," he replies, bowing his head slightly.

Even though he's new to the lifestyle, submissive behaviors come naturally to him. His abusive past plays a role in that, something I remain vigilant about. I never want him to silence himself or allow his wants and needs to go unmet because of carryovers from his past trauma. Through his submission, I want him to find freedom.

"And you," she says, turning to me, tears shimmering in her eyes. "I'm so happy that you've found love once again. No one deserves happiness more than you—both of you," she adds, looking between us.

I lean in, placing a kiss on her cheek. "Your friendship was a lifeline for me when my life fell apart. I'll always be grateful for it," I whisper, my words meant only for her. "But what you've done for Leopold. You found him when he was lost and brought him back to me." My voice wavers with emotion. "Your unwavering support and role as a mentor in his life. I can never repay you, my friend."

Star brushes away a tear that escapes down her cheek as she exits the stage.

Motioning toward Owen, who waits at the back of the club, I signal for him to lower the lights and start my chosen playlist. Then, I turn to Leopold and command, "Take off your robe."

"Yes, Master," he whispers, allowing the robe to fall open, exposing his nude frame.

Stepping back, I fix my gaze upon the man standing before me. Leopold's captivating blue eyes shimmer with an undeniable intelligence, their depths hinting at the wisdom he carries within. Set against his fair complexion, they gleam like sapphires against porcelain. Each glance he casts exudes a quiet strength, a silent reminder of the challenges he's faced and conquered. Through the beauty and harshness of life, Leopold's emerged stronger than ever before.

Society often perceives submissive men as weak, but Leopold challenges that notion. Inside, he's a warrior who's battled demons that would break the spirit of most. Yet, in his demeanor, there's a tranquility that speaks to the inner peace he's found despite the storms he's weathered. It's a rare quality that draws others to him like moths to a flame, eager to bask in the warmth of his aura.

On the outside, his body is a masterpiece. Broad shoulders taper to a narrow waist, every sinew meticulously sculpted. The swell of his biceps and the tautness of his abdomen hint at hours dedicated to physical fitness. A tattoo adorns his chest, weaving the narrative of his triumph over adversity and the role he feels I played in it. It steals my breath when I look at it.

Despite the strength evident in his muscular frame, there's a softness in his mannerisms, a compassionate aura that defies conventional notions of masculinity. This contradiction adds depth to his character, portraying him as a man of both power and empathy. He's journeyed through the labyrinth of his own soul and emerged finally at ease with himself and the world around him.

"You're perfect," I say in amazement. "There's no one else I'd rather share this moment with."

Extending my hand, Leo willingly intertwines his fingers with mine as we walk to the bed that awaits him. With a gentle ease, he reclines onto the soft surface, his eyes fixed on me with a mixture of trust and anticipation. Leaning closer, I murmur words meant for him alone, our connection deepening in the quiet intimacy of our exchange. *"Sei la vita mia. Sei il mio cuore.* You are my life. You are my heart."

His sapphire eyes shimmer with unshed tears as our lips meld in a passionate kiss. I step back, breathless. "Are you ready?"

"I've been waiting for this moment my whole life."

This past week, I've spent every free minute sketching the design I intend to create on my canvas tonight. It's important that I capture not only Leopold's unbreakable spirit but also the significance of this moment.

Grabbing the bottle of body oil, I pour a generous amount into my palm. This step is crucial to ensure the wax lifts cleanly from Leo's skin once the design is complete. Taking my time, I massage the oil onto his body, starting at his shoulders and moving downward to cover his chest in a smooth, even layer.

"Your body was made to be worshipped," I murmur, my hands trailing down his abdomen to his waist. His eyelids flutter closed, his breath hitching as I follow the defined V leading to his erection. With a firm grip, I wrap my hand around his cock, eliciting a guttural groan. "Do you like that?" I ask.

"Very much, Master," he responds, his tone laden with longing.

"So do I," I say, feeling the urgent pulse of my own desire pressing against the constraint of my zipper.

I glide my hands over his well-defined thighs, causing a ripple of sensation to cascade through his body. Although doing this scene in public was Leopold's idea, a part of me remained concerned with how he'd cope once we were under the spotlight. However, seeing his responsiveness and hearing his moans of pleasure assures me that he relishes this exhibition as much as I do.

Once I'm sure his skin is fully coated, I briefly pause to cleanse my hands before turning my attention to the candles. Selecting several, I ignite their wicks, giving them a minute to burn.

With precision, I tilt the candle over Leopold's calf, watching the warm liquid pool against his fair skin, painting it a rich crimson. "Considering this is your first foray into my world," I note, a sense of anticipation coloring my words. "I'm eager to hear your initial thoughts."

"It's silky and warm," he responds.

As I guide the liquid higher, allowing it to trickle over his thighs and onto his groin, a sharp gasp escapes Leo's lips. "Is it too much?" I ask, mindful of our ongoing exploration of his boundaries.

"No, Master," he assures me. His gaze is filled with a profound devotion that nearly overwhelms me. "It feels different in each place—different in a good way."

"Let yourself surrender to the sensations," I encourage, my voice laced with seduction. "Imagine the wax as my touch, my lips caressing every inch of you."

Leo inhales deeply as he shuts his eyes, immersing himself in the scene. Silently, I blend shades of red, orange, and yellow, their fusion swirling into a raging fire that engulfs his lower body.

Across his chest, I carefully dribble streams of blue and purple, setting the stage for the centerpiece of the design—a phoenix, fierce and majestic, emerging triumphantly from the fiery inferno below. Every drop of liquid wax must be placed with precision as I coax the avian form into existence. Gradually, its contours begin to take shape.

This design is undoubtedly the most intricate I've ever

embarked upon. From the moment the concept ignited within me, I knew I had to bring it to fruition. It symbolizes my Leopold perfectly—he's the phoenix, rising unscathed from the ashes. The life he now possesses, forged amidst the hottest flames, is a testament to his unwavering resilience. Each day, he continues to astound me.

With a soft breath, I extinguish the candles, casting the stage into shadow. Stepping back, I take a moment to appreciate what I consider my greatest artistic achievement. Then, turning to face the audience, I extend an invitation. "For those interested, please join me on stage to appreciate my canvas up close."

Excited murmurs fill the room as club members eagerly approach to inspect Leopold and the intricate artwork gracing his skin.

"Your talent with wax knows no bounds," Owen remarks, his tone filled with awe. "But this surpasses anything you've done before. It's truly magnificent."

"Thank you," I reply, gratitude swelling at his heartfelt praise.

"I need to say something, and please understand, it's not meant to undermine your bond with Kameron," Owen says carefully. "But in all the years I've known you, I've never seen you as content and fulfilled as you are with Leo. There's a connection between you two that transcends anything I've seen. He completes you in a way Kam never could."

My love for Kameron will always endure. Even after his passing, a piece of my heart will forever belong to him. But the dynamic with Kameron was distinct from what I share with Leo. When I met Kam, he was already established in his career and accustomed to being the one in control.

Throughout our vetting process, Kameron and I navigated discussions surrounding the roles in our dynamic. It was challenging for him to accept nurturing from another. Kameron's submission will always hold a special place in my heart because I knew he didn't need me to care for him, but he allowed it nonetheless. It's different with Leo. He craves the nurturing I freely give.

"I genuinely believe Kameron guided Leo to me. The day he walked into my restaurant was the first time I felt alive since Kam's passing," I confess, my gaze unwavering from Leo, who lies peacefully on the bed. "He's everything to me, Owen. He's the forever I've been waiting for."

Leopold

FIVE YEARS LATER

While Star was mentoring me, I suggested that Fire and Ice should do classes for people looking to get involved in the lifestyle. Star liked the idea so much that she and Owen developed a curriculum for a six-week intro session and began offering them. Over the years, they've been an overwhelming success both with bringing new members into the club as well as providing general information and hopefully diminishing the stigma about the BDSM lifestyle.

Last year, Star approached me with a proposal of her own. She and Owen wanted to add a mentor portion to the classes. Starting in week four, they planned to pair the prospective Dominants and submissives with someone living the lifestyle. Star asked me to be one of the mentors. At the time, I was taking extra credits to finish my hospitality management degree and had to decline. Now that I've graduated, I have more free time and can get involved.

"Do you know who I'm going to be mentoring?" I ask Tony as I walk down the street.

"I do," he chuckles, the warmth in his voice palpable.

"Will you tell me?"

"No."

"Not even a little hint?"

His laughter rings through the phone. "I think we need to work on delayed gratification," he teases.

"You're cruel." I can't help but laugh in return.

"But you love me."

"Yes, I do," I reply tenderly.

"I have to go, *cuore mio.* It's a mad house here tonight."

The restaurant's popularity continues to soar, establishing it as one of the most sought-after venues in New York City.

"I'm about to walk in anyway. I love you, Master."

"And I love you."

I toss the phone into my bag and pull the door open.

"Good evening, Leo," Star greets me as I enter. "Are you all ready for tonight?"

"I could be more ready if you tell me who I'm going to mentor," I say, leaning against the counter.

"And ruin all the fun? No way."

I pout playfully. "You're as bad as Tony."

"And you love every second of it." She smiles. "You're going to be in room seven."

"Yes, Mistress."

"Leo," she calls after me. I pause and turn back. "The name of your mentee is in there."

I quickly return to her side, planting a kiss on her cheek. "Thank you, Mistress."

Room seven, the boudoir chamber, greets me with a vibrant red envelope resting on the bed's center. With anticipation coursing through me, I tear it open. "Natalie Clark," I read aloud. Why does that name sound familiar? Then, I have a flicker of recognition. She's Svetlana Solonik's roommate. I met her a few weeks ago at the club. She was with Alex Montgomery.

After evaluating the room's arrangement, I decide to make a slight adjustment. With purposeful movements, I reposition the chic, black armchairs to the room's center, flanking them with a delicate table. "Perfect," I remark. "Much cozier." I retrieve a notebook and pen from my bag and place them on the table before stowing the bag away. Now, all that remains is to await her arrival.

A short time later, the door opens, and Natalie hesitantly walks in. When she sees me, she squeals, "Leopold."

"The one and only," I say, pulling her in for a big hug. "I hope you're not upset you got paired with me."

"I'm thrilled to be with you." A smile lights up her face.

"Me too. Come on and sit down so we can get started." I say warmly, indicating the seating area I've prepared. Trying to be professional, I take the pen and notebook from the table and turn to Natalie. "The first thing we need to do is list any questions you have. That'll give us a starting point."

She bites her lip. "I can't think of anything off the top of my head."

I wasn't prepared for that, but I can still work with it. "That's okay." I set the items back down and opt for a more natural approach. "Tell me about yourself, and we'll go from there."

"There isn't much to tell," she says. "I'm originally from Northmeadow. It's a very small town in Missouri."

"How did you end up here?"

"Much to my parents' dismay, I came here for school," she remarks, her tone tinged with a hint of amusement. She then shifts her gaze to me. "Have you always lived here?"

I shake my head. "No. I'm originally from California."

She raises an eyebrow. "Wow. You're a long way from home. Do you miss it there?" she asks, genuine curiosity evident in her tone.

"I haven't thought about that in a long time. I used to consider California my home, but that seems like a lifetime ago," I muse, feeling a twinge of wistfulness. "Nope. There's nowhere else in the world I'd rather be than right here," I assure Natalie, offering her a warm smile. Natalie plays with her hands in her lap, a nervous habit I recognize immediately. "Do you have any siblings?" I ask, and her smile fades, making me instantly regret bringing up the topic.

"I had an older brother, Michael. He passed away a few years ago," she shares, her voice trembling slightly. "My parents didn't accept him when he came out as gay. He and his boyfriend took their lives within a few weeks of each other."

"Oh my God. I'm so sorry," I offer quietly, my heart aching for her. "I know a bit about that. My family didn't accept me either. They sent me to a conversion therapy center to try to cure me of my gay ways. Clearly, they failed," I add with a soft chuckle, which elicits a smile from Natalie.

"Do you have any brothers or sisters?" she asks.

"I have two younger sisters, but I haven't spoken to them in years," I confess, feeling a pang of regret and sadness. "I used to be close with London, my youngest sister. I miss her a lot."

"Are they still in California?"

"I really don't know," I admit with a shrug. "London would be twenty-four now, so she could be just about anywhere."

"She's the same age as me," Natalie remarks and then offers, "I can volunteer as a stand-in."

"I'd love that," I respond warmly. Despite our brief conversation, it feels like we've known each other for ages.

Natalie tells me more about her small town and her parents. They sound just as marvelous as my own. Every pun intended.

"So, what brings you to the BDSM lifestyle?" I probe.

"That's a bit of an embarrassing story," she admits, her cheeks flushing a vibrant shade of pink.

"Don't hold out on me. Spill it," I urge, a playful grin tugging at my lips.

"You already know that Svetlana and I are roommates," she states, her tone slightly resigned. I nod in understanding. "I was supposed to be home visiting my family and my now ex-boyfriend. That's a story for another time," she explains with a roll of her eyes. "Anyway, I cut my trip home very short, but I didn't tell Lana. Oh God, I can't believe I'm telling anyone about this," she groans.

"It was the middle of the night when I got home. I just wanted to crawl into bed and forget everything that happened. On the way to my room, I heard something. Lana was begging for help. I thought she was being attacked," she recounts, her eyes meeting mine. "So, I called 911 and then went to stop whatever was happening."

I pull my feet up under me and settle in, eager to hear the rest of her story.

"I threw open her door and flipped the light on while I yelled at the person to stop. I figured I'd startle whoever it was, and boy, was I right," she admits, shaking her head in disbelief. "Except Lana wasn't being attacked. Brandon was there, and they were doing what I've since learned is a consensual/non-consensual scene."

"Are you making this up?" I inquire, my eyebrows raised in disbelief.

"I wish," Natalie replies with a resigned sigh.

"Wait. You said you called 911. Did the police show up?" I ask, leaning forward in anticipation. Natalie nods slowly. "I wish I could've been a fly on the wall. What happened next?"

"The cops had Brandon at gunpoint while Svetlana did her best to explain that it was all a horrible misunderstanding," Natalie recounts, her voice tinged with disbelief. "It took some doing, but she finally convinced them of Brandon's innocence. After he left, she told me about BDSM and her involvement in it."

"And you wanted to know more?" I ask, my interest growing with each revelation.

"Not exactly. It took months before I brought it up to her again," Natalie admits. "Lana asked me to come to the club to see her first scene with Brandon. I agreed, not knowing that she and Brandon had gone behind my back to set me up."

"This story keeps getting juicier," I remark with a grin.

Natalie laughs softly, her eyes sparkling with amusement. "They arranged it so Alex and I would have to spend the evening together." She then shifts the conversation. "What about you? How did you get involved in the lifestyle?"

The jovial atmosphere dissipates as I delve into the darker chapters of my past. "Life hasn't always been good to me," I confess, the weight of my words evident in my somber tone. "I met Anthony at one of the lowest points." Briefly, I touch upon the trauma of the therapy center, glossing over the painful memories and choosing to focus on the pivotal moment when Tony entered my life. "I was in a bad place, ready to end it all when Tony found me. He saved me. He taught me it was okay to trust again."

Before I realize it, the hour has slipped away, and our session draws to a close. Natalie kindly assists me in rearranging the furniture, a gesture of camaraderie that warms my heart. As she reaches the door, she hesitates, a glimmer of uncertainty in her eyes. "Would you like to grab a bite to eat with me?" she asks tentatively.

"I'd love that," I respond with genuine warmth, touched by her invitation.

Leopold

DECEMBER *9*

I don't know by what stroke of luck Star paired me with Natalie, but I'm so thankful. When she volunteered to be my sister, I melted. We've become very close in a short amount of time. We text every day and have made dinner and drinks after class—a new tradition. The only negative is that I've thought about London more in the past few weeks than I have in years. That's a boundary that cannot be broken.

Last night was the last training class. Natalie and I went out for margaritas and discussed Alexander Montgomery. She's head over heels for the guy—who wouldn't be. He's tall and fit with dark hair, and the most beautiful blue eyes. His alpha male energy is everything. I'm pretty sure everyone at Fire and Ice would gladly submit to that man. But I digress...

Natalie told me Alex asked her to consider a Dom/sub dynamic with him. She's hesitant because she has to return to Northmeadow, her hometown, in a few months. Natalie came to New York for school on a full-ride scholarship with one caveat—in exchange for the scholarship, she had to agree to return to Northmeadow and work for the school district for five years.

Alex has offered to buy out her scholarship so she can stay in

Manhattan. I'm fully in support of that, by the way. Natalie, on the other hand, is not. She feels a sense of responsibility to the youth in her hometown and is insisting she go back and see it through.

As an alternative, I suggested asking Alex to put a time limit on their contract to help manage expectations. The problem is that she's falling for him as more than just a potential Dominant. Distance complicates things when the heart is involved.

I really hope fate intervenes and they find a way to be together.

Anthony

Leo's sitting in the kitchen with his laptop open when I walk in. "Who's that?" I ask, looking over Leo's shoulder.

He slams his laptop closed. "It's no one," he says, a bit too hastily. "I didn't hear you come in."

I raise an eyebrow at his abruptness. It's not like Leo to be secretive. "I see," I say, walking over to the fridge to grab a bottle of water.

"How long have you been home?"

I crack the seal and take a drink. "I just walked in."

"You're home early," he says as he fidgets his hands nervously.

"I thought I'd surprise you. Seems I did just that," I say, taking a seat at the kitchen table behind him.

Leo drops his head into his hands and admits, "I was looking at my sister's profile."

I knew if I didn't push, he'd eventually tell me what he was looking at, but his sister wasn't any of the answers I would've ever guessed. "London?"

"Yes," he says, opening his computer and turning the screen to face me. Looking back at me is a petite young woman with honey-gold hair and eyes that match Leopold's. "She's studying to be a doctor," he adds with a hint of pride.

"Are you thinking about contacting her?" I probe.

"No," he says firmly. "That can't happen."

"London's an adult now, Leopold. She's free to decide who she wants in her life."

"I can't risk my father hurting her," he admits, his voice strained. "It was just a stupid search. How was the restaurant?"

"Busy," I answer and move to sit beside him at the island. "As usual. How was your night?"

"Ramiro called. He wants me to visit him," he murmurs. "To celebrate my graduation."

Leopold had been a busser at *Italiano Desiderio* for several years when my floor manager, Ryan, approached me about promoting him to host. He pointed out how natural Leo was on the restaurant floor. In addition to clearing tables, Leo was engaging with the patrons—who often sought him out to chat. When I approached Leopold with the idea of promoting him, he revealed his aspiration to pursue a college degree in Hospitality Management.

He threw himself into his studies, taking on extra courses each semester, and finally graduated magna cum laude earlier this year. Despite my suggestion of throwing a big graduation party for him, he begged me not to. "I think a trip to California would be the perfect way to celebrate," I suggest.

His lower lip is caught between his teeth for a moment before he finally asks, "Would you come with me?"

"Of course," I answer without hesitation. Despite the fact that Leopold and I have been together for a little over five years, Ramiro's acceptance of me remains uncertain. This trip could offer me the opportunity to gain an understanding of why he still distrusts me.

"Maybe we can arrange to see Donnie and Lindsay, too?" he asks excitedly. "You can finally meet them in person. They'll love you."

"Talk to Ramiro and let me know when he wants you to visit,

and we'll make it happen." Leo watches me, his expression filled with questions. "What is it, *cuore mio*?"

Silently, he moves and lowers himself to his knees, resting his head on my lap. I run my fingers through his hair, comforting him.

"How is it that even though you know Ramiro isn't your biggest fan, you didn't even think about it before agreeing to go with me?"

"Ramiro's important to you, so I'll continue to do everything I can to extend friendship to him," I reply. I'm hopeful he'll give in and accept me as part of Leopold's life. Not for my sake, but for Leo's.

"Have I ever told you what initially attracted me to you?" he asks curiously.

"Not that I recall," I admit.

Leo raises his head, a soft smile forming. "It was your eyes and the kindness they held. It was as if you could see straight into my soul and understand my every need without a word.""From the instant I saw you all bundled up in your hat and scarf," I reflect with amusement. "My heart felt an instant connection. I knew then that I had to take care of you however I could."

Memories of a younger and more vulnerable Leo play in my mind. There was something about him that day, a silent plea that resonated with my soul. Despite knowing little about him, I felt an innate desire to nurture and shield him from the world. With each encounter, that urge grew stronger. But I never dared to hope he'd return my affection.

"I spent so much time fearing you'd never feel the same way," I confess.

"Why would you ever think that?" Leo's voice carries genuine confusion.

"Our age gap. I couldn't shake the feeling that you, being much younger, wouldn't be interested in someone older," I admit with a soft laugh.

"When I look at you, age is the last thing on my mind," Leo insists, rising higher on his knees.

I spread my thighs, making room for him. "What do you see, Leopold?" I ask, lowering my voice.

"I see a man who's capable and sure," he whispers, deftly unfastening my leather belt and letting it drop to the floor. "A man who isn't afraid to show tenderness," he continues, undoing the button and easing down the zipper. "I see a man who gives of himself so freely," Leo says, slipping his hands beneath my shirt to trace the contours of my abdomen before gripping the waistband of my pants and boxers. "A man who rescued me when I was drowning." Lifting my hips, he gently pulls my pants off my legs. "A man whose body I plan on worshipping so he never doubts my desire for him."

Leo takes hold of my throbbing erection, his touch deliberate and enticing. I release a low groan as he teases the tip. He then trails his tongue along the length of my shaft, his movements sending waves of pleasure through me. I tilt my head back, surrendering to the intoxicating sensations. Finally, he lowers himself until my cock hits the back of his throat. He gags slightly but doesn't pull away.

Understanding that, at times, oral can still be a challenge for him, I lift my head and offer, "You don't have to do this."

"I want to," he mumbles around my cock, his lips continuing their diligent work. His head bobs up and down my length, his tongue skillfully teasing and licking. He takes me deep into his throat once more.

"That feels incredible," I manage to utter, overwhelmed by the sensations. Leopold guides my hand to his head, silently signaling his readiness to relinquish control. "Are you absolutely sure?" I ask, concerned about pushing him beyond his limits. He nods, his eyes determined. "Tap my leg if you need to stop. Understand?" Once more, he nods in agreement.

I begin to gently thrust my hips upward, watching as my erection slides in and out of his throat. He gags with each movement.

"Are you alright?" I ask, concerned about pushing him beyond his limits. Once again, he nods, lowering himself until his face meets my groin.

Firmly grasping his hair, I intensify the rhythm and force of my thrusts, penetrating deeper with each motion. He emits a soft hum around my cock, his efforts unwavering. Saliva cascades from his mouth, coating me, while tears trickle down his face. "You look absolutely stunning——powerful, with my cock in your mouth."

Leopold meets my gaze with his captivating blue eyes, and at that moment, I'm overwhelmed. Unable to restrain myself any longer, I release with a final thrust. He swallows every drop before diligently cleaning my cock. "You taste exquisite. Thank you, Master."

"You never stop amazing me, *cuore mio.*"

Leopold

Me: I'm going to miss you, girlfriend.

Natalie: I'm going to miss you too, but we'll keep in touch.

Me: Did you get on the plane yet?

Natalie: No. We're still waiting to board.

Me: It's not too late, then. Change your mind and come back to me.

Alex hasn't stopped begging her to allow him to buy out her scholarship. Lord knows he has the money to do that, but she refuses to give in. I'm convinced they're soulmates. Except right now, she's sitting at JFK, ready to return to Missouri instead of being with Alex, where she belongs.

"You're supposed to be packing. Who are you texting?" Tony asks, a hint of frustration in his tone.

"Natalie," I sigh, a hint of sadness coloring my words. "She's at the airport with her parents. I wish she would've let Alex buy out her contract so she could stay here."

"I'm sure she has her reasons," Tony remarks calmly while folding a shirt.

"She does, but she belongs here—with Alex."

"Alex is a big boy. He'll handle it," Tony replies firmly.

"But—" I begin to protest.

"Leopold," Tony interrupts with a warning tone.

"I know. I know. Don't butt into their relationship." My shoulders fall in defeat. "It's partially selfish. I don't want her to leave because I'm going to miss her," I confess, feeling a pang of guilt as I admit my true feelings.

"There's video chats and airplanes. We can go visit," Tony suggests, tossing a shirt at me. "Right now, you need to pack your suitcase, or we won't make our flight tonight."

Tony and I are flying to California to spend time with Ramiro and his family. Surprisingly, he didn't give me grief when I told him Tony was coming with me. I'm hopeful that means he's finally ready, after all these years, to accept that Tony's a permanent part of my life.

While we're there, we'll also get to spend time with Donnie and Lindsay—something I'm very much looking forward to. We've kept in touch over the years, but I haven't seen them since I came to New York. It's not for lack of trying. Whatever Donnie's job is, and it's something he refuses to answer questions about, he can't be away for long.

Initially, I was concerned about the safety of visiting, given the issues with Krew. I don't know how long people like him might hold a grudge. Donnie reassured me that Krew's been taken care of, and there's no need for me to worry. He brushed it off when I pushed for more details, telling me to trust that he handled everything.

"Seriously though," Tony adds, his tone thoughtful. "Natalie's commitment to the school district is something she values deeply. Her reasons for not letting Alex intervene with money are significant to her. If she and Alex are meant to be, they'll find a way."

"I know," I acknowledge while I fold the last of my clothes and place them inside my suitcase.

"You and Natalie will always be friends, regardless," Tony reassures, leaning in to plant a kiss on my forehead.

"I truly hope so. I cherish her friendship," I admit, a fond smile gracing my lips.

Natalie's presence highlighted a longing I tried to keep buried deep inside. The closer we became, the more I wondered about my sister. Natalie's presence highlighted a longing I tried to keep buried deep inside. The closer we became, the more I wondered about my sister. Eventually, curiosity got the best of me, and I caved. I promised myself it would be a one-time thing, but it quickly turned into a weekly occurrence.

Thankfully, London isn't particularly cautious with her privacy settings, granting me access to her posts and photos. It fills my heart with happiness to see that she's grown into a confident young woman who's currently in med school.

There are many pictures of her surrounded by friends. One thing I don't see is any photos of London and the rest of our family. There's not a single picture of them. I don't know what to make of that. In each image, London's smile is radiant. It appears she's surrounded by friends and is happy. In the end, that's all that matters.

Anthony

Opting for a short-term beachfront rental house instead of a hotel was a decision I don't regret. We've only been here for two days, and I've already grown accustomed to the calm, serenity beachfront living offers. For the first time in my life the allure of Manhattan begins to fade, and I question the possibility of living somewhere other than the city. But today isn't the day for such contemplation. We're expecting a visitor — one Leopold remains unaware of.

Ever since seeing Leopold's sister's social media profile, I haven't stopped thinking about it. I know he misses her, but his fear of their father prevented him from reaching out. Taking a leap of faith, I contacted her, introducing myself and providing Leo's profile, where he goes by my last name. It was the only way I could think of to prove my identity since she never would've found Leo on her own. I gave her my phone number and asked if she was open to seeing her brother that she would please call me. Two days later, my phone rang.

Thankfully, Leo was out with Natalie when she called. We spent over an hour talking. She's as sweet as he described her. She was eager to learn everything about Leo's life and where he'd been all these years. I shared that he's been living in Manhattan for seven years but added anything else she'd have to ask him.

I did mention his reluctance to reach out because of their father but that he and I would be making a trip to California. She expressed the desire to see him while we were on the West Coast. London knows Leopold is unaware we've spoken.

Glancing at my phone, I anticipate her arrival any minute.

Leo and I are sitting on the deck, watching the waves roll in.

"Is everything okay, Master?" he asks, concern evident in his voice.

"Yes," I reply, though the truth lingers unspoken. The closer this reunion gets, the more I question if I did the right thing.

"How about we go for a walk on the beach?" he suggests, trying to ease my tension.

"Maybe later. I'm enjoying just watching the water from here."

"Okay," he sighs, sensing my unease. "Are you sure you're okay?"

I don't have a chance to respond because the doorbell rings. "Can you get that?"

"Sure," Leo responds, standing up. "It's probably just the wrong address for a delivery."

I allow him to enter before quietly trailing in his wake, my phone ready to capture the scene. I'm concerned at first that he's going to be angry at me for going behind his back. But I hold onto the hope that he'll eventually appreciate having this moment preserved on video.

Leopold

T**ONY'S BEHAVIOR TODAY IS BIZARRE. H**E **CLAIMS TO BE** enjoying the opportunity to unwind before we meet up with Ramiro later this week. But instead of relaxing, he's noticeably tense and kind of cranky.

I was trying to convince him to go down to the beach when the doorbell interrupted us. He's not getting off the hook. As soon as I send this person away, I intend to make Tony tell me what's going on.

I pull the door open and squint in the sunlight. "I'm sorry, I think you have the wrong address."

"Leo," a familiar voice says my name and launches into my arms.

Instinctively, I close them around the girl who's sobbing. "London? How—" I look up and see Tony holding his camera with tears pouring down his face. "You knew about this?"

"I reached out to her," Tony admits.

"London." I take her by the shoulders and hold her back to get a good look at her. "Is it really you?" She nods, unable to speak from crying. I pull her back against me, afraid if I let her go, she'll disappear. "I can't believe you arranged this. Why didn't you tell me?" I ask.

"I was afraid if I did that, you wouldn't come." Tony slides his phone into his pocket.

"Please don't be mad at him." London pulls away from me. "I've looked for you for so long. I'm so glad he messaged me."

"I could never be mad at him," I say, focusing on my Master.

"I'm going to go upstairs and make a few calls," Tony offers.

"Wait." I hurry over to him and wrap my arms around him. "Thank you for doing this."

"You don't have to thank me."

"I know. I want to." I press a kiss on his lips. "I love you."

"I love you too, *cuore mio*." He glances over my shoulder. "Go spend some time with your sister. She's a pretty incredible young lady." With that, Tony walks up the steps and disappears down the hall.

London comes up next to me. "That man is crazy about you," she whispers conspiratorially.

"I feel the same about him," I say, putting my arm around my sister. "Are you hungry or thirsty?"

"I'd love some water," she responds.

"Go on outside. I'll get you a drink, and then we can sit and talk," I suggest, motioning toward the door.

"Can we go down to the beach?" London asks, her eyes bright with anticipation. "Do you remember when we were younger, and Mom and Dad would take us on vacation to the shore? We'd sit on the sand for hours planning out our lives."

Even though I tried not to dwell on those memories, they were always there, lurking in the recesses of my mind. "Of course, I remember."

London and I walk down the weathered wood steps to the private beach. We settle onto the soft, sun-warmed sand, the rhythmic pulse of the waves providing a soothing soundtrack to our impending discussion.

"Tell me about you," I prompt, hoping to steer the conversation away from my past for as long as possible. "I saw on your social media that you're studying to be a doctor."

"I'm currently in my third year of med school at the University of California San Diego," she replies confidently.

"What's that like?"

"This year is crazy. We started our rotations. I'm in pediatrics right now," London explains, excitement lacing her voice. "It's great because I intend to do my residency in pediatrics."

"I can't believe my baby sister is all grown up and is going to be a doctor," I say, my chest swelling with pride.

"What about you? What happened to you after you left Walking in the Light?" she asks, curiosity evident in her tone.

There's no way I can tell her the things I went through. My hand scoops up sand, letting it run through my fingers as I contemplate what to reveal.

Sensing my discomfort, she asks, "Do you want to know how I ended up at UCSD?"

"Yes," I reply quietly.

"My senior year of high school, I did dual enrollment at Rolling Hills Community College. I applied to a bunch of schools and got accepted at all of them. I was also awarded scholarships at most of them," she adds, a smile tugging at her lips. "But Dad insisted I stay close to home my first year. Since I was still seventeen when I graduated high school, I had no choice but to do what he wanted."

She pauses, gazing out over the water for a brief moment.

"Once I turned eighteen, I secretly applied to UCSD and made all the arrangements to live on campus," she grins mischievously. "Dad was furious when he found out."

"Did he hurt you?" I ask, panic creeping into my voice.

"Not anything I couldn't handle," she responds calmly.

My face snaps to look at her. "What do you mean not anything you couldn't handle? Did he touch you?"

"He hit me," she says softly, her words barely audible.

"How many times?"

"What do you mean?"

"How many times did he hurt you?"

"It happened a lot," she admits, her voice tinged with sorrow.

"I'm going to kill him," I declare, my anger rising.

"No, you're not." She puts her hand over my fist. "It was a long time ago." When I don't relax, she persists. "Please, Leo. It's over. I haven't seen him since that night. I walked out and never looked back."

Maybe I was wrong for not going back for her? If I had, I could've spared her from being hurt by our father. I can't go there, though. I was barely surviving myself. I would never have been able to take care of London, too. "Out of everywhere, why did you choose San Diego?"

"I wanted to find you," she says softly, then continues, "I was so happy when David called Dad to tell him you got kicked out of the facility."

"He told them I got kicked out? What exactly did he say?" I inquire, curiosity tinged with a hint of anger coloring my tone.

"David said they found you and another boy having sex— rough sex, to be exact and that because you forced the other person. So, they expelled you from their program."

"David's a damn liar," I mutter, my frustration evident in my tone.

"What really happened?" London persists, her voice soft yet insistent.

I deflect her question with one of my own. "Did Mom and Dad try looking for me?"

"Mom wanted him to," she responds, her voice tinged with sadness. "She cried for weeks, but Dad refused. Said you were beyond saving, and he needed to protect Arianna and me by never letting you near our family again."

Hearing it confirmed hurts more than I anticipated.

"What really happened?" she presses further.

"Nothing. I just left," I lie, the words tasting bitter on my tongue.

"That's not true. There was a reason David emphasized the *rough* part of his story. What did he do to you?" London's voice is gentle, yet there's a firm resolve behind her words. I pull my knees up to my chest and wrap my arms around them. I can't do this. "Leo, please don't shut down on me," she pleads. "I'm not a kid anymore. You don't have to protect me now." She tugs at my arms until I drop them.

"David raped me," I admit, the words heavy on my tongue.

London sucks in a breath, her eyes widening with concern.

"Just once?" Her voice is barely a whisper. I shake my head. "How many times?"

"I don't know for sure," I confess, feeling the weight of uncertainty pressing down on me.

"Everything I read about that place was true," she mumbles, her tone filled with sadness. "Why didn't you go to the police?"

"I did," I reply. "But David lied to them, too."

"And they believed him over you." Her words hang in the air like a heavy cloud of injustice, and I can only nod in silent agreement, feeling the sting of betrayal all over again. "I had a bag packed so I'd be ready to run away," she continues, her voice soft but resolute. "I fell asleep every night with my phone in my hand, waiting for you to call me."

Her words cut me to my core. "I'm so sorry, Lulu," I say softly, wrapping my arm around her as she rests her head on my shoulder. "I didn't want to risk Dad finding out and doing something to hurt you. I'm so sorry he did. I'll never forgive myself for what he did to you, but you were safer there than with me."

"You would've made sure I was safe."

"I wish that were true, but it isn't," I admit, my voice heavy with regret.

London turns to me, her eyes searching mine. "How did you end up in New York?" She isn't going to let me get away with not telling her. I owe her the truth, especially knowing she waited for me to rescue her, and I never came. She was hurt because of me.

"When I got away from Walking in the Light, I stayed at a

center for homeless LGBTQ youth. It was a nice place with people who were helping me get on my feet. Things were good until I met a guy, Krew. He was dangerous," I explain but leave out details she can never know. "I went to New York for safety."

London's eyes grow wide. "Why are you back here then? Are you still in danger?"

"No, I'm not."

"Tell me about New York and about Tony. I'm jealous, by the way," she giggles. "He's stunning."

I glance back at the house. "He is," I admit, a smile tugging at my lips. "Tony saved me—literally and figuratively."

"What do you mean?"

"I was in a bad place, Lulu. I didn't deal with everything that happened with David and then Krew. Then, I found myself in an unfamiliar city. Things were okay. I had an apartment and a job. That's how I met Tony," I explain, recalling those difficult times. "I was delivering groceries to local restaurants. One of them was the restaurant he owned. He always made something for me to eat on delivery days."

"Didn't you have enough food?" she asks, concern lacing her words.

"No," I admit, a hint of vulnerability in my tone. "Until Tony, I often went hungry."

"Is that how he saved you?" Her question is gentle, probing for deeper understanding.

I shake my head solemnly. "My boss died suddenly. I lost my job and my apartment on the same day. I gave up. I tried to kill myself." London gasps, her eyes welling with tears. "Tony found me and brought me to his home. He cared for me."

She wipes her cheeks with the backs of her hands, visibly moved. "How long have you been together?"

"Six years," I reply, my voice tinged with gratitude. "We fell for each other long before we took the next steps. He wanted to make sure I was healthy emotionally before we got involved with each other. Tony's the kindest person I've ever met. I love him more than I have words to describe."

"I'll forever be indebted to him," London says, emotion thick in her voice. "He brought you back to me." She throws her arms around me.

Out of the corner of my eye, I spot a shadow. Looking up, I see Tony walking our way.

"I don't mean to interrupt," he says, his tone gentle. "I thought you two might be getting hungry."

"What time is it?"

"It's going on six." I had no idea several hours had passed since we came outside. "Are you hungry, Lulu?"

"I could definitely eat," she says, getting to her feet and wiping off the sand. "But first, I have to hug you." She wraps herself around Tony. "I don't know how to thank you for loving Leopold."

"You don't need to thank me. Loving him is easy," Tony says, his eyes never leaving mine.

TONY COOKS DINNER WHILE LONDON AND I SIT AT THE expansive island. The three of us talk and catch up on years of missed time. She updates me on our sister, Arianna. Not surprisingly, Arianna remains closely tied to our parents. She married a man of my father's choosing, and they now have two children—a boy and a girl. London hasn't seen or spoken to her since she left our parents' home.

"Tell me more about you," I encourage. "Are you seeing anyone?"

Her cheeks turn pink. "Not really." She shrugs.

"Something tells me there's more to that answer." I elbow her playfully. "Keep talking, Lulu."

"He's my professor," she confesses, her voice muffled as she buries her face in her hands.

"Sweetheart," Anthony says, a spatula in his hand. "There's nothing you can say that would bother us."

"Is it consensual?" I ask.

"Yes," she says and lifts her head. "It's completely mutual. He's a good man, and he treats me well." She glances between Tony and me. "We have to be careful, though. He could lose his job if he's caught with a student."

"Can we meet him before we go back to New York?" I ask.

"If you want, you can meet him tonight. He brought me here. He'll be back to pick me up."

"Why don't you call him to see if he wants to come for dinner?" Anthony suggests.

"Are you sure?"

"I'm positive. We'd love to meet him."

"Okay," she agrees and pulls out her phone.

"If you want privacy—"

"I don't need privacy from you," London reassures, squeezing my hand. "Hey, baby," she says into the phone, her smile evident in her voice. "Everything's great. They want to know if you'd like to join us for dinner." She nods. "Great. We'll see you soon." Setting the phone down on the counter, she turns back to us. "He'll be here in a few minutes."

"How far away do you live?" I inquire.

"About ten minutes," London responds with a grin.

The evening sky paints a vibrant sunset backdrop as we gather around the deck table for dinner. Patrick, London's boyfriend, effortlessly blends into our conversation, fielding every question Tony and I toss his way.

"London, can you give me a hand in the house?" Tony's request momentarily breaks the flow of our conversation.

"Sure." She gives Patrick a quick peck on the cheek. "I'll be right back."

"Take your time," Patrick says, his eyes following her as she disappears indoors.

I'll thank Tony later for giving me this time to talk to Patrick alone. With no time to waste, I dive straight into the heart of the matter. "How many other students have you dated?"

"None," he responds without hesitation.

"Have you ever been married?"

"I have," he admits. "We met towards the end of my residency. It was a whirlwind romance. We got married after only knowing each other for six months," he explains. "After my residency, I started working in an emergency room. We found out we were having a baby. I thought things were great until I came home and found her in our bed with another man." His shoulders sag. "Lisa, my ex-wife, had been having an affair with him for nearly a year. I was devastated."

"So, you have a child, too?"

"No." He shakes his head. "The baby wasn't mine. Apparently, Lisa had taken a paternity test without me knowing."

"That's rough. I'm sorry."

"It was hard. I lost my wife and my baby all at once. I don't blame her, though. I had responsibility there, too. I was so focused on work—too focused. I didn't pay enough attention to my wife, and I lost everything. It's a mistake I won't make again."

"Fair enough."

"I love your sister," Patrick admits, leaning forward. "I tried not to. She didn't need to get involved with her professor. There's too much for her to lose."

"What do you mean?"

"She could get kicked out of school if anyone finds out," he explains. "Your sister is a force to be reckoned with." He laughs softly.

"What are you two talking about?" London asks as she steps back outside.

"You," I say, fixing her with my gaze.

Tony joins us on the deck, his eyes shifting between London and me. "What's going on?"

"Patrick is just telling me that London could get kicked out of school for being with him," I say, focusing on my sister.

"Get over it, Leo. I have." She places her hand on Patrick's shoulder.

"Forgive me if I'm worried about you."

"Were you aware of the consequences of getting involved with your professor?" Tony inquires.

"Of course I was." London crosses her arms. "He did everything he could to get me to stay away. He didn't want me to jeopardize my residency. But I told him, and I'll tell you both, I love him." Her expression softens. "I have one more year, and then we'll be free to go public."

"You could lose everything you've worked so hard for," I argue.

"Being together is worth any risk," she insists, taking Patrick's hand. "Patrick finally accepted that, and I hope you both will, too."

"Love has no boundaries and doesn't follow rules," Tony adds.

"You're happy?"

"More than happy."

"And you're going to make sure London doesn't get kicked out of school?" I ask, pinning Patrick with my stare.

"London agreed—"

"Grudgingly," she interjects.

"Grudgingly," Patrick confirms. "If our relationship were to be exposed, she'll let me take the blame. I'll tell them I forced her. Whatever I need to do to protect London." She rolls her eyes. "And you're not going to break your promise to me, are you?"

"As much as I hate it. No, I won't," she agrees. "But we aren't going to get caught, are we?"

"I'll do everything in my power to ensure we don't."

"Doesn't living together increase the risk?" Tony asks.

"Yes and no," Patrick explains. "On the record, London rents a small apartment close to campus. We live more than a half hour from the school."

"We don't go out together, and I Uber back and forth to campus," she adds.

"It bothers me that I can't take her on dates and do things she deserves in a relationship."

"I've told him I don't care about that stuff. I only want him."

"It sounds risky," I say, looking between the two. "But I can see how much you love each other. As long as you're happy, then I'm happy."

"Thank you, Leo." She beams.

We spend the next few hours talking. I have to stop several times and pinch myself. I can't believe I'm sitting here with my sister. This is more than I could've ever imagined, and Tony's responsible for making it happen.

"I don't want tonight to end," London says, grabbing my hand, her voice tinged with regret. "But I have to be at the office for seven in the morning."

"I understand," I respond, sympathizing with her busy schedule.

"I know you're only in town for a few more days, and London's schedule is crazy, but we'd both like to see you again before you leave," Patrick suggests warmly. "Would you be willing to come to our house for dinner?"

Glancing to Tony, he replies, "We'd love that."

After a final emotional embrace with my sister, we confirm our plans to visit their home later in the week. Tony and I stand together in the doorway, silently watching London and Patrick head toward his car. Patrick opens the door for her, and she gives him a tender smile before getting in.

"Thank you, Tony," I express, squeezing his hand gratefully.

"You aren't mad at me?" he asks, seeking reassurance.

"Having my sister in my life is something I never dreamed possible," I confess, overcome with emotion from the evening's events. "You gave her back to me. I don't deserve you."

"*Cuore mio*, I'd pull the stars from the sky and lay them at your feet. You're deserving of every good thing, and I plan to be the one to give them all to you."

"The only thing I want is you."

"I'm yours. I'll always be yours," Tony pledges.

Anthony

OUR DRIVER PULLS UP IN FRONT OF A SINGLE-STORY stucco home at the end of a cul de sac. Before we get out of the car, the front door opens, and an older version of the Ramiro I met years ago in New York steps out and meets us on the sidewalk.

"I can't believe you're actually here," he says before hugging Leopold.

"It's been far too long," Leo responds.

"Yes, it has," he agrees.

"Good to see you again, Tony." He offers his hand.

I accept his gesture of friendship. "You as well."

"Come on. Jacinta can't wait to finally meet you in person." Entering the house, we're greeted by an unexpectedly spacious interior, bathed in natural light pouring through large windows. The rooms feel airy and expansive, inviting us to explore further.

"Everyone's out back," Ramiro says as he opens a set of glass doors.

We step out onto a concrete patio situated under a stunning pergola. Encircled by flourishing trees, the backyard exudes a sense of tranquility and privacy. On one side, a well-appointed outdoor kitchen beckons, while across the yard, an inviting inground pool and bubbling hot tub tempt us with promises of relaxation. The sound of children's laughter fills the air as they splash around, adding to the lively ambiance. Beyond the pool, a sprawling deck extends into the distance, offering ample space to unwind and enjoy the outdoors.

"This place is stunning," I comment, admiring the picturesque surroundings.

"The backyard is what drew us to this property. With the canyon, we'll never have neighbors overlooking us," Ramiro explains. "Come on, there are some people here who are eager to see you."

"Leo!" a young woman calls out excitedly, dashing across the yard.

"I had no idea you guys were coming!" he exclaims as he lifts the girl from the ground.

"We wanted to surprise you," she replies with a grin as he sets her down.

"You clean up well, Leo," a man in a black T-shirt remarks. "It's great to see you."

"You too," Leo responds before introducing us. "Tony, this is Lindsay and Donnie."

"It's a pleasure to finally meet you face-to-face," I say warmly.

"The pleasure's ours," Donnie replies.

"Leo, Tony," Ramiro interrupts, drawing our attention. "Meet my wife, Jacinta." We exchange greetings, and Ramiro continues, "And these are our children: Camila, Marisol, and Dante."

"I can't believe we're all here," Leo says as he looks around at everyone who's gathered to see him and presses the heels of his palms against his eyes. "I promised myself I wouldn't cry anymore, but I just can't help it," Leo admits, his voice choked with emotion. He reaches for my hand, and I draw him close, wrapping my arm around him for comfort.

Seeing the questioning look on Ramiro's face, I explain,

"We've had an emotional week. Unbeknownst to Leopold, his sister London came to see him two days ago."

"How did she find out you were here?" Ramiro questions.

"I've been curious about her," Leo interjects. "I showed Tony her social media a few weeks ago."

"After that, I reached out to her and introduced myself," Tony adds. "Once our travel plans were finalized, I arranged for her to surprise Leo."

While the adults engage in conversation, the children splash and laugh joyfully in the pool. Leopold's face radiates with joy as he recounts his time spent with his sister.

While I've communicated with everyone through video calls over the years, today marks the first occasion I'm meeting all but Ramiro in person. They form the chosen family who provided care and support for Leopold before he entered my life.

Donnie and Lindsay played a pivotal role in rescuing him from Krew's grasp. I'm confident they all experienced worry for his safety when he ventured to New York. Yet, it was that brave decision that paved the way for him to find his way to me. Each person present holds a piece of my gratitude.

"You should start cooking," Jacinta prompts her husband gently. "The children will be getting hungry."

"I didn't realize what time it was," Ramiro admits with a sheepish grin. He turns to Donnie, an invitation in his eyes. "Care to help cook?"

Donnie tilts his beer up in response, a smirk on his face. I don't know much about their story, only that Ramiro and Donnie share a somewhat tenuous past.

"Fine. I'll do it myself," Ramiro concedes, his tone tinged with annoyance as he trudges across the yard towards the grill.

Sensing an opportunity to assist, I wait a few minutes before excusing myself from the group and approaching Ramiro.

"I can give you a hand if you'd like," I offer, extending my assistance with a friendly smile.

Initially, I expect him to decline, but his response catches me off guard. "That would be great." We work silently for a few prolonged minutes before he speaks up again. "I owe you an apology for the way I've treated you. When Leopold came to Safe Haven, I knew there was something different about him—something special," he explains. "I don't typically get personally involved with the residents we have with us, but Leo's profile caught my attention. He never had anyone in his corner."

Ramiro deftly flips the sizzling burgers before continuing, "When he came in that day and was with Krew, my stomach sank. I knew Krew and that Leo was in trouble, but my hands were tied." His shoulders slump. "I offered to open my home to him, but Krew had his attention. I couldn't get through to him."

Knowing the hell Leopold lived through after this, I can't imagine how helpless Ramiro felt recognizing the danger he was in.

"I have so many regrets for letting him walk away that day," he confesses, the pain evident in his voice.

"You did the best you could," I offer, trying to reassure him.

"When Donnie called and said Leo was with them, I was so relieved. He didn't tell me his condition," Ramiro adds, his voice trembling. "Tony, if you saw him. He was so thin and strung out. I was afraid he wouldn't make it through the night."

"Why didn't you bring him to a hospital?" I ask.

"They would've asked too many questions. Ones we wouldn't have been able to answer. Donnie had experience getting guys through withdrawal, and Lindsay's a nurse. He was safer with just us."

"I understand."

"Once we knew he would be okay, the next problem I needed to address was where Leo would live. He couldn't stay in San Diego; even California was a risk. Sending him to New York killed me," Ramiro explains, his voice pained. "I knew the amount of help and support I could give him from here would be limited." He looks at me. "Then he called that night, and you were with him, I'll admit," he says regret lacing his tone. "I saw another Krew situation. I was scared."

Ramiro glances over to where Leo's laughing and talking with the small group. "I know I've not been the most accepting of you, and for that, I'm sorry. You've beyond proven that you only have Leo's best interest at heart," he says, softening his tone. "I know you love him."

I'm not sure what sparked this change of heart in Ramiro, but I'm not complaining. Up until now, he's merely tolerated me. Whether or not our relationship will evolve into friendship remains to be seen. Still, his newfound acceptance of me as part of Leopold's life is reassuring. "I do love him very much. Leopold is everything to me, and I intend to spend the rest of my life showing him that."

The hours melt away as I find myself enveloped in the warmth of togetherness, seamlessly blending into the fabric of what now feels like *our* extended family. Admittedly, I was nervous about this trip to the West Coast. I wasn't sure how receptive this group would be to me. With each shared laugh and exchanged story, any lingering misgivings between us are swiftly dispelled, replaced by a sense of unity and understanding. It's a heartwarming reminder of the power of human connection to bridge differences and foster deep bonds, reaffirming that we're united in our affection for Leopold.

Leopold

DECEMBER 1

I can't describe the enormity of my emotions over the past few months. Having London back in my life has been remarkable. Despite being on opposite coasts, we text daily and try to have a video call at least once a week. Her schedule at school and now at the emergency room, where her current rotation is, is absolutely crazy. I don't know how she does it.

Natalie and I also talk every day. I wish I could go fly to Northmeadow and bring her back here. She's been positively miserable. Her parents are the most close-minded, judgemental, and just plain awful people I've ever heard of.

From the second she arrived back in Northmeadow, they were trying to set her up with her ex-boyfriend, Tommy—the same one who cheated on her with her best friend. Natalie, being the sweetheart she is, didn't have the heart to rat him or the girl out to anyone. I'm not as nice as her. I was ready to take out an ad in The New York Times. I still think she should make it public, by the way.

Anyway, everything came to a head on Thanksgiving. That crazy ass ex of hers proposed to her at dinner. Obviously, she said no. Her parents freaked out. It sounds like it was complete chaos. The one good thing that came out of the mess was that Natalie finally *found the courage to stand up for herself to her parents. She told them Tommy cheated on her but still kept the secret of with whom.*

She tried to get them to understand that she's in love with Alex, but that didn't happen. The bad thing is that her father blew a gasket and gave her an ultimatum. Either follow their rules or leave their house. They must've read the same parenting manual my parents did.

I was so proud of her when she called and told me she packed up and left. She couldn't find an apartment, so she's staying at a motel. It's not ideal, but I was hoping it would be a positive step forward.

But things can never be easy, can they? After the Thanksgiving dinner debacle, she went off the radar for a while, which freaked Alex out. He nearly lost his shit. Alex is still in Russia doing some top-secret work with Maxim Solonik. Since he couldn't get to Missouri, he sent Viktor, his scary Ukranian bodyguard, to stay with her. The good thing is I don't have to worry about her safety.

I hate knowing she's going through so much. I miss my best friend. I wish she'd give in and come back to New York, where she belongs.

Anthony

"THE SHOW WAS AMAZING," LEO SAYS, STILL WIDE-EYED after tonight's performance of *Wicked*.

"It's one of my favorites," I reply.

"*What's next on the list?*" he asks, curious.

"The Lion King," I respond with a grin. Pulling my cell phone from my pocket, I pretend to check my messages. "We need to stop at the club. Owen asked if I could check something in the café."

"Okay," Leo agrees.

Me: Is everyone at the park?

Owen: Yes. We're waiting for you to get here.

Me: We're on our way. Be there in a few minutes.

The Dominant/submissive dynamic Leopold and I share has grown and evolved over the past five years. In the beginning, I was cautious, probably overly so. Leopold was in the beginning stages of healing from his traumatic past. I didn't want the power shift between us to hinder that in any way. Since the beginning of our relationship, we've discussed the significance of being collared. Leo's expressed that he desires to wear my collar—to be owned by me.

I'm not and never have been a Dominant who makes a lot of

demands of their submissive. I don't get off on cruelty or power trips. I'm fulfilled knowing my submissive is provided and cared for. That he allows me to nurture him. Some might say our dynamic is unconventional, and perhaps they're right, but it's perfect for us.

With each passing day, Leopold's grown stronger and more sure of himself. Watching this metamorphosis and seeing him develop into the outgoing and capable man he is today has been an honor. He's the perfect example of a self-confident submissive.

Tonight holds the promise of a transformative moment in our dynamic. I'll present Leopold with my collar—an elegant piece crafted from a thick silver chain and embellished with a symbolic O ring. Its locking mechanism at the back signifies a permanent bond.

I've been planning this ceremony for the past several weeks. Knowing how close Leopold is to Natalie, I reached out to Alexander to see if they'd be back in town soon. Turns out he's planning to surprise Natalie by flying into Northmeadow for Christmas. He expressed his regrets that they would have to miss the ceremony.

"How about we take a walk along the river before we go to the club?" I suggest, intertwining my fingers with Leo's.

"Sounds perfect," Leo replies, a smile playing on his lips as our hands meet.

Leo and I often walk this path. I think we both have our reasons for being drawn here. For me, it serves as a gentle nudge to heed the soft whispers of intuition and a reminder of the fragileness of life. Of how blessed I am to have this remarkable man beside me.

Unlike our usual walks, I lead Leo from the riverwalk onto the pier.

"Is there an event tonight?" he asks, his eyes scanning the surroundings with curiosity.

"Not sure," I respond.

As we approach the gathering, Leo furrows his brow. "Tony?" he asks softly. "What's everyone doing here?"

"They're here for us," I reveal, a rush of excitement coursing through me.

Upon reaching the gathering, we pause. Leo's gaze is fixated on Owen as he ignites his candle, its flame a beacon of light in the gathering dusk. Astrid's candle meets his, the flickering flames intertwining. Slowly, the light is passed from one candle to the next, the circle around us glowing brighter until every candle flickers in unison, their glow harmonizing with the soft whisper of the breeze.

"We're truly grateful to have you all here with us despite the chill in the air," I express warmly. "Each one of you has been with us through thick and thin, and we're honored you're here to share this special night with us," I add, feeling a swell of emotion.

"This park is more than just a location," Anthony says, his voice soft yet resonant. "It holds the echoes of our past from the darkest depths of despair to the moment you offered me your submission. It's witnessed our laughter, tears, and everything in between. And tonight," he continues, a hint of anticipation in his tone, "it becomes the backdrop for another significant moment in our lives."

"I'm not going to have you kneel. The ground is too cold."

"Thank you, Master," he replies respectfully.

"Leopold, we stand here tonight surrounded by the warmth of our friends, others who share in the lifestyle. I find myself humbled by the strength and solidarity of our community—our family," I breathe, my voice filled with emotion. "Together, we'll celebrate not only the love you and I have found but also a commitment that is unique to our lifestyle. The offering and wearing of a collar."

Turning my attention to my submissive, I continue, "For the submissive, wearing a collar is more than wearing a piece of jewelry. This collar," I say, reaching into my pocket to retrieve the silver chain. "Represents a deep commitment between us. It's an outward sign of your willingness to submit to my authority and guidance. Do you understand what agreeing to wear my collar means?"

"Yes, Master. It's a symbol of my trust and devotion to you," Leopold answers, his voice resonating with devotion.

"At the same time," I say softly, the weight of the words heavy in the air, "the collar serves as a constant reminder of the power dynamic within our relationship—a reminder of the roles each of us has chosen to fulfill and the responsibilities that come with them. It's a symbol of ownership and possession, not in a controlling sense, but rather a mutual acknowledgment of our bond."

"I understand, Master," Leopold murmurs, his tone laced with sincerity. "It's a constant reminder of our dynamic, of the roles we've chosen to embrace."

"As your Dominant," I explain tenderly, my voice carrying the weight of my commitment, "when I see my collar on you, it's a daily reminder of the sacred trust you've placed in me. I hold the responsibility of cherishing, protecting, and caring for you. Your well-being is in my hands, and I do not take that lightly."

Leopold's eyes soften, a silent acknowledgment of the depth of my words as he responds, his voice barely above a whisper, "I know you'll always have my best interests at heart," he murmurs, his gaze never leaving mine. "I trust you completely, Master,"

"This collar," I assert gently, my fingers tracing the silver chain as I speak, "is a symbol of the deep connection and mutual respect between us. It's a tangible expression of our dynamic and the love that binds us together. It's a symbol of strength, vulnerability, and profound intimacy—a reminder of the beauty found in surrendering to love and trust." Leopold's eyes glisten with emotion as he listens to my words, his expression reflecting the gravity of the moment. "And I promise to always honor that trust," I continue, my voice steady with sincerity, "to guide you with love and respect. Will you accept my collar?"

"Yes, Master," Leopold declares, his words ringing with conviction. "I'm yours, now and always."

Moving closer to Leopold, I am acutely aware of the significance of this moment—the culmination of a journey that has led us here. Leopold has captured my heart in a way no other ever could. With trembling hands, I place the collar around his neck. It's as if time stands still, and in that moment, our souls intertwine. The ends come together and lock, sealing our bond in a moment that feels both surreal and inevitable.

I know with absolute certainty that Leopold is the one who I've been waiting for. He completes me in ways I never thought possible. He's the man who brings light to the darkest parts of my soul.

Leopold is my forever.

Leopold

As the ceremony concludes, I'm overcome by a flood of emotions swirling within me. The weight of the collar around my neck is both grounding and liberating, a tangible symbol of the commitment I've made to Anthony, my Dominant, and the journey we've chosen to take together.

I meet Anthony's gaze and am filled with overwhelming gratitude and love, my heart overflowing with emotion. Everything has fallen into place, and I'm exactly where I'm meant to be—wrapped in Anthony's embrace and bound by the unbreakable bond we share.

With a sense of profound contentment, I intertwine my fingers with Anthony's as we walk back to Fire and Ice, surrounded by the people who witnessed our ceremony. Their presence is a comforting reminder of the love and support that surrounds us.

"Natalie's going to be so upset she missed this," Svetlana says, coming up next to me.

Svetlana Solonik has undergone a remarkable transformation from when I first met her—when she wore Alex's collar of protection. She was infamous for her stubbornness and strong-willed nature. I wasn't sure anyone could ever tame her or if she really even wanted to submit. That all changed when she met Alex's best friend, Brandon.

"I wish she was here, too," I say, my voice tinged with longing.

"Hopefully, Alex will be able to convince her to let him buy out the remainder of her contract so she can finally come home," Lana says wistfully.

"I hope so," I say, though deep down, I know the likelihood is slim. It's not just a matter of fulfilling the terms of her scholarship. It's about Natalie's deep-seated obligation to advocate for the youth in Northmeadow. She experienced firsthand the repercussions of inadequate services, particularly for LGBTQ+ teenagers, in the wake of her brother and his boyfriend's tragic deaths. Natalie's determined to ensure nothing like that ever happens again. As much as I miss her, I was once one of those kids without a voice or support. I know they need her there more than I need her here.

"Are you two staying for a while?" Star asks Tony.

"Just for a little bit," Anthony replies, a mischievous glint dancing in his eyes. He inches closer, the warmth of his breath sending shivers down my spine as he whispers, "I have plans for us tonight."

Throughout the evening, Tony keeps me on edge with his teasing touches and lingering caresses, heightening my arousal with each passing moment.

"Let's go home," he says, his voice carrying a potent mix of authority and desire.

"I've been waiting for you to say that all night, Master," I confess, my voice trembling with need.

***

The subway ride home is a test of restraint that only serves to heighten the anticipation. But the moment we step into the apartment, Tony's desire ignites. He spins me around and pins me against the door.

As we stand there, pressed against the door, the heat between us explodes into a fiery passion. Tony's hands roam eagerly over my body, igniting sparks of pleasure with every touch. He captures my lips in a fervent kiss, and his tongue moves with mine in a sensual dance.

I moan softly against his mouth, my hands tangling in his hair as I pull him closer, desperate for more. Our bodies meld together, fitting perfectly as if they were made for each other. My erection presses against him as our bodies move together, seeking the friction we crave.

With practiced skill, Tony begins to divest me of my clothing, each piece falling away to reveal the eager flesh beneath. His touch is electric, sending jolts of pleasure coursing through me. When I'm finally bare before him, he steps back to admire the sight, his eyes dark with desire.

"My collar around your neck is the most erotic thing I've ever seen," he murmurs. "Do you see what you do to me?" My eyes drop down to the bulge in his pants.

"Yes, Master. I do," I gasp, my voice thick with desire.

"I'm going to fuck you so hard," he whispers in a low growl that sends shivers down my spine. "Get in the bedroom, now," he commands.

Before I realize it, my feet are already in motion, carrying me to the bedroom. Tony's gaze pierces mine as he sheds his clothes with a sense of urgency.

Stepping closer, his hands explore my body, setting my skin ablaze with anticipation. Our lips meet in a passionate kiss, causing both of us to moan with longing. Reluctantly, he pulls away, leaving me breathless. "Get on all fours on the bed," he orders, his tone commanding yet filled with desire before he turns to his dresser.

Tony returns to the bed and settles behind me, placing nipple clamps, a slender rod, a ring, and lube within reach. Then, I feel his hands on my ass. Spreading it open, he leans in to tease my entrance with his tongue. A low moan escapes my lips as I push back against his tongue as he fucks me.

"That feels incredible. Please, don't stop," I plead, the sensation driving me wild.

With a swift motion, he withdraws his tongue and slaps my ass hard, eliciting a surprised yelp. Another stinging slap follows, even harder this time, sending a jolt of pleasure through me.

"Do you enjoy that?" he asks, his voice filled with authority.

Tony and I have experimented with spanking. At first, I was tentative yet curious. He started with light taps that gradually heated and got stronger until any hesitation was gone, and in its place was only undeniable pleasure. It was a profound awakening that transcended the purely physical sensation but was, more importantly, a testament to the trust and intimacy of our relationship.

"Yes, Master. Please, I want more," I reply eagerly.

Tony obliges, his hand meeting my skin repeatedly in a rhythmic pattern. He suddenly stops and reaches for the bottle of lube, coating his fingers before sliding one into my waiting heat. With expert precision, he adds a second finger, plunging them into me, igniting a fire of desire within me.

"Are you up for trying something new?" Tony's voice is filled with anticipation, his eyes locked on mine.

"Anything," I respond, breathless.

"Lie on your back," he instructs, his tone firm yet gentle.

"You're absolutely breathtaking," he murmurs as his gaze traces my body with admiration. He reaches for the nipple clamps. "I need you to remember your safewords tonight," he reminds me. "Don't be afraid to use them."

"Yes, Master."

With practiced skill, he attaches the clamps, each sensation sending waves of pleasure through me. Linking them with a chain, he pulls lightly, eliciting a gasp of delight.

"Are you ready for more, *cuore mio*?" Tony's voice is filled with desire, his gaze smoldering.

"I want to do everything with you," I whisper, surrendering to the allure of our shared journey.

Tony lifts the thin metal rod. It glistens in the dim light. I watch intently as he traces it along my skin, each touch sending shivers of pleasure down my spine. "This is a sound rod. I'm going to insert it slowly, he explains, guiding me further into the realm of ecstasy and trust.

Excitement had bubbled within me during our discussions, but as Tony readies it with a generous amount of lube, a sudden wave of apprehension washes over me.

"Color?" Tony checks in.

"Nervous but green," I reply.

With a firm yet gentle touch, he cradles my erection as he guides the rod toward me. As it begins to slide inside, I can't help but gasp at the unfamiliar sensation.

"It's... it's bigger than I expected," I admit the blend of discomfort and pleasure, creating a heady mix of sensations.

"Do you want me to keep going?" he asks, seeking my consent.

"Yes," I reply, my voice betraying my desire, a needy edge to its tone.

Tony proceeds to insert the rod further until it's fully inside me. "Are you prepared?" he teases, a playful glint dancing in his eyes. I nod, rendered speechless by the anticipation. He begins to move the rod in and out, starting slowly before increasing the pace.

"Oh, it feels incredible," I breathe, overwhelmed by the sensation.

Once again, he comes to an abrupt stop, and I groan.

"We're far from done, Leopold," his voice oozing with desire as he retrieves the cock ring and slides it down my rigid length. Securing the chain from the clamps to the end of the sounding rod, he adds, "I'm eager to witness you unravel beneath me."

Tony dispenses more lube onto his hand and begins to stroke his own erection while teasing my entrance with his other hand. A whirlwind of sensations overwhelms me, yet I stay fixated on the sight of his self-pleasure.

"Is this what you want?" he asks, and I respond with eager nods.

"I ache for you," I plead, my voice trembling with desire. Tony positions himself at my entrance. I gasp at the sensation of his thick, hard length pushing past my tight muscles. "More, please," I whimper, yearning for a deeper connection.

Tony chuckles softly as he drives all the way in. "Like this?" he asks, his tone playful yet commanding.

"Yes, Master."

He withdraws, and I groan at the loss. "What's the matter, Leopold?" he teases, playfulness evident in his voice.

"I need..." My plea is cut short as he switches on the cock ring, sending intense vibrations through me, leaving me panting and desperate for more.

Tony thrusts inside until our bodies are pressed together, then pulls back slowly before plunging in again. "You're so responsive tonight," he moans, increasing his pace.

"I'm close," I rasp, the urgency evident in my voice.

"There is no coming without permission," he commands firmly. "Do you understand?"

"Yes, Master," I reply, biting my lip to suppress the rising tide of pleasure.

With renewed determination, Tony increases the force of his thrusts, the sound of our bodies colliding filling the room as he drives me closer to the edge.

"Please, may I come?" I plead, desire consuming me.

"Not yet," he murmurs, withdrawing momentarily. He reaches for the lube, coating his cock once more before plunging back into me with force. "You feel incredible, Leopold," he growls, eliciting a moan from me in response.

As he thrusts into my ass, Tony simultaneously moves the

sounding rod in and out of my dick. "Oh, fuck," I gasp, overwhelmed by the intense sensation, my breaths coming in ragged pants.

"This is unbelievable," he moans, his voice filled with ecstasy. "I've never experienced anything like this."

"Please, Master, let me come," I plead, on the brink of release without permission.

He pauses, his cock buried deeply inside me. "I'll count down from ten," he says, his gaze piercing into mine. "You must wait until I reach zero to come. Do you understand?" I whimper in frustration as he begins the countdown.

"Ten," he starts. "Nine, eight..." With each number, he withdraws and thrusts back in, the anticipation driving me wild.

"Please," I beg, tears welling in my eyes as my climax nears. "I'm not going to make it."

"You can do this. Focus on my words," Tony encourages as he continues the countdown. "Seven, six, five."

Tears cascade down my cheeks, each breath a struggle as I teeter on the brink of oblivion, the promise of release tantalizingly close yet agonizingly out of reach.

"Four, three," he counts, his movements becoming more urgent.

"I'm so close," I whimper, my voice barely above a breathless murmur. My entire being pulses with raw, visceral need. The ache in my core is almost unbearable, a delicious torment that twists and coils with every movement. Every fiber of my being screams for release, pulling me closer to the edge of oblivion.

"Two," he says, pulling almost entirely out. "One. Come for me, now," he commands, pulling on the chain and sending me spiraling into ecstasy.

As the nipple clamps release, a wave of intense sensation floods my senses, the simultaneous removal of the sounding rod from my cock pushing me over the edge. "Oh fuck... Tony...

Master," I cry out as ecstasy consumes me, experiencing a climax more intense than anything I've ever felt before.

Observing my reactions, Tony remarks, "You've never looked more beautiful," his voice husky with desire as he maintains his steady rhythm. "Your ass is clenching so tight around my dick."

"Please fill me, Master," I implore.

With a final, powerful thrust, he drives into me. With a primal growl, he stills as his release fills me completely. Tony's body trembles with the force of his climax. His touch is tender yet possessive, a silent declaration of ownership and devotion.

He slams into me one last time and stills as his cock twitches deep inside me. Tony collapses on top of me. "You were magnificent," Tony murmurs softly, his words carrying a depth of emotion that resonates within me.

"That was..." I search for the right words.

"Perfect," he whispers, his words a soothing balm to my soul. "You were meant to be mine, *cuore mio*."

"Everything I am belongs to you, Master," I pledge, my commitment unwavering.

Leopold

FEBRUARY 18

I had my last session with Sarah yesterday. To say it was bitter-sweet is an understatement. My treatment lasted far longer than it does for most people. Sorting through my messy, complex trauma wasn't a walk in the park. But Sarah and I tackled each issue head-on. Some things were difficult to process and took extra time. I had some rough panic attacks in her office, but Sarah was there every step of the way, helping me push through.

From the beginning, the goal was clear—to attain a state of wellness where therapy is no longer needed. And yes, that's copied straight from my treatment plan.

My plan was to be completely off anxiety medication before being discharged. But Sarah explained complete independence from medication may not always be feasible and that taking medication isn't wrong, nor does it mean I'm a failure. It took a lot of exploration of that topic to get to the bottom of why I felt that way.

Not surprisingly, it went back to when I was an inpatient at Walking in the Light. They drilled it into my head that if a man was on medication to control his anxiety, then he wasn't a 'real' man. I didn't realize it then, but that was their answer to anything they didn't want me to do. Why? Because even though I'm a gay *man, I still identify as a man. I want to be looked at as a man. If they wanted to control me, all they had to do was play on my insecurities—and they did.*

Sarah helped me reframe what I believe a 'man' is. It isn't something defined by sexual orientation or the medications a person takes but rather by the strength of his character, the depth of his compassion, and the courage to live authentically. For the first time ever, I didn't feel shame for who I loved. I felt worthy of being called a man.

With each day that passed, I shed the shackles of society's expectations and forged a new path for myself. One that was paved with self-love, acceptance, and unyielding pride.

Still, goodbyes are never easy. Although Sarah's my therapist, she's been a part of my life for the past five years. It's hard to say farewell to someone who's played such a pivotal role in my life. But I'm no longer a broken man. I'm walking away with my head held high. I have a newfound confidence and the knowledge that no words, no matter how cruel, could ever dim my light.

Still, it's going to feel odd when next Wednesday comes, and I don't have an appointment.

If you'd asked me a few years ago what my life would be like, I would never have guessed I'd be involved in BDSM, let alone be a willingly collared submissive to the kindest Master. Tony's surpassed everything I could've ever asked for in a partner. He's been patient and so unbelievably kind. Tony's taught me what it's like to be loved unconditionally—something I'd never experienced before.

Tony's impact on my life goes beyond what he and I share together. He's been the driving force behind some of the most significant changes in my life. It's because of him that I not only have London in my life but also a new family. A family of choice.

These are the people who have welcomed me with open arms, embracing me as one of their own without question. They've stood by me through thick and thin, offering me their unwavering support and love. They've supported me through my darkest moments and celebrated with me in times of joy. Tony's the thread that binds us all together, and for that, I'll always be grateful.

The past few months have been a rollercoaster of emotions. Tony and I were still riding the high from my collaring when I got a text from Natalie with a picture of her and Alex. She was holding up her hand. On her ring finger was a stunning diamond engagement ring.

It's kind of a crazy 'Gift of the Magi-esq' story. Natalie talked Viktor into helping her surprise Alex by flying back to New York City without telling him. Meanwhile, Alex was planning to surprise Natalie by coming back from Russia early and flying to Northmeadow. But when he got there, she wasn't there. So, he flew back and planned an even bigger surprise—he proposed to her in Central Park.

Unfortunately, their happiness was short-lived. Natalie got a phone call in the early morning hours of Christmas morning that her father had been shot in a robbery gone wrong at his pharmacy. Her crazy ex-boyfriend, Tommy, who apparently has an addiction, was trying to steal some pills when her father showed up. Stanley was shot in the lung. It was touch and go for a while, but thankfully, he survived. He's been in the hospital for months, but he's still in the hospital with a long road to recovery.

In the middle of all that, Alex went CRAZY. Without telling Natalie, he bought out her contract. I don't blame him. If Tony would've let me, I would've done the same thing. Except Natalie didn't see it the same way. She was furious and broke up with him.

They were miserable. For months. There was nothing I could say or do to help cheer her up. I offered to go stay with her, but she refused. Natalie said it would be too much with her traveling back and forth between the hospital in Branson and Northmeadow while she tried to keep her parents' store.

Fortunately, Brandon and Lana staged an intervention to get Natalie and Alex in the same room together. They were able to talk about their issues with communication and re-negotiate a contract. Thankfully, they're back together.

The other good thing to come out of this near tragedy is her parents apologized for their behavior and now accept Alex with open arms.

I was hopeful that, with her contract bought out, they'd be coming back to the city. But they're not. They've decided to stay in Missouri until further notice to help her parents.

Once again, I'm struggling with the selfish wish that Natalie would just come home.

Anthony

"NATALIE'S FATHER'S FINALLY BEEN DISCHARGED," Alex explains, relief evident in his voice. "So now we can move forward with our wedding plans."

"I know it was touch and go for a while there. I'm so glad to hear the good news. Leo will be, too," I remark, my tone filled with genuine happiness.

"I have a special request," Alex adds hesitantly.

Alex is never one to ask for frivolous things, so now I'm paying attention.

"We had the chance to discuss the bridal shower with Natalie's parents. Charlotte's insisting that we have the bridal shower in Northmeadow," he says, a note of exasperation evident in his voice.

I'm catering the shower, so I understand his concern. "That's fine. We don't mind traveling," I reply, hoping to alleviate some of his stress.

"That's not everything," he adds cautiously.

"Okay," I reply, noting the change in his tone.

"This is our wedding. It's supposed to be a time of fun and anticipation," Alex laments. "I wanted Natalie to enjoy planning this, but Charlotte's giving her a hard time with everything. I thought if we gave in and agreed to have the shower in North-meadow, she'd calm down. But nope," he sighs loudly.

"She disapproves of us getting married in Manhattan. Forget about the fact that we're having it at your restaurant and not a church. Charlotte was carrying on because she doesn't know what your food tastes like—"

"How about Leo and I take a trip out there and do a tasting?" I offer, trying to be helpful.

"You wouldn't mind?" he asks tentatively, seeking reassurance.

"Not at all. Natalie deserves the wedding of her dreams. And so do you, of course," I add, chuckling softly. "If I can help make that happen by coming out there to cook for her parents, then I'm all in."

"Do you and Leo have plans for the Fourth of July?" he asks with genuine curiosity.

"We don't," I reply.

"Would you like to come out for the holiday? My father and Luna, as well as Brandon and Lana, will be here. We can make a party out of it," Alex suggests, his tone much lighter now.

"That sounds like a lot of fun. We'll be there," I confirm.

"Natalie's going to be so excited," Alex says.

His excitement is contagious, which gives me an idea. "How about we do a scene when we get there?"

"What do you have in mind?"

"Something for both our subs." Leo enters the room and casts a curious glance my way. "I'm going to have to text you the details. My sub just walked in." Alex laughs. "I'll be in touch soon." We hang up, and I turn to Leo, who's practically bouncing with excitement. "Go ahead and ask."

"Where are we going, Master?" Leo asks eagerly.

"Northmeadow," I reveal, watching as Leo's eyes widen in excitement. "Alex invited us for the Fourth. Sam and Luna will be there. So will Brandon and Svetlana."

"Really?" Leo's excitement is palpable.

"We'll be doing a tasting for Charlotte and Stanley. She's giving Natalie a bit of a hard time about the shower and the wedding," I explain.

"Shocking," Leo responds dramatically, placing a hand over his chest.

"Leopold," I caution, sensing where his thoughts are going.

"I know. Natalie does everything she can to please them, but Charlotte's always giving her a hard time. It's not right."

"Right or wrong, it isn't any of our business," I assert firmly.

"But—"

"There are no buts. If you can't promise to behave, you won't go," I state, setting the boundary.

"I'll be on my best behavior," Leo assures me, flashing a charming smile.

"You better be. For Natalie's sake."

⌇

Me: We're signing the papers for the rental car.

Alex: Excellent. It's only about twenty minutes to get to the lake.

Me: We'll see you soon.

Our flight landed at a small airport just outside Northmeadow not long ago. After sorting out the paperwork, we locate our rental car, a white Volkswagen Jetta, in the parking lot. Leo and I stow our bags in the trunk, and he heads towards the passenger seat.

"Here." I toss the keys to him. "You're driving."

"I am?" he questions, eyebrows raised in surprise.

"You're the one who loves to drive," I jest, a playful smirk tugging at my lips.

Living in the city, driving isn't something we often do, but when we do, Leopold always jumps at the chance to drive. I don't

222

mind at all. I've had plenty of driving experience and am more than happy to relax in the passenger seat.

"It'll help keep my mind occupied," Leo answers enthusiastically. "I can't wait to see her."

"Soon enough," I reply, a soft smile gracing my lips.

As we make our way from what was already a fairly remote location to a lake nestled in the Ozark Mountains, the breathtaking beauty of the surroundings captivates me.

"Now I understand why Alex and Natalie have a cottage here," I observe, marveling at the picturesque scenery.

"But it's so far away from everything," Leo muses quietly.

"It's a bit secluded," I concur, nodding thoughtfully. "But I'm certain you'll find a variety of local businesses that offer everything you might require."

"I've never lived in a small town. Rolling Hills, where I grew up, was a pretty big area, and then I lived in San Diego. This—" He motions around us as we drive. "—is not like anything I've ever experienced."

Guided by the GPS, we make a turn onto a gravel road that leads us straight to Alex and Natalie's charming cottage. Leo's anticipation is evident as he quickly brings the car to a stop, practically bounding out of the driver's seat.

The front door of the cottage swings open, and Alex steps out onto the porch, with Natalie following closely behind. With a bright smile, Natalie rushes towards the car, presumably eager to greet Leo, but I quickly step forward, intercepting her path.

"Pixie," I say affectionately, pulling her into a tight hug. She's so tiny that lifting her off the ground is effortless.

"I can't believe you guys are here," she squeals in delight.

"You can put my sub down any time now," Alex teases, his laughter filling the air.

"She's cute," I comment, gently setting her down. "But I brought my own sub with me." Leo steps forward, holding our bags.

Natalie throws her arms around him, exclaiming, "Leo! I can't believe you're here." "I can't believe we're here either," Leo responds, leaning in to plant a kiss on her cheek. He then takes a look around. "You really live in the middle of nowhere."

"Wait until nighttime," she suggests, her gaze drifting upwards. "It gets so dark you can see all the stars."

"And risk getting eaten by a wild animal," Leo scoffs, shaking his head. "I'll take a pass," he quips, eliciting a giggle from Natalie.

"Let's go inside," Alex suggests. "Natalie will show you to your room so you can get settled in."

As we make our way into the house, I lean in and whisper, "I'd like to ask you to keep an open mind while we're here."

"I'll try my best, Master," Leo replies in a hushed tone.

Leopold

"It's this way." Natalie hooks her arm through mine, and I let her lead me through the contemporary yet inviting interior. Sunlight streams in through the skylights, creating an open and expansive atmosphere.

"This place is gorgeous. Your pictures don't do it justice, girl."

"Alex has a great eye for design," she says as she opens the door to what I assume is our room. "I'll miss this place when we go back to the city."

Stepping inside, I release the bags and immediately gravitate towards the windows, captivated by the panoramic scenery. "Look at that view," I marvel as I look out the expansive windows that showcase the lake.

Natalie joins me at the window, and together, we soak in the warm breeze drifting through the open window.

"I've missed you," I confess, pulling her close. "But I can see why you've been holed up here. Even I might be able to get used to this."

"You guys are welcome here anytime," she says softly, resting her head against my chest.

We share a moment of silence, gazing out over the tranquil

water. Two boats glide past, their wake creating gentle ripples along the rocky shore. It's a scene straight out of a storybook.

"Natalie. Leopold. We need you both out here," Alex's voice interrupts the moment.

"Coming," she replies.

"That sounds suspicious," I remark with a playful grin.

"It sure does. I wonder what's going on?"

"Let's go find out," I suggest, taking her hand.

As we step into the living room, we're met with a sight that hints at something more. The furniture has been moved aside, creating an open area in the center of the room. A black blanket lies on the floor. Tony's candles have been arranged next to it. Alex and Tony stand poised and confident, exuding dominance as they take control of the space.

"Go change," Alex instructs, handing Natalie some clothes.

"Yes, Sir," she responds with a smile before making her way past me.

"You, too," Tony directs, offering me a pair of spandex shorts.

"Yes, Master," I reply, hurrying to join Natalie. "Looks like we're about to have some fun."

Somehow, Natalie changed and made it back to the living room before me. When I get there, she's already on her knees. I join her, spreading my legs slightly and resting my hands with my palms up on my thighs.

"Anthony has graciously offered to give us an early wedding present," Alex says as he steps in front of Natalie. "Are you willing to allow him to create a wax design on you?"

Engaging in public scenes has become a thrilling aspect of my dynamic with Tony. Each one has been exhilarating. The idea of sharing a wax scene with another couple, especially that it's Alex and Natalie, is a tantalizing new adventure, one that promises to be both intense and exhilarating.

"Yes, Sir. I'd love that," Natalie responds eagerly.

"You and Leo will lie next to one another, and you will remain clothed," he continues, and I bite my lip to keep from laughing.

Alex and Natalie don't do public scenes—ever. He's extremely territorial where she's concerned.

"Leo, I want you on your stomach," Tony directs. "Pixie, lie on your back with your arm and leg against Leo's." While Tony lights the candles, he carries on speaking. "Alex tells me you two have played with wax."

"Yes," she replies respectfully.

"My wax is similar in burn temperature to what you've used. However, if you're uncomfortable in any way, you are to use your safewords. What are they?" he asks.

"Yellow and red."

"First, we're going to prepare your skin. It'll help with removing the wax later," Tony explains, kneeling beside me.

Drizzling warm oil down my spine, Tony's fingers work the liquid into my skin, his fingers dipping beneath the waistband of my shorts. Leaning towards me, his voice soft against my ear, he whispers, "Are you hard for me?"

"Yes, Master," I reply, licking my lower lip. "Very."

"Ready?" Anthony asks.

"I'm ready," Natalie answers.

"Let's have some fun," Anthony announces with a grin as he reaches over me. The scent of bergamot and cedar fills my nose, and I close my eyes, savoring it. "Your Dominant is going to be my assistant. I'm going to teach him how to be an artist," he adds, sharing a laugh with Alex.

Tony patiently guides Alex's hand, showing him where to drip the wax. Together, they work in harmony, covering us in the warm, cascading liquid. With closed eyes, I surrender to the sensation, letting myself drift into a state of deep relaxation.

"Head down," Alex admonishes sternly. "You'll see it when it's time."

"May I have a hint?"

"No," they echo in unison.

I chuckle, well aware of Natalie's impatience with surprises.

"Patience, little pixie," Anthony reassures with a gentle tone. "Relax and enjoy this."

Tony steps in, focusing on the delicate nuances of the design he's creating, while Alex assists with the broader strokes. Soft strains of music filter through the room, enveloping us in a cocoon of calmness. With a contented sigh, I shut my eyes and surrender to a blissful drowsiness, letting myself drift into a peaceful slumber.

"It's done," Tony announces, bringing me back to awareness. Natalie turns her head to look at me and gives me a sleepy smile. "Alex, can you grab the black light from my bag?"

Tony dims the lights and closes the curtains, casting the room in darkness. Then, he activates the black light, casting an ethereal glow across the space. Beside me, Natalie lets out a soft gasp of awe at the magical display.

"Shh," Anthony corrects her gently.

The air is charged with anticipation as I lie motionless, eagerly awaiting the reveal of Tony's handiwork. Meanwhile, Alex diligently photographs the scene from various angles, each click of the camera capturing the essence of the moment. Despite the meticulous preparation, a sense of apprehension lingers, knowing that the fragility of the wax designs leaves them vulnerable to breakage upon removal.

"I think I got enough," Alex states, satisfied with his photography.

"It's time to lift the wax. Hopefully, we can get it off in one piece."

He and Tony take their positions on each side of us. Alex whispers to Natalie, "You look gorgeous covered in so many colors, baby girl."

Side by side, they methodically remove the wax from our skin, handling it with utmost care. It appears mostly intact, but I continue to watch with bated breath until they set it safely on the dining table.

Alex returns to Natalie, helping her get to her feet. "Ready to see it?" he asks.

"I'm so ready." Something tells me there's a double meaning to Natalie's words, suggesting an underlying truth about the transformative power of hot wax. It's impossible to experience the sensuality of hot wax without being affected.

Alex leads Natalie to the table while I linger behind with Tony.

"As usual, you looked beautiful as your skin turned pink," Tony croons softly, his voice carrying a hint of desire. "The things I want to do to you. I can't wait—."

"Is that glitter?" Natalie's voice breaks through the moment.

"It is," Tony replies, moving away from me. "Do you like it?"

With my erection straining against the spandex shorts, I inch away, my thoughts turning to the predators lurking outside. A definite mood killer.

"Like it? It's the most beautiful thing I've ever seen," Natalie exclaims. "Thank you so much. I'll treasure this always."

"I have a custom frame for it in the car," Tony explains. "Leo and I will arrange it in the frame for you before we leave."

Alex clasps Tony's shoulder. "Thank you. This means a lot to both Natalie and me."

"It's my pleasure," Tony replies warmly before turning to me. "You two go get cleaned up so we can eat."

"Come on in," Natalie invites, her voice welcoming. "I'll wash your back off."

I follow Natalie into her room.

"I don't know how Tony does that," Natalie muses.

"It's something that comes naturally to him," I explain. "And I'm glad. I love being on the receiving end."

"I can see why."

"Thank you, sweetheart." I kiss her forehead. "I'm going to go get dressed or hopefully undressed."

"Go get 'em, tiger," she giggles.

Entering our room, Tony's sitting on the edge of the bed waiting for me. "Lock the door."

I follow his command. When I turn to go back, Tony's behind me. His hands gently frame my face as he kisses me softly, the tenderness gradually giving way to passion. "Take your shorts off," he instructs between kisses, his voice husky with desire.

With fluid grace, I slide the spandex down my legs, letting it drop to the floor without a sound. Stepping out of it, I kick the garment aside before focusing on his belt. "May I, Master?" I request permission as I reach for it.

With a subtle nod, he consents, and I swiftly unbuckle it, letting his pants fall away. Tony sheds his shirt and discards it. He stands before me, his boxer briefs straining against the evidence of his arousal.

Gliding my hands down his torso, I feel the defined contours of his abdomen beneath my fingertips, trailing lower until I reach the waistband of his underwear. With deliberate slowness, I ease them down, freeing his pulsing erection.

Dropping to my knees, I wrap my fingers around his thick shaft, applying gentle pressure as I stroke him. With my other hand, I cradle his balls, relishing the weight of them in my palm.

With a gentle yet firm grip on the back of my head, he guides me closer. "Suck my cock, Leopold," he instructs, his tone laced with urgency.

I part my lips and ease him into my mouth, gradually sliding his length deeper. He lets out a low groan, holding me still for a moment before granting me air. "Damn," he breathes out. "You're incredible at that."

When we first met, this scenario, willingly giving a blow job, seemed impossible. But I'm not the same man I was back then. I've reclaimed everything stolen from me. I have complete trust in the Master I've chosen to submit to.

I maintain my rhythm, gradually intensifying my efforts until he signals for me to stop. "Get on the bed," he instructs.

Tony drops to his knees behind me, spreading my cheeks to

expose my waiting entrance. His tongue dances around the rim before pushing inside, evoking unrestrained moans of pleasure from me. With each sensual caress, I'm reminded of just how much I love it when Tony pleasures me this way, his every movement driving me wild with desire.

With his hand wrapped firmly around my throbbing cock, Tony continues to expertly tongue-fuck me, sending waves of pleasure coursing through my body. "Master, I'm so close," I pant desperately, the need for him overwhelming me. "I need you inside me, please."

"You want this?" he asks as he rubs his cock against my hole.

"Yes," I plead, my voice trembling.

With a slow, deliberate motion, he eases the head of his cock into me, gradually sinking deeper until I'm completely filled. The sensation elicits a mutual groan of ecstasy. Tony's hand snakes around my waist, finding my throbbing cock and wrapping around it, adding an extra layer of pleasure as he jerks me off. His other hand finds purchase on my waist, anchoring himself as he increases the speed and intensity of his thrusts.

"Feels so good," I say through gritted teeth.

"Come for me, Leopold," Tony commands as he ruts into me with furious abandon.

Waves of ecstasy crash over me, my body trembling as I release onto the bed. Tony's unwavering rhythm only intensifies the pleasure, sending tremors of delight coursing through me. With one last, powerful thrust, he fills me completely, his cock pulsing with warmth inside me.

Breathless, we sink onto the bed, our bodies spent from the intensity of our passion.

"Do you think they heard us?" I ask, and Tony chuckles heartily. "What?"

"Alexander had these rooms soundproofed when he remodeled," Tony explains with a grin.

"Phew," I exclaim, dropping my arm over my forehead. "I wouldn't want them to think we're bad guests."

"Come on," Tony says, still chuckling. "Let's go get cleaned up."

After a quick shower, we rejoin Alex and Natalie in the living room, where they're already tidying up.

"Here, let me help," I offer, bending down to collect the leftover bits of wax from the floor.

"Thank you," Natalie responds appreciatively as she carefully folds the blanket and picks it up. "Shall I put this in the washer, Tony?"

"That would be great," Tony confirms, nodding his head.

While Natalie starts the laundry, Alex, Tony, and I quickly restore the furniture to its original position. With the house back in order, Alex suggests ordering takeout for dinner, and we all agree. Outside, we enjoy our meal together, captivated by the beauty of the night.

When Tony asked me to try to keep an open mind, I anticipated a struggle, yet here, beneath this vast expanse of stars, I'm spellbound. The stars shimmer with an intensity I've never witnessed before, casting a radiant glow upon the earth. Fireflies dance in the meadow, adding to the enchantment. All around, the night is alive with the harmonious chorus of bullfrogs, crickets, and the occasional bird. Amidst the symphony of nature's nocturnal chorus, I feel a profound sense of peace and connection.

This place exudes magic.

Leopold

As the new day dawns, a flurry of anticipation and apprehension fills the air. Alex's bodyguard, Viktor, appears particularly tense, his usually composed demeanor slightly strained as he keeps a watchful eye on the surroundings. Despite Viktor's unease, the other guests seem unaware. They're immersing themselves in the joyful atmosphere and eagerly anticipating the festivities ahead.

Tony and I spend most of the day prepping for this evening's dinner.

"Go on outside," Tony urges, wiping his hands on a kitchen towel. "I'm just about done."

"I'm fine here," I reply, enjoying the familiarity of the kitchen and the comforting routine of helping Tony.

"I want you to go outside and enjoy yourself," he insists, his tone gentle but firm.

"Are you sure, Master?" I ask, torn between staying and going.

"Yes," he replies, pressing a quick kiss to my lips before nudging me towards the door.

As I step outside, I notice the only empty seat is next to Natalie's mom, Charlotte. With a deep breath, I approach her. "Is this seat taken?" I ask politely.

"No, it isn't," she replies, gesturing for me to sit.

"Perfect," I say with a smile, settling into the seat beside her. Leaning closer, I whisper, "I never thought I'd say this, but I think I'm starting to love it here."

"You are?" she asks, clearly surprised.

"Trust me. It shocks me more than you. I've never been to a lake," I reply with a chuckle."Never?" Charlotte repeats, sounding incredulous.

"Nope," I shake my head, a hint of nostalgia creeping in. "My parents would only take us to the shore when we were young."

"Where did you grow up?" she asks, curiosity piqued.

"California," I answer.

"Whatever made you move to New York City?"

"That's a long story," I reply, glancing around. "But I think we have time. Would you care to join me for a walk?"

"A walk?" she asks tentatively, then surprises me when she says, "Sure."

I rise and extend my arm, offering it to her. She hesitates before sliding hers into mine. Natalie shoots me a questioning glance, and I respond with a reassuring wink before leading Charlotte away.

What am I doing? This woman rejected her own son for being gay. Yet, something inside me urges me to talk to her, and I've learned from Tony's experiences not to ignore such impulses. Everything happens for a reason.

"How I ended up in Manhattan isn't a happy topic. I don't want to bring all that negative energy to the table," I explain.

"That's very thoughtful," she says softly, patting my arm.

I wait until we're out of earshot from the group before continuing.

"When I came out to my parents, they had me pack my bags and sent me to live at a conversion therapy center," I begin my tale. Charlotte keeps her eyes forward as I speak. "I was there for two years until I escaped."

"Escaped?" she questions. "Do you mean until you were discharged?"

"No, I mean escaped," I repeat before continuing, "My therapist regularly abused me," I explain. "It wasn't until he drugged me and raped me for several days that I couldn't take it anymore," I explain. "Even though I was eighteen, they had no plan to discharge me. So, in the middle of the night, when no one was watching, I made my move. I had to threaten the woman at the front desk to let me out. Then, I ran."

"I'm very sorry the people who were supposed to help you hurt you," she says, her tone laced with sorrow. "Did you go back home when you escaped?" The word sounds almost foreign this time.

"No. I've not seen or spoken to my parents in nearly ten years."

"Oh," she says, her voice barely above a whisper.I continue my story. "I went to the police to report the rape. They took my statement and set me up in a program for homeless LGBTQ+ youth."

"Was that in New York?"

"It was in San Diego. It was a good place with good people, except I was so desperate to be loved that I messed up. I met someone and even though I was warned he was trouble, I didn't listen." We stop walking when we get to the water's edge. "His name was Krew. He pretended to care about me enough that I let my guard down. He drugged me, got me hooked on heroin and other drugs all so he could invite people in to rape me," I admit. "More people than I can count. I looked forward to the next time he'd drug me so I could stay numb."

"Please, Leo. I can't hear any more," Charlotte says, her voice quivering and tears streaming down her face. "I had a son, Michael. I'm sure Natalie told you about him."

"She did."

"You remind me so much of him. Your blonde hair and blue eyes and your gentle soul." She pauses to catch her breath, her words laden with guilt. "It's my fault he's not here. When he told us he was gay and was in a same-sex relationship, we rejected him —I rejected him. I was his mother, the person who was supposed to love him unconditionally, but I failed him."

"If we didn't kick him out. If we tried to understand him, he'd still be here," she says, her voice trembling with regret. "If I could go back and do things differently, I would." She looks up at me, and I see a familiar brokenness reflected in her eyes. "I'd give anything to have my boy back. I want to tell him that even though I don't like the lifestyle he chose, I love him."

"I'm sure he knows." I offer what comfort I can.

"I'm a Christian woman, Leopold. I believe God works in mysterious ways—ways we often don't understand," she says, attempting to regain her composure.

"Admittedly, I haven't gone to church in many years."

"That's okay. God still loves you," Charlotte says tenderly. "And I believe he sent you to me so I can love you, too." Her unexpected words catch me off guard, and she notices. "I'm the last person you thought you'd ever hear that from, right?"

"To be honest, yes," I admit.

"Ever since Natalie and Alex told us about you and Tony, I couldn't get you, in particular, off my mind," she explains, her voice filled with sincerity. "I've prayed for you for months, and I've asked God why He's bringing you into my life. The answer I kept getting is love heals." Tears trickle down my cheeks as her words sink in. "I'm not your mom, and I wouldn't try to replace her, but I will do my best to show you the kind of unconditional love I should've shown to my son and the kind your mother should've shown to you."

"I don't know what to say, and I'm rarely ever speechless," I admit, my voice thick with emotion.

"I'm not perfect, and I'm going to make mistakes. But I ask that you give me a chance."

Inviting Charlotte for a stroll had seemed like a simple

gesture. But as we walked and I began to bear my soul to her, I realized the profound impact it was having on both of us. Setting aside her long-held convictions, she embraced me with a mother's love, filling a void that had long haunted me. It was a moment of catharsis, a healing journey shared between two souls unexpectedly brought together by circumstance.

Wordlessly, I wrap Charlotte in a gentle embrace, feeling a rush of gratitude and emotion surge through me. She responds immediately with a silent promise of understanding and compassion. "Thank you, Charlotte," I murmur, my voice trembling with emotion. "This... this means everything to me."

After regaining our composure, we make our way back to the table just as Tony begins to serve the food. It's no surprise that everyone thoroughly enjoys the meal.

"Anthony, dear," Charlotte gushes, her eyes sparkling with delight. "Your food is exquisite."

Tony, seated next to me, beams with pride. "Thank you, ma'am."

"Our wedding guests will be getting a real treat."

Sam stands, raising his glass. "I'd like to propose a toast to the future, Mr. and Mrs. Montgomery."

Glasses clink together as everyone raises a toast to the soon-to-be-wedded couple.

The awareness of being gay dawned on me from a young age. It was accompanied by the knowledge that legal marriage in America was reserved solely for heterosexual couples. It was a bitter pill to swallow, a reminder of the systemic barriers that stood in the way of LGBTQ+ individuals. Unless I somehow magically turned straight, marriage was a privilege that wouldn't be afforded to me.

Until now.

With the recent legislative changes, the tide has turned. Gay couples are now afforded the legal right to marry in every corner of the U.S. While it's a milestone worth celebrating, the fight for acceptance and equality is far from over. Yet, the mere fact that we have the right to marry—to be seen as equal in the eyes of the law—fills me with hope for what lies ahead.

Except for one small or rather large detail. I don't know if Tony would want to get married.

Anthony

Leopold pulls our car into a mundane parking lot, the crunching of the gravel beneath the tires echoing softly. I can't help but envision the potential lying in this unassuming space. The picture in my mind is so clear—smooth pavement accented by lush greenery. A flagstone path lined by bursts of colorful blooms invites guests to wander toward the three-story log cabin.

"Wow," Leo marvels, his eyes sweeping across the scene. "This place is gorgeous."

"It is," I agree, still lost in my daydream of how much better Water's Edge could look with a little TLC.

We retrieve our bags from the trunk, and my eyes are drawn to the shimmering lake that's only steps away. As we approach the front porch, the gentle marks of age become more apparent in the building's weathered exterior. Yet, it doesn't detract from the allure. Together, we walk up the natural stone steps. I'm delighted to discover raised flower beds lining the space, their blossoms adding bursts of color to the weathered wood.

Rocking chairs line the porch, their well-worn surfaces inviting us to rest awhile, while ceiling fans, some of which no longer seem to work, continue their slow rotation. A few strategic improvements could evolve this area into a true gem. An elderly woman appears from around the corner, a watering can in her hand.

"Good afternoon, you must be the guests I was waiting for," she greets us warmly, a smile spreading across her face. "Anthony and Leopold, right?"

"Yes, ma'am. Can I help you with that?" I offer, stepping forward to lend a hand.

"That would be wonderful," she says, passing me the metal can with a grateful nod. "It seems to get heavier each day."

"Your flowers are breathtaking," I comment, pouring water into the closest container filled with geraniums and evening primrose before tending to the hibiscus.

"When my husband Carl was alive, gardening was his passion. Having them helps me feel close to him," she shares, her voice tinged with nostalgia.

"That's a beautiful way to honor his memory," Leo adds, his tone empathetic.

"Come on inside," Mrs. Wilson says. "Let's get you checked in."

As we follow the woman into the foyer of the home, she takes her place behind the desk, slipping on wire-rimmed glasses before reaching for a notebook. That's when I notice the absence of a computer or any other modern technology to check us in. "Anthony and Leopold Genovese. You're Italian," she remarks, glancing up at me.

I offer a nod in response, attempting to maintain my usual calm demeanor. "Yes, that's correct," I confirm and notice a flicker of surprise dance across Leo's features.

The contrast between the commitment of our D/s relationship and the possibility of legal marriage weighs heavily on my mind, leaving me to wonder if Leopold would ever desire such a conventional bond.

I catch his gaze for a moment before quickly returning my attention to the woman at the desk.

"You'll be my guests for the next six nights. Until Sunday," she confirms, her tone conveying a sense of hospitality as she reads from the page before her. "I've arranged for you to stay in my largest room on the third floor. You'll have a view of the water from your balcony.""That's perfect. I'm just glad you had vacancies," I say with a grateful smile.

"You boys are my only guests this week," she states, her tone carrying a sense of resignation. "Unfortunately, business gets slower each year."

"How is that possible in such a beautiful place?" I wonder aloud.

My gaze sweeps across the space, taking in the meticulous craftsmanship of the natural woodwork that graces every corner, from the polished floorboards to the intricately carved beams overhead. My gaze then drifts toward the expansive windows that dominate the walls, offering uninterrupted views of the tranquil lake just a stone's throw away.

"I don't keep up with all the fancy on-the-line things those big hotel chains have," she comments, and I suppress a chuckle at her charming term for the internet. "No one knows this place is here."

"That's a shame," I sympathize, and she offers a casual shrug in response.

"Here's the key to your room," she says, presenting a physical key with a slight flourish. "You just missed lunch, but if you're hungry, I can throw something together for you."

"We actually ate before we arrived, but thank you for the offer," I decline politely.

"Dinner's at five thirty," she adds, her tone hospitable.

"What's on the menu?" Leo asks.

"Stuffed haddock," she replies.

"That sounds delicious. I'll definitely come hungry," Leo responds eagerly.

Mrs. Wilson's face lights up with genuine delight. "I look forward to seeing you boys later," she says warmly, her eyes twinkling.

Looking around, I inquire, "Is there an elevator?"

"There isn't. Are you okay with the steps? If not, I can move you down to the ground floor," she offers, her voice filled with concern.

"The steps are just fine," I assure her.

Making our way up the grand oak staircase, I'm struck by the craftsmanship of the hand-carved railing, each curve and twist a testament to the artistry of its maker. The details are exquisite, something you don't often find in modern fixtures. Along the walls, picture montages depict scenes from years past, each labeled with the corresponding year—a poignant reminder of this place's vibrant history. It's disheartening to witness the emptiness that now pervades, especially during the peak of the summer tourist season.

After settling into our room, Leopold and I are eager to take advantage of the sun-soaked day. We venture down to the lake, where the bed and breakfast boasts a picturesque sandy beach. There, a young family with three playful children catches our eye, their laughter mingling with the gentle lapping of the waves. Nearby, a dock extends into the water, its sign tempting us with the promise of boat rentals, but there's no attendant.

"Would you care for a walk?" I suggest.

"That would be great," Leo agrees.

As we set off, the gentle lapping of the water against the shore accompanies our steps, a soothing rhythm that guides us forward. Sunlight filters through the canopy overhead, dappling the ground with patches of golden warmth. With each twist and turn of the path, we uncover new vistas and hidden nooks, each one a testament to the beauty of this tranquil oasis.

"This place is a hidden gem," I remark, casting a thoughtful glance around. "She just needs the right tools to get it seen."

"Something tells me it's all a bit too much for her," Leo adds, his expression reflecting a mix of sympathy and concern.

"You might be right." We continue our stroll in contemplative silence for a while. "I wonder when the last time was that someone cooked for Mrs. Wilson?"

"What are you thinking, Master?" Leo's voice carries a note of curiosity.

"I'd like to find her before she starts cooking and see if she'll let me make tonight's meal," I suggest, my voice laced with determination.

"This is one of the many reasons I love you," Leo replies, admiration shining in his eyes. "Your kindness knows no bounds."

The late afternoon sun filters through the windows as I seek out Mrs. Wilson. I find her in the kitchen peeling potatoes. She stops every few minutes to rub her hands, which appear sore from a lifetime of work.

"May I take over for you?" I ask, extending a helping hand.

"Don't be silly," she chuckles, waving off my offer. "This is just part of the job."

"When's the last time someone cooked for you?" I inquire gently.

She takes a moment to reflect before replying, "It's been quite a while, I reckon."

"Did I mention I'm a chef?" I interject, hoping to sway her decision.

"His food is absolutely divine," Leo chimes in with a smile. "You should come visit us in New York."

"I've never been out of Missouri," Mrs. Wilson admits wistfully.

"I'd be honored if you'd allow me to cook for you this evening," I press once more, my determination unwavering.

"Okay. I'd like that very much," she concedes, passing the potato peeler over to me. "Would you care to join me on the porch?" Leo suggests, offering a change of scenery. "We can relax for a while."

"I'll pour us some sweet tea," Mrs. Wilson announces, her voice carrying a hint of Southern hospitality as she retrieves three glasses from the cupboard. "The fish is in the fridge. So is the broccoli." With practiced efficiency, she pours the drinks. "The spice cabinet is the one on the end. The utensils are all in the big drawer." She offers a thorough rundown of the kitchen before excusing herself and disappearing with Leopold.

I set my phone on the counter and cue up my favorite playlist, the familiar tunes serving as a comforting backdrop as I dive into preparations for tonight's meal.

An hour later, the three of us gather around the table, plates filled with the fruits of my labor.

"This isn't my stuffing recipe," Mrs. Wilson remarks, taking another bite with evident curiosity.

"It isn't. I hope you don't mind," I reply, my tone tinged with a touch of uncertainty.

"Mind? It's scrumptious. Would you be willing to give me the recipe," she insists, a warm smile gracing her lips.

"I can do that," I agree, relief flooding through me.

We continue to eat in companionable silence, the clink of cutlery against plates the only sound filling the room until Mrs. Wilson breaks the quiet. "What brings you two boys to Finn Lake?"

"Friends of ours have a cottage here. We came to join them for the holiday," I explain, hoping to satisfy her curiosity.

"Oh, who are they?" Mrs. Wilson asks, her interest clearly piqued.

"Alex Montgomery and Natalie Clarke."

"Yes, Natalie Clarke. I heard she was getting married," Mrs. Wilson remarks, taking a sip of water. "I remember when she and that handsome fiancé of hers stayed here."

"I've known Alex for a long time. He's a good guy," I assure her.

"How do you two know each other?" Mrs. Wilson asks innocently, her curiosity catching me off guard.

"Leopold and I are a couple," I confess, gauging her reaction carefully. "We've been together six years."

"No one around here knows," Mrs. Wilson confesses quietly, her voice tinged with a hint of sadness. "My grandson, Lance, is gay, and I love him unconditionally." Despite her candidness, her words hold a sense of grace, reflecting her deep-seated acceptance. "People around here might not understand," she confides further, her tone gentle yet resolute. "But for me, it's simple. He's my grandson, and that's all that matters. Love knows no bounds."

"I hope Lance knows how lucky he is," Leo remarks sincerely.

"I'm sure he does," Mrs. Wilson replies with a warm smile.

"How many children do you have?" I ask.

"Just one. A son."

"Does he live close?" Leo inquires.

"No. He and his family live in Florida. He's a marine biologist," Mrs. Wilson explains, a hint of pride in her voice. "He wants me to retire and move in with them," she adds.

"I'm sure they miss you. Why don't you do that?" Leo presses gently.

"I'd love to," she says wistfully.

"But?" I prompt, sensing there's more to her hesitation.

"I'd have to close this place," she confesses.

"Have you considered selling it?" I ask.

"Not seriously. Who'd want to buy a bed and breakfast that has no boarders?" she asks, gesturing around with a resigned expression. "And I don't have the heart to see it shut down," she adds, rising from the table to gather the dishes. "You cooked, so I'll wash."

"I didn't cook," Leo says, jumping up from his seat. "I'll help you."

Leopold and I lose ourselves in the rhythm of lazy days spent by the lake and leisurely strolls through quaint streets lined with colorful storefronts. But beneath the surface of our carefree exploration, Mrs. Wilson's words weigh heavily on my mind. *No one would want to buy a bed and breakfast that has no boarders, and I don't have the heart to see it shut down.* Her heartfelt sentiments tug at my conscience.

On the eve of our departure, a wave of reluctance washes over me, and I find myself not wanting to leave.

"We've had a truly wonderful time this week," I say to Mrs. Wilson, who's dabbing at the tears in her eyes.

"I have too. I'm going to miss you boys," she replies, her voice tinged with genuine affection.

"We'll be back in a few weeks for Natalie's bridal shower. Can we make reservations to stay here now?" I inquire eagerly, already anticipating our return to this beloved retreat.

"Oh yes, that'll be wonderful," she exclaims, a smile brightening her tear-streaked face as she hurries to retrieve her notebook. After providing her with the necessary information, she embraces us both warmly. "Have a safe trip back to New York."

"Thank you," I respond, returning her hug and planting a gentle kiss on her cheek. "We'll see you soon."

Leopold

RECLINING ON THE SOFA NEXT TO TONY, MY MIND drifts back to our recent stay in Northmeadow. Memories of lazy mornings by the lake, leisurely walks through the quaint downtown, and heartfelt conversations with Mrs. Wilson flood my thoughts. It's hard to believe that when we first got there, I was ready to turn around and come back to the city, but by the time we had to say goodbye, I didn't want to leave.

I'd intended to bring up the topic of marriage to Tony while we were there. The romantic atmosphere and picturesque surroundings seemed like the perfect backdrop for such a conversation. But as each day passed, I found myself hesitating. Now that we're back in the city, it feels like I missed my chance.

A text from an unknown number interrupts my lamenting.

Unknown: It's Lana. Natalie's postponing her bridal shower. We'll be in touch.

The cryptic nature leaves me feeling uneasy. I attempt to text back, but my message fails to send.

"What do you think this means?" I show Tony the peculiar message.

"It sounds as though they're extending their Russian vacation," Tony muses, glancing up from his book to examine the text on my phone.

"Natalie wouldn't postpone her bridal shower for a trip to Russia," I reply, a note of concern lacing my words. "I've tried calling Natalie a million times, but my calls go straight to voicemail, and my texts are all unread."

"They don't have cell service where they're staying," Tony responds, his gaze returning to the book in his hands.

"Then how did Lana text me, and why was it from an unknown number?" I press, a sense of unease settling in the pit of my stomach.

"Why does Svetlana do anything?" Tony suggests with a nonchalant shrug. "She probably lost her phone. I'm sure it's nothing."

"I have a bad feeling," I confess, my apprehension growing with each passing moment.

"Viktor's with them, and they're at Maxim's, so all of his security is there too. I'm sure they're fine," Tony reassures, though his words do little to ease my concern.

Scanning through my social media feeds, I hope to find an update from either Natalie or Lana, but there have been no recent posts. I toy with the idea of reaching out to Charlotte but decide against it. She was upset enough when Alex and Natalie left in a hurry. I don't want to cause her any more distress. I'm sure Tony's right. Given Maxim's affiliations with the Russian Bratva and his extensive security, they're probably safer in Russia than they are in New York City.

Anthony

A QUICK GLANCE AT MY CELL CONFIRMS THAT MY UBER has just pulled up.Leo and I have to be at the airport in three hours. But I'm stuck at the restaurant meeting with the architect. We're ironing out the intricate details for the installation of wrought iron gates that will mark the entrance to our highly anticipated garden wedding venue.

However, our permits hit a snag. There were some bureaucratic hurdles dealing with logistical issues impeding our progress. My architect worked diligently to make the necessary adjustments to obtain the permits. He's here now reviewing the changes with me.

"Is there anything else you need from me?" I ask, my irritation thinly veiled.

"Your signature on the proposal," the architect replies, tapping a few screens on his tablet. "Here's the final design."

"And this will meet the city's requirements for the permit?" I seek confirmation.

"Yes, Mr. Genovese."

With a swift motion of my finger, I sign the screen. "I apologize for any abruptness. I have a flight to catch and am on a tight schedule."

"That's all I need from you at the moment," he acknowledges.

"Excellent. I'll be reachable via text if any issues arise."

"Safe travels," he bids farewell.

Me: I'm getting into the car now. We'll be there shortly.

Leopold: Perfect. I'll grab the bags and head down to the lobby.

The sluggish progress through Manhattan's bustling streets affords me plenty of time to peruse the detailed spreadsheet crafted by Emersyn, our newly hired wedding consultant. She's meticulous with her details, listing all the couples who are looking to celebrate their special day at the new venue.

It was Leopold's suggestion to hire someone to oversee this part of our business. It seems he was correct. Emersyn has appointments every two hours all weekend to show the space to interested couples. Our venue is in high demand, with bookings likely extending well into the upcoming year.

Italiano Desiderio is the culmination of years' worth of dreams and hard work. After Kam died, I almost walked away from it. Let it die with him. But as I healed, I rediscovered my purpose and passion. The restaurant served as my sanctuary, the place where I could still feel close to Kam on the days the pain of his loss seemed too much to bear.

Leopold has thrived here, as well. In those early days, bussing tables, although a menial job, was a means for him to find direction—something to help give him a purpose in life when he didn't have one. But as time went on, and he found healing, his charm and charisma captivated diners. Promoting him to a full-time host was a natural progression. From there, he earned a college degree, and now he helps me run the business.

Today, this restaurant embodies not just my dream but Leopold's as well. So, why do I feel so unsettled lately?

It all stems from my recent discussion with Mrs. Wilson about her wish to move to Florida to be with her son and his family and her resignation from being unable to sell the bed and breakfast. I haven't been able to stop thinking about Northmeadow, the serenity of the lake, or the quaint yet failing inn. I'm hoping this second trip is what's needed to dispel these nagging thoughts. After all, our life is here, not in Northmeadow.

When the car is a block away, I text Leo.

Me: We're about to turn onto our street.

Leopold: I'll be outside.

Several hours later, we find ourselves back at the bed and breakfast. This time, the lot is not as empty as before. Two other cars are already parked there, hinting at the presence of other guests.

"It looks like there's some other people here," Leo points out, nodding towards the other cars in the parking lot. "Mrs. Wilson must be thrilled."

"I'm sure she is," I reply, noting the increased activity with a smile.

With our bags in hand, we make our way to the entrance, where Mrs. Wilson greets us warmly.

"Good afternoon, boys," Mrs. Wilson beams as she rounds the desk to greet us.

"How are you?" I ask, giving her a friendly kiss on the cheek.

"No use complaining," she says with a grin. "How was your flight?"

"Uneventful," Leo responds.

"I'm told those are the best kinds, she replies and turns to me. "Tony, dear, I have a favor to ask."

"What is it?"

"Would you be willing to make that haddock dish for dinner tonight? There are two other couples here this weekend, and I hate to admit this," she confesses, casting a cautious glance around. "I haven't been able to get the stuffing to taste the same as when you made it.""I'd be delighted to," I assure Mrs. Wilson.

"Do you mind if I stayed and watched? Maybe I can figure out what I'm doing wrong," she inquires, her eyes reflecting a mix of curiosity and determination.

"Of course. I can walk you through it if you'd like," I offer, eager to assist.

"That would be wonderful." She retreats behind her desk. "Let's get you checked in so you can get yourselves settled. I put you boys in the same room. Is that okay?"

"That's perfect," I reply with a smile.

After we get the key, Leo and I start the walk upstairs.

"I'm jealous, Master," Leo remarks with a soft laugh.

"Jealous?" I echo, raising an eyebrow.

"I'm pretty certain Mrs. Wilson was flirting with you," Leo pouts playfully.

"I know the perfect cure for jealousy," I tease, turning the key in the lock to our room. "Take your clothes off and get on the bed, ass in the air, so I can remind you why there's no need for such feelings."

Leo wastes no time, dropping his bag to the floor and kicking off his shoes with casual ease. Then, he indulges in a tantalizing striptease, shedding his clothes with deliberate sensuality, piece by piece.

As Leo gradually reveals more of his skin, I find myself mesmerized by the canvas of his body. Over the past few years, he's gotten several more tattoos. But none hold the same significance to me as the phoenix rising from the flames gracing his back.

He used my sketches for the wax art I created on him from our first scene and had it recreated into something permanent. To know he chose to immortalize that memory upon his skin still leaves me breathless and fills me with a profound sense of connection.

He saunters by me, and his fingers dance lightly over the bulge in my pants. I'm transfixed as he seductively crawls onto the bed, lowering his face to the mattress and baring himself to me. I waste no time grabbing the lube from my bag and opening my pants to free my erection.

"There will never be anyone else for me," I breathe, my voice laden with desire as I enter him. "Every damn breath I take is for you," I gasp as I thrust into him.

"I love being yours, Master," he whispers, his voice laced with devotion.

"Say it again," I demand.

"You own every piece of me, Master," he exhales, his words heavy with desire. "Take me. Use my body for your pleasure," he pleads, his tone submissive yet eager.

His words ignite a primal need within me, a desire I hadn't realized was there. I grab his hips firmly, knowing my fingers will leave a mark—my mark, a testament to my ownership. I pound into him relentlessly, ensuring he feels every inch of me. I crave the sensation of claiming every part of him as my own. Leo's moans turn into screams, his fingers clawing at the sheets as he eagerly pushes back against me.

"That's right, Leopold. Let me hear how much you love your Master's cock in your ass," I growl.

"Yes, Master. I do," he moans, his voice a mix of pleasure and desperation.

I slam into him, the force causing our bodies to collide, our skin slapping together. My orgasm builds as he begs for more, his words fueling my desire. Reaching around, I grab his hard length, pumping fast. "You're going to come for me while I fill your ass."

Leo tenses as he climaxes, his ass clenching around my cock, driving me over the edge. "Fuck," I roar, the intensity of the moment overwhelming.

I pull out and collapse on the bed next to him, my chest heaving with exertion.

"Is it always like this?" Leo asks, his voice laced with awe.

I know what he's asking but not saying.

"No," I reply without hesitation. "It's never felt like this with anyone." I prop myself up on my arm, meeting Leopold's gaze. "I want to spend forever with you. Make me the happiest man ever, and marry me."

Leo's eyes widen in disbelief. "What did you say?"

"I want you to share my life. My last name. I want you to marry me."

"Oh my God, yes." He pulls me close, his legs straddling my waist as he leans down, his lips meeting mine. "Yes," he says between kisses. "A million times, yes."

After a refreshing shower where we both have another mind-blowing orgasm, Leo and I make our way downstairs, eager to find Mrs. Wilson and start the dinner preparations.

Leopold

Lost in a whirlwind of emotions, I find myself grappling with the reality of the moment. Tony asked me to marry him, and I said yes. For so long, I doubted whether Tony truly wanted marriage, whether he saw a future with me beyond our Dom/sub dynamic. Now, as I bask in the glow of his proposal, those doubts feel like distant echoes. I have a fiancé. I'm engaged. It's a surreal realization, one that fills me with a mixture of joy, disbelief, and excitement. How did I get here? How is this my life? Every dream I never dared to entertain is suddenly within reach, coming true in ways I never imagined possible.

As I drift through the haze of my daydream, I'm vaguely aware of Tony's presence nearby, his voice mingling with the sound of Mrs. Wilson's laughter as he guides her through the process of making his famous crab meat stuffing. Their conversation drifts in and out of my consciousness, overshadowed by the magnitude of the moment. Yet, even as I revel in the euphoria of our engagement, a part of me remains grounded in the simple beauty of this ordinary moment – the clinking of utensils, the aroma of spices in the air, and the warmth of companionship shared in a cozy kitchen.

"Did you say you were coming in for Natalie's bridal shower this weekend?" Mrs. Wilson asks.

"Some of Alex's family lives in Russia," Tony explains, his tone tinged with understanding. "They wanted to celebrate with both families, so they're currently there with them, and they're going to reschedule the shower here."

"Oh, that's very nice," Mrs. Wilson replies, her expression softening.

"Yes, it is," Tony agrees, with a hint of warmth in his voice.

It's been over a month since I last spoke with Natalie. My mind swirls with all sorts of unsettling scenarios about what could be happening, but I choose to keep those thoughts to myself. I can only hope that Maxim is as powerful as Svetlana claims and that whatever's going on, he's keeping them safe.

"How serious were you when you said you've considered selling so you could move to be with your family?" Tony inquires, steering the conversation in a new direction.

"Why do you ask?" She sets her knife down, her expression curious.

"If you're serious about selling, I'm serious about buying and keeping Water's Edge open," Tony declares.

My head snaps up in surprise. I had no idea he was considering purchasing this place.

"Are you joking with me?" she asks, her tone incredulous.

"No, ma'am. The last time I was here, I fell in love with this place. I haven't been able to stop thinking about it," Tony responds earnestly.

"And how do you feel about this, Leo?" she asks, turning to me.

"Leo and—"

"Being here and operating a bed and breakfast together is a dream we share," I reply, my gaze shifting between Tony and Mrs. Wilson.

"We understand this is a lot to process at all once," Tony adds diplomatically.

"Like you, I, too, haven't stopped thinking about our conversation the past few weeks," she says, smiling. "If you didn't bring this up, I was going to."

"Really?" Tony asks, visibly surprised.

"I spoke to my son, and he thinks it's a great idea," she confirms.

"Don't feel you have to make any decision today," Tony reassures.

"Right now," she says, pointing at the clock on the wall. "We need to get this food made, or our guests will start getting rowdy. Before you leave, we'll discuss numbers."

"It's a date," Tony agrees, nodding.

The dining room is alive with chatter and laughter as Mrs. Wilson's guests relish the delicious meal. Tony reclines in his seat, a grin of satisfaction tugging at his lips as he observes her enjoying the praise.

As we linger over coffee and dessert, my phone vibrates on the table, signaling an incoming text.

Natalie: We're back in New York.

Me: Where in the world have you been?

Natalie: It's a long story, one that I can't get into on a text.

Me: I've been so worried about you. Are you okay?

Natalie: I am.

The following notification brings with it a picture. My breath catches as I open it.

"Is everything okay?" Tony inquires, and I turn the screen

toward him. He leans in closer before asking, "Whose ultrasound is that?"

"Natalie's," I reply, barely containing my excitement. "She just texted me that they're back in New York."

"I'm glad they're home," he says, relief evident in his tone. "Send my congratulations."

Me: OMG, I'm going to be an uncle! Congratulations!

Natalie: Thank you.

Me: I have news for you, too.

Natalie: Spill it. 😊

Me: Tony and I are engaged.

Natalie: Oh, Leo, I'm so happy for you!

Me: When can I see you?

Natalie: In a few weeks. I had some complications and am on bed rest.

Me: I'm just so glad you're safe and home.

Natalie: Me too. We'll talk soon. Love ya. <3

Putting away my phone, a sense of relief washes over me, knowing Natalie's safe, allowing me to fully engage in the conversation at the table.

As I reflect on my response to Mrs. Wilson's question from earlier in the kitchen, I realize I hadn't given it much thought. All I knew was that if running this place was Tony's dream, then it would be something I would support. However, at this moment, as I sit here sharing a meal with individuals who were strangers mere hours ago, I come to the profound realization that this dream belongs to me just as much as it does to Tony.

Perhaps this is why I felt drawn to earn my degree in Hospitality Management. I thoroughly enjoy my role as host at *Italiano Desiderio* and working alongside Tony in the restaurant. I also know I'm not fully utilizing the skills and knowledge I've acquired.

The idea of us owning a bed and breakfast, both of us putting all of our skills to use, excites me to no end.The prospect of managing both a restaurant in New York City and a bed and breakfast in Northmeadow, Missouri, seems daunting. But I have every confidence that we'll navigate the challenges together and make it work.

NOVEMBER 23

The past several months have been a rollercoaster of emotions. After we returned from our trip to Northmeadow, I learned the truth about what Alex does with Maxim Solonik—a revelation that shook me to my core.

Svetlana revealed she had an older sister, Jelena. Years ago, when Svetlana was a little girl, Jelena was kidnapped and sold to traffickers. Despite Maxim's connections in the Bratva, he wasn't able to save his daughter. Since then, he's assembled a network of individuals around the world who work on busting trafficking rings. Alex uses his marketing firm as a cover, helping relay covert messages for Maxim.

A data breach in Alex's company sent them to Maxim's safe house in Russia. While they were there, Natalie found out she was pregnant, but she needed to leave the safety of Maxim's compound to see a doctor. Even though Maxim took every precaution, she and Alex were taken by a trafficker. They were brought to Mexico, where they were tortured for weeks. Thankfully, Viktor was able to find them and get them back safely. The trafficker—I'm told he's no longer breathing.

After nearly losing each other, Alex's perspective on life seemed *to shift. He didn't want to wait any longer to get married. He, along with everyone's help, planned a surprise wedding at their cottage. Seeing my bestie get her happily ever after with the love of her life was nothing short of breathtaking.*

They exchanged their vows with the backdrop of the sun setting behind the lake. The love radiating between them was palpable, filling the air with a sense of hope and promise for the future.

While we were there, Tony and I took a leap of faith. With only Charlotte privy to our secret, we signed papers taking ownership of Water's Edge Bed and Breakfast. Mrs. Wilson agreed to stay on for one more summer, giving us the breathing room needed to plan our next steps. There are a lot of logistical decisions we have to make. Managing businesses in both Manhattan and Missouri will undoubtedly pose challenges, but we're prepared to tackle them together.

For the next few weeks, we're putting all of those concerns aside so we can celebrate the holidays with our friends and loved ones.

Anthony

FROM CHILDHOOD, WE'RE TAUGHT TO BELIEVE IN THE myth of 'happily ever after,' a fictional construct woven into the fabric of fairy tales. It's a beguiling fantasy that whispers sweet promises, enticing us to chase after an unattainable ideal.

It makes us wish for—believe in something that isn't possible.

The reality is that life is unforgiving and unpredictable. The childhood dream of "happily ever after' is an elusive dream that will forever be out of reach.

This past week brought with it the heavy burden of hosting another memorial service at *Italiano Desiderio*. I'm tired of saying goodbye to loved ones who were taken from us too soon, their untimely departures leaving behind a trail of shattered hearts.

The restaurant that was once a place of joy has become a haunting reminder of loss and sorrow. Stepping into the restaurant, I am met with an oppressive weight that threatens to suffocate me.

"I can't do this anymore," I confess, my voice heavy with resignation, as I pull up Charlie, my realtor's contact.

The phone rings several times before he answers.

"This is Charlie. How can I help you?" he answers professionally.

"Charlie, this is Tony Genovese," I identify myself.

"Mr. Genovese, how are you?" Charlie greets me warmly.

"I'm well," I respond mechanically.

"What can I do for you?" Charlie prompts, sensing the seriousness in my tone.

"I want to put my restaurant on the market," I state firmly.

A long pause follows, hanging in the air like a weight.

"That wasn't what I was expecting to hear," Charlie admits, his surprise evident.

"It's time for a change," I reply, trying to maintain composure. "When can we meet to get the process started?

After arranging to meet next week, I end the call, knowing I have to face the daunting task of telling Leo when I get home.

"You're home early," Leo says, peering over his laptop screen.

"We need to talk," I announce.

"I can't take any more bad news," he groans as he closes his computer and sets it aside.

"I want to get married. Right away," I announce. "As soon as we can."

"I'd like that too," Leo agrees.

"You don't care if we skip the big wedding?"

"Where's all this coming from?" Leo asks, concern lacing his voice.

"If the past few weeks have taught me anything, it's that we're not guaranteed a tomorrow. If there's something we want to do, we can't wait," I explain.

Leo searches my face, and I know he sees I'm not done. "What else?"

I take a deep breath. "I called Charlie, my realtor. I'm putting the restaurant on the market. I want to focus our attention on running the B&B." Leo's quiet for too long. "Say something, please."

"Wow. That's a lot," Leo responds, swiping a hand over his mouth. "Where are we going to live?"

"Northmeadow."

"I need a minute to process all this," he says, standing up and walking over to the window. "I figured that's where we'd eventually end up. But I didn't think it would happen so soon."

"I didn't either," I admit, going to him and wrapping my arms around his waist. Leo leans against my chest. "After everything that's happened, I just can't do it anymore. I can't breathe when I'm in the restaurant. There are too many sad memories here," I explain, my voice cracking with emotion. "I want a fresh start for us as a married couple. I want a home that only holds memories of you and me." Leo turns in my arms. "Unless you don't want that."

"I want you, Master," Leo says, enveloping me in his arms. "Wherever you are is my home." He leans in, pressing his lips against mine. "And we'll fill that home with nothing but love."

"Yes," I murmur, gently resting my forehead against his. "With nothing but love and happiness."

Leopold

The past few days stretched on endlessly as I anxiously awaited the moment when Tony and I would make our way to the city clerk's office for our civil ceremony. Now, at last, we're stepping through the doors with Star and Owen, our accomplices in this clandestine affair.

We're guided to a modest room and informed that the clerk will join us momentarily.

"Can you believe we're about to get married?" Tony's voice carries a mix of excitement and disbelief.

I don't get a chance to answer because there's a knock on the door a second before it opens. "Mr. Genovese and Mr. Wagner?"

"That's us," Tony responds, rising from his seat.

"I'm Mr. Lewis," he introduces himself and shakes our hands. "I'll be conducting your ceremony today. Are you ready to get started?" he asks, his gaze shifting between us.

"We are," we both answer in unison, our voices filled with nervous anticipation.

"We're gathered together to celebrate the marriage of Anthony Genovese and Leopold Wagner. If there's anyone who knows of any reason this couple can't be legally married, please speak now." He looks between Star and Owen, giving them a chance to object before continuing, "Perfect. I was told you've written your own vows."

"Yes, we have," Tony confirms.

"Mr. Genovese, would you like to go first."

"From the moment we first met," Tony begins, his voice filled with warmth and affection. "I knew there was something special about you. Something that called to the deepest recesses of my heart and soul. Together, we've weathered storms that would've shattered lesser souls," he continues, his eyes never leaving mine. "We've laughed, we've cried, we've celebrated, and we've mourned, but through it all, one thing has remained constant—our love for each other."

"Leopold, you're my greatest blessing," Tony says, his voice soft and tender. "In you, I've found my soul's true counterpart, my perfect match in every way. With you, I've discovered a love that transcends time and space, a love that knows no bounds and only grows stronger with each passing day. I promise to nurture and cultivate this love," Tony pledges, his gaze filled with adoration. "To water its roots with patience and understanding as it continues to blossom in the years to come."

"I vow to cherish and honor you. I promise to be your unwavering support, your constant companion, and your greatest ally. I vow to be your confidant, your shoulder to lean on, and your safe harbor in the storm. I'll celebrate your victories and share in your sorrows as though they were mine own. I pledge to listen to you with an open heart," Tony promises, his words filled with sincerity. "To communicate with honesty and kindness, and to always treat you with the utmost respect and tenderness."

"Together, we'll build a life filled with laughter, adventure, and unwavering devotion. We'll create a home," Tony says, his eyes shining with love. "That's a sanctuary for our souls, a place where we can always find solace and comfort in each other's arms."

"Leopold," Tony whispers, his voice filled with love and longing. "You're my heart, my soul, and my everything. I'm grateful beyond words for the love we share and for the opportunity to spend the rest of my days loving and being loved by you. Today, I give you not only my vows but also my heart, my hand, and my eternal devotion. I give you not only my love but also my commitment to always strive to be the best husband I can be."

"I promise to learn and grow alongside you, to support your dreams and aspirations, and to stand by you as we navigate the highs and lows of life's journey. I'll treasure every moment we share together," Tony promises, his voice filled with emotion. "Knowing that our love is a precious gift that must be cherished and nurtured each and every day. With you, I've found my home and my happiness. I love you now and always."

With a steadying breath, I center myself before reciting my vows.

"Tony," I say, my voice trembling with emotion. "As I stand here on the threshold of forever with you, my heart overflows with gratitude and love. In your eyes, I see the reflection of a love that has transformed my life in ways I never thought possible."

"In your presence," I continue, my gaze locking with his. "I feel a sense of peace and contentment that I've never known before. It's as if the chaos of the world fades away. You're my refuge, my anchor in the storm. You're a warm embrace, wrapping around me and filling me with a sense of security and belonging. It's in your eyes that I find home, in your smile that I find hope, and in your touch that I find healing."

"In your love, I find a strength that empowers me to face life's challenges with courage and grace. With you, I feel empowered to embrace my true self," I murmur, feeling my heart swell with emotion. "To embrace my flaws and imperfections, knowing that you love me all the more for them. Your love gives me the courage to be vulnerable, to let down my walls and share my deepest fears and insecurities, knowing that you'll always be there to catch me when I fall."

"You've taught me the true meaning of love," I reflect, my

words carrying a depth of understanding. "It's a love that's patient, allowing us to grow and evolve at our own pace, never rushing or demanding, but always understanding and accepting. It's a love that's kind, showing compassion and empathy even in the face of adversity, always choosing understanding over judgment, forgiveness over resentment. And it's a love that's selfless, putting the needs and desires of the other before our own, sacrificing without hesitation, and giving without expecting anything in return."

"Tony," I say, my voice filled with love and reverence. "You're my rock, my confidant, and my greatest love. You are my heart's desire. My true north. The love of my life and my partner in all things. Today, I give you my heart, my soul, and my unwavering devotion."

Finally, I whisper, "I promise to love you fiercely. To honor you deeply and to cherish every moment we share together. To support you in all that you do and to walk hand in hand with you through the journey of life. I am blessed beyond measure to call you my husband."

"As a symbol of your promise, please place your ring on Leopold's finger," Mr. Lewis instructs, his voice steady and solemn.

Tony gently slides the platinum band over my ring finger, his touch warm and reassuring.

Mr. Lewis then turns to me. "As a symbol of your promise, please place your ring on Anthony's finger."

My hand trembles slightly as I carefully slide Tony's matching platinum band onto his finger, our eyes locked in a moment of profound connection.

"In as much as you both have consented, by the power vested in me by the State of New York, I now pronounce you married. You may kiss."

Tony takes a step closer to me, anticipation evident in his gaze. Our lips meet in a tender yet passionate kiss as Owen and Star erupt into applause and cheers.

"I love you, Leopold Genovese," Tony whispers against my lips.

"And I love you, my husband," I reply, my heart overflowing with joy and love.

Anthony

IF YOU ASKED ME TEN YEARS AGO IF I'D EVER BE A married man, I probably would've told you that you were crazy. Yet, here I am walking out of the City Clerk's office holding Leopold's—my husband's hand, I've never been happier.

"There's something I didn't tell you," I admit.

"Oh?" Leo raises an eyebrow inquisitively.

"I rented a cozy cottage on Lake Ontario for our honeymoon," I reveal, hoping he'll share my excitement.

"That sounds wonderful," Leo's smile widens. "When do we leave?"

"Tonight," I reply, a sense of anticipation tingling in the air between us.

Following our wedding ceremony, we celebrate by having a leisurely lunch with Star and Owen. Their unwavering friendship and support have been a constant in our relationship. It only feels fitting to have them share in the joy of our special day.

Now that the vows have been exchanged and we're officially married, we take the opportunity to spread the news by sending out text messages to our friends and family with pictures from the ceremony.

Me: Surprise! Leopold and I are overjoyed to announce that we're now officially married!

The soft hum of the small plane's engines fades as we touch down in Rochester, signaling the beginning of our honeymoon. As we step onto the tarmac, the late afternoon sun envelops us in its warm embrace. With the rental car ready and waiting, we set out on the winding roads that lead us further from the populated town and closer to our secluded haven. Finally, we arrive at our destination—a cozy cabin perched on the shores of Lake Ontario.

"How did you find this place?" Leo asks as we gather our bags from the trunk.

"Keirnan, a friend of mine from Fire and Ice Hamptons, owns it," I explain. "They only rent it to club members." With a cautionary tone, I add, "Fair warning. There's a lot of bondage equipment in here that we won't be using."

Leo's unexpected question catches me off guard. "What would you say if I wanted to try it?"

"Bondage?" I ask, taken aback.

"Yes."

I swipe the key card, and the front door unlocks. "Let's see what you think when we go inside."

Leo's gaze sweeps across the main room of the cabin, taking in every detail of the seductive décor with a mix of intrigue and fascination. His fingers trace the intricate stitching of the red leather tantra chaise.

A smile plays on my lips as I imagine Leo reclining on it, bathed in the soft glow of candlelight, his body relaxed and inviting. We're lost in a world of sensual pleasures, our bodies entwined in a dance of desire. I can almost feel the weight of Leo's touch, his hands trailing along my skin with a gentle yet insistent caress. I can taste the sweetness of Leo's lips as they meet mine, the heat of our passion building with each breathless sigh. The idea ignites a flicker of longing deep within me, but I quickly push it aside, focusing instead on giving Leo the freedom to explore at his own pace.

"How does this work?" he asks, his attention captured by a sleek black pole nestled in one corner of the room.

Wanting to give him space, I don't approach when I answer, "It's a restraining pole. There are countless positions to put a sub in," I explain. "The dildo, well, that's self-explanatory."

"I think I'd like to try that," Leo remarks before striding towards the bedroom door and disappearing inside. "Tony?"

"Yes, *cuore mio*?" I reply, closing the distance and positioning myself in the doorway.

"Why is there a cage under the bed?"

"Some Dominants use it for their submissive who craves bondage. Others use it for their human pets. We will not be using it," I state matter-of-factly.

He runs his hand over the spreader bar lying on the foot of the bed. On one side of the room, a black leather sex swing hangs from hooks in the ceiling. Across the room, leaning against the wall is a St. Andrews Cross. "That." Leo points. "Is a hard limit. I've seen Brandon do impact scenes with Lana. No. Just no."

"Fair," I reply, crossing my arms as I lean against the doorway.

A large oak armoire sits adjacent to the cross. Leo opens the doors, revealing a vast array of impact tools, sensory toys, travel containers of lube, and condoms. "Wow. This is a lot of stuff," he remarks before closing the doors.

"Yes, it is," I say as I advance towards Leo, each step deliberate. Reaching in, I pull out a silicone sleeve and a remote. "Are you up for trying something different?" I whisper.

"What are you suggesting, Master?"

Leopold

"Kiernan owns over a hundred acres. We can do what we want where we want, and no one will bother us," Tony explains, watching me closely. "I have a fantasy of knowing you're out there, exposed and being hunted by me."

A thrill shoots through me. "I like the sound of that."

"Tell me to stop, and I will," he reassures.

"Don't stop, Master," I reply, my heart racing at the promise of what's to come.

"Strip for me," Tony commands.

There's something in the tone of his voice and the hungry look in his eyes that awakens a part of me that seeks to be his prey. My hands tremble as I slowly remove my clothes. The cool air of the cabin caresses my skin as I stand before my Master, naked and vulnerable.

"Good boy," Tony purrs, his eyes drinking in every inch of my exposed body. He wraps the black silicone around my cock. It's a snug fit that sends a delicious shiver down my spine. "I can control this from anywhere," he explains. My cock twitches in response. "I'm going to give you a head start to find a hiding spot in the forest," he explains, his voice low and filled with lust. "Then I'm coming for you. Go now, Leopold. Run."

Without hesitation, I dart into the trees, the thrill of the hunt fueling my every step as I seek out the perfect hiding spot. My heart pounds at the thought of being chased through the forest by Tony. It doesn't take long for me to find a place that conceals me.

Now, I wait for Tony to find me.

Anthony

As I wait for Leo to get his head start, I can't help but feel a surge of excitement coursing through me. The anticipation of the chase, the thrill of the hunt, it all stirred something primal within him that I couldn't ignore.

With each passing moment, my anticipation grows, my senses tingling with the promise of adventure. Outside, the sun dips below the horizon, casting a warm orange glow in the sky. The air is heavy with the scents of pine and earth. As I stand here, poised and ready to give chase, a surge of adrenaline courses through my veins, knowing this is unlike anything I've ever experienced before.

I move at a leisurely pace, my senses on high alert, attuned to every sound and movement around me. Each step I take brings me closer to my elusive prey, and I can't help but feel a surge of excitement at the prospect of finally catching him.

The forest is alive with activity, the air thick with the scents of pine and earth. I move with purpose through the dense foliage, my eyes scanning the shadows for any sign of movement. Every rustle of leaves, every snap of a twig, sets my heart racing with anticipation.

After what feels like an eternity, I finally catch sight of Leo's naked form pressed against a tree, but he doesn't see me yet. Reaching into my pocket, I press a button turning on the vibrations around his cock. He gasps from the sensation as he looks around. When he spots me, his eyes widen in anticipation. A predatory smile curves my lips as I close in on him, a primal energy coursing through my veins as I close the distance between us.

Without a word, I grab Leo's wrists and pin them above his head, holding him in place as I capture his lips in a heated kiss. Leo moans against my mouth, his body arching into my touch as our tongues tangle in a fierce dance of desire.

My free hand roams over Leopold's body, taking in every contour as I explore his form with reverence. Leo's breaths come in ragged gasps as my mouth trails down his neck, leaving a trail of heat in its wake. My teeth nip at his sensitive skin, causing him to cry out in pleasure.

"Turn around and bend over. Keep your hands on the tree," I order as desire surges through me.

Leopold's body quivers with anticipation as I open my pants, allowing my erection to spring free. Leaning in close, I ask. "Are you ready to be fucked by your husband?"

"Yes. Oh god, yes," he says through panting breaths.

Positioned behind him, I take my time, relishing the moment as I tease his entrance with feather-light touches. With a flick of my fingers, I turn up the intensity of the vibration as I ease inside him, sending a jolt of desire through both of us. The raw intensity of our connection takes over, and I begin thrusting into him.

"Fuck, Leo. I'm not going to last," I pant.

"Don't hold back, Master," Leo rasps, glancing over his shoulder. "Fill me. Use me."

My movements grow more forceful and possessive. With each thrust, I fall deeper into our shared desire. "You're mine in every way, Leopold," I grunt as I thrust into him. "Your collar bound your soul to me, and now our marriage seals that union."

"I'm yours," Leo repeats, his voice filled with conviction. "Only yours. Forever yours."

Our connection reaches a fevered pitch, and I feel an urge I've never experienced before—a need to mark Leopold as mine. Leaning over his back, I press my hot breath against his skin before sinking my teeth into his shoulder in a display of desire and ownership.

"Fuck," Leopold gasps at the sharp sensation, his pleasure mingling with pain. My fingers find the remote, and I turn the vibrations higher, adding another layer of stimulation.

Leo's gasp of desire and need fills the air, and my control falters. I release my raw, unbridled passion as I rut into him with a fierce urgency, igniting a fire that brings us closer to the brink.

As my climax approaches, Leopold's body tightens around mine. With a final thrust, I let go with a roar, succumbing to the overwhelming pleasure coursing through my body. Leo follows soon after, his cries of ecstasy mingling with mine and echoing through the trees.

I withdraw from Leo and remove the vibrator, slipping it into my pocket as we sink to the ground. Leopold's body is slick with sweat as I cradle him against me.

"I know this stretched your boundaries," I whisper, tracing my fingers along his spine. "You're so fucking brave."

"There was no fear because I knew it was you coming for me," Leo confesses. "I'm yours, Master. In whatever way you want me."

The stars above us shimmer with a radiant brilliance as we lie together, spent and breathless. The beauty of the night sky serves as a silent reminder of the bond that binds Leopold and I together. It's stronger and more powerful than anything I have ever known.

Leopold

THE SUN IS BEGINNING TO CAST ITS GOLDEN HUES OVER the horizon, painting the sky with hues of pink and orange. Our week here is coming to an end. I can't help but feel a pang of regret that it's passed by so quickly, and I find myself cherishing the final moments of our honeymoon.

Beside me, Tony is still sleeping, his expression peaceful. Running my fingers through his now salt and pepper-colored locks, I'm struck by how age has only added to his allure, leaving me marveling at the passage of time.

"Good morning, *cuore mio*," he greets before even opening his eyes.

"Good morning, my husband," I reply with a smile, the endearment bringing a flutter to my heart.

"Did you sleep well?" he inquires, his fingers already finding their way through my hair as I rest my head on his chest.

"I had the most vivid dreams," I share, feeling the warmth of his embrace comforting me.

"About what?" he asks, his touch gentle and reassuring.

"A child. Our child—a son," I admit, the concept of having children together quietly taking root in my heart.

"Do you want to start a family, Leopold?" he asks, his voice filled with sincerity and longing.

"I'd love for us to have a child. Maybe more than one," I respond without hesitation, the thought bringing a sense of excitement and anticipation. "What about you?"

"Yes. I want to have children with you," he affirms, his gaze meeting mine with unwavering determination.

"How do we do it?" I inquire, curious about the practicalities of starting a family together.

"If we want a biological child, we can look for a surrogate," he suggests, his tone thoughtful and considerate.

"What about adoption? It's just an idea, but... do you think it's something we could explore?" I propose hesitantly, aware of the complexities involved but curious to see if he shares my willingness to explore non-traditional routes to parenthood.

"I think adoption would be a wonderful avenue to explore," he replies warmly, his words filling me with a sense of reassurance and possibility. "There are many children waiting for a family to love them, and we have a lot of love to give."

"Yes, Master. We do," I agree softly, my heart filled with love and determination.

"When we get back to the city, we'll look up an agency and get the process started," he promises, his words infused with a sense of purpose and determination as we embark on this new chapter together.

This week surpassed all of my expectations. Each moment has been an exploration of my soft limits. Tony approached each new experience with careful consideration. The bondage pole quickly became a favorite of mine. The sensation of being bound and helpless while knowing I could stop it at any second was an exhilarating experience. Tony already ordered one for our apartment.

At my urging, we tried using a blindfold, a seemingly innocuous piece of fabric that promised to heighten my senses and intensify the experience. However, as Tony gently secured it over my eyes, I found myself engulfed in a suffocating darkness that sent panic coursing through my veins. As soon as I uttered my safeword, Tony removed it and gathered me in his arms until my senses returned to normal.

I didn't think I could feel closer to him than when we arrived, but as the cabin door closes behind us, our bond is inexplicably stronger—unbreakable.

Leopold

MARCH 13

I've lost count of how many times we've flown back and forth between New York City and Missouri. Trying to juggle the responsibilities of running Italiano Desiderio and planning for a complete remodel of the bed and breakfast is exhausting.

One positive about spending time in Northmeadow is getting to spend more time with Charlotte. Currently, she's the only person in our circle who knows we've purchased Water's Edge. Her unwavering support has been invaluable as we navigate the complexities of our new endeavor.

I've had to stay behind in Northmeadow on several trips. Instead of allowing me to stay at the bed and breakfast alone, Charlotte insisted I stay with her and Stanley. They welcomed me into their home with open arms, immersing me in the rhythm of family life, from sharing meals around the kitchen table to watching movies together in the evening with a bowl of popcorn. It healed a part of the little boy Leopold, who desperately needed to feel the love of a Mom and Dad.

For Charlotte, my presence offers a chance at redemption, an opportunity to rewrite the narrative of motherhood. Despite her initial discomfort with my sexuality, she's embraced the journey of *acceptance and understanding. She's found peace by willingly offering unconditional love and acceptance to a 'son' who has embraced his identity as a gay man and who has chosen to love someone outside of her deeply ingrained beliefs.*

Our conversations about God, spirituality, and the meaning of love have been both challenging and enlightening, allowing us to navigate the complexities of our relationship with honesty and respect.

I even attended church with her as I tried to understand where her beliefs came from. It wasn't a particularly wonderful experience, as I was clearly unwelcome, but Charlotte didn't flinch. She proudly stood by my side in support and love. Through all of these experiences, we've found common ground and a deeper appreciation for each other's perspectives.

One particularly poignant moment etched itself into my heart when Charlotte brought me to Michael's grave, her eyes heavy with the weight of grief and loss as she introduced me to her son. As we sat in the cemetery, Charlotte shared stories of her beloved son. Through her words, she painted a vivid picture of his laughter, his quirks, and his dreams.

With each memory shared, I found myself feeling an unexpected connection to Michael, as if his spirit hovered nearby, reaching out to touch my own. It was a profound sensation, one that stirred a mixture of emotions within me—a sense of longing mingled with sadness for a life lost too soon.

Charlotte and I have formed a bond that goes beyond mere biology. We've discovered kindred spirits willing to extend unconditional love and support in a world that is often unkind and anything but predictable.

Things here in the city are also moving along. Several weeks ago, Tony received a call from Charlie, letting him know a full-price offer for Italiano Desiderio came in. Of course, Tony accepted it right away. If all goes well, the closing could be in as soon as two months.

In between the whirlwind of planning a move and navigating the intricacies of selling the restaurant, there's another crucial aspect of our lives that demands attention—the adoption process. From filling out mountains of paperwork to undergoing thorough home studies, it's been a painstakingly slow process, completing the necessary steps, but we're finally making progress.

Cora, our adoption worker, called several days ago to let us know she has information on waiting children for us. We'll be back in Manhattan tomorrow and plan to stop by her office on the way home from the airport. Everything suddenly feels so much more real.

Looking from the outside, one might think our lives, at the current moment, are in complete chaos. But do you want to know something? Despite the uncertainties and challenges that I'm certain await us, I'm not afraid.

I'm exceedingly happy and eager to embrace this next chapter in our lives.

Anthony

Due to tornado-producing storms sweeping across the country, our flight from Missouri faced delays, pushing our arrival time to an unfathomable four am. Despite the exhaustion, I managed to reach out to Cora, explaining our predicament and apologizing for missing our appointment. Thankfully, she understood our situation and kindly dropped off the sealed envelope containing information about waiting children at our building, ensuring we could review it at our convenience.

Despite our bubbling excitement, we made the mutual decision to prioritize a few hours of sleep before delving into the contents of the envelope. Recognizing the gravity of the moment, we wanted to approach it with clear minds and open hearts.

While Leo finishes making our coffee, I settle at the kitchen table, eyeing the envelope containing the children's pictures and information.

"Can you believe our future child is in that envelope?" Leo's voice is filled with a mix of wonder and disbelief.

"Yes and no," I admit as I carefully pull the stack of papers out of the manilla envelope. "It still feels surreal."

"How are we supposed to choose just one?" Leo's brows

furrow in concern, and as he passes me my coffee mug, it slips from his grasp.

Reacting quickly, I shove the papers away, preventing them from being drenched in coffee.

"Are you okay?" Leo's immediate reaction is to ensure my well-being.

"I am," I reassure him, grabbing paper towels to help clean up.

"I didn't ruin any of the children's profiles, did I?" Leo's remorse is evident in his tone.

"Only the edge of the top one, but it's okay," I reply, offering him a reassuring smile.

Leo crouches down to pick up a fallen paper. "We dropped one," he remarks, lifting it from the floor and pausing to read it. "This is him." With a solemn expression, he hands it to me.

On the paper is a photo of a baby boy with dark hair and striking blue eyes.

Leo moves closer. "It says he was born at twenty-nine weeks to a drug-addicted mother," he murmurs, his voice tinged with sorrow. "He's too young to tell, but they suspect he'll have neurological problems because of it. He's the one, Tony."

My heart races as I fixate on the picture. "How do you know?" I manage to ask, my voice barely above a whisper.

"The same way I knew when I looked into your eyes the first time. My heart recognized yours," he murmurs, his voice gentle and sure.

Feeling overwhelmed, I choke out, "His birthday... September eleventh." A tear trails down my cheek, my voice thick with emotion. "I don't need to look through the other profiles, do you?"

"No, Master. This is our son," Leo declares, his voice steady and sure.

As soon as the clock strikes nine, we dial Cora with the phone on speaker. "We found him," I announce eagerly.

"That was fast," she remarks.

"Perhaps, but we knew the second we saw him," Leo adds confidently.

"What's the name and his number?" She asks, her tone almost callous, as if these aren't living, breathing children.

"It's baby boy September," I respond, noting the lack of a given name. "Number 36125."

"He's brand new on the waiting child list," she elaborates, her voice tinged with clinical detachment. "He was born preterm and went through withdrawal. There's no way to know the extent of any neurological disabilities he may have. Are you sure you want to take that risk?" she questions.

"Leopold and I are certain," I answer firmly. "What happens next?"

"I'll send your dossier to my contact in Columbia. It could take quite some time," she says matter-of-factly. "I'll be in touch when I have more information."

Anthony

I'VE BEEN A BUNDLE OF NERVES WAITING TO HEAR FROM Cora about the status of our potential adoption. Yesterday, I couldn't hold back any longer and called her. She informed me there's a backlog on the Colombian end, and it could be upwards of six to eight months before we hear anything.

Leopold and I will be leaving New York to relocate permanently to the lake in two weeks. While the idea of raising a child in the city holds its own appeal, we're both eager for the slower pace of life that awaits us at the lake, a setting we believe will be more conducive to raising a child. Knowing our apartment will always be here provides comfort, allowing us the flexibility to return and stay whenever we feel the need.

While we were in Northmeadow a few months ago, we consulted with an architect regarding some major renovations for the building. Since we'll be living there full-time, we need to have a private living space. The architect proposed an extension to the current structure. Alongside modernizing all the plumbing and wiring, we're also installing an elevator to ensure the entire property is accessible to guests with varying abilities.

We're completely overhauling the third floor, which currently consists of six smaller rooms and two shared bathrooms. Our vision is to transform this space into two spacious, soundproof suites, each equipped with its own private bathroom. Additionally, we're customizing these rooms with BDSM furniture, catering to guests seeking a kinkier vacation.

We have an extensive list of renovations planned, including paving the parking lot and planting flowering dogwood trees to line the edges. The building, with its current log cabin appearance, is a bit misleading—I've discovered that the logs are actually manufactured and serve as a façade. We're opting for a more authentic look by replacing them with cedar siding.

Our wraparound porch, already a striking feature, will undergo enhancements. We're installing large, southern-style fans to amplify its charm, and custom-made rockers will offer the perfect spot for guests to relax. The built-in stone planters, a nod to Mr. Wilson's memory, will continue to grace the porch, overflowing with vibrant flowers to add a touch of natural beauty.

Leopold and I approached Charlotte with the idea of her joining us in this venture. Her enthusiastic acceptance was a welcomed relief. Since then, she's been an indispensable asset, helping to oversee the ongoing renovations while we're in New York and assisting us in selecting new linens and décor for the rooms. When we're ready to re-open, she plans to continue her involvement, transitioning to a part-time role to ensure the smooth operation of our establishment.

As I look ahead to the future, I'm filled with excitement at everything that lies ahead. However, before I can fully embrace it, I must navigate the emotional hurdle of informing my staff that I'll be stepping down as the owner of *Italiano Desiderio* by the end of the month.

While I try to reassure myself that this announcement will be straightforward, deep down, I know it will stir up a mix of emotions. Yet, amidst the uncertainty, I'm filled with an overwhelming sense of peace that accompanies the decisions Leopold and I have made together.

Tonight has been unusually busy for a weeknight. We had patrons lingering until half an hour past our usual closing time. The staff is well aware that we'll be holding a brief team meeting as soon as the last of our guests clear out. Additionally, I've asked the off-duty staff to join us for this important announcement.

"Master," Leo announces as he strides into the office. "We're ready for you." Seeing my hesitation, he gently closes the door and approaches me. "Are you having second thoughts?"

"No," I admit, my gaze fixed on the distant horizon outside. "But leaving behind the memories that led me to sell... it's harder than I anticipated."

"Memories don't get left behind. They journey with us wherever we go," Leo murmurs softly, his hand resting over my heart. "Kameron will always be with you. Right here."

"How is it that my love for Kameron has never bothered you?" I ask, turning to face him.

Leaning against the desk, Leo meets my gaze. "I could never be jealous of the relationship and bond you shared with Kameron. Your love for him is why you can love me so deeply."

Drawing him closer, I embrace him, feeling his heartbeat against mine. "Do you know how much I love you, *cuore mio*?"

"I do," Leo replies, his lips meeting mine in a tender kiss.

"Let's go share the news," I suggest, intertwining our fingers as we leave the office to address the staff.

Anthony

LEO'S DISAPPOINTMENT AT MISSING THE RESTAURANT closing today is palpable as we said goodbye earlier. Before we had the closing date, Star asked him to speak at today's submissive training class, a responsibility he's grown fond of. He was going to back out, but I encouraged him to go ahead, knowing how much he values these opportunities to share his knowledge and experience. It's moments like these that make leaving Manhattan bittersweet.

As I pull open the door to my attorney's office, my stomach churns with nerves. Today marks the moment I'll sign the papers and hand over the keys to the new owner of *Italiano Desiderio*.

"Tony, wait," Leo's voice calls out, and I turn to see him running down the street.

"What are you doing here?" I ask, surprised.

"Something told me I needed to be here," he explains breathlessly. "I apologized to Star, but I couldn't miss this."

"Thank you, *cuore mio*," I say, thankful to have my husband by my side.

"Good afternoon," William, the receptionist, greets us as we enter the office. "Can I get you both something to drink?"

"Coffees would be wonderful," I reply.

"If you want to come with me, I'll take you to the conference room," he offers.

"Thank you."

"Tony. Leo." our attorney says, joining us in the hallway. We exchange handshakes. "This is a big day. Are you ready?"

I glance at Leopold, who offers me a reassuring smile. "We are."

"Let's do it, then," he says, opening the door to reveal Charlie and three other men seated at the table. "Thank you for your patience, gentlemen," he adds as we take our seats. "This is Brett Neilson, counsel for the buyer, Cassius Williams, and this is Christopher Young, the young man who's about to be a new restaurateur."

"Good to meet you all," I reply.

"We have a lot of paperwork to get through. Let's get started," our attorney suggests as William hands me my coffee.

For the past hour, I've observed Christopher Young, racking my brain to figure out why he looks so familiar, yet I'm drawing a blank. Finally, I interject, breaking the silence. "I have to ask," I address Christopher directly. "What inspired you to buy my restaurant?"

"You don't recognize me, do you?" the young man inquires.

"I feel like I should," I respond, my mind racing to place him.

"We first formally met about ten years ago in a courtroom," he reveals, and suddenly, the memories come flooding back.

"Levi Young?" I whisper, the realization dawning on me.

"Yes, Sir," he confirms with a nod. "Although since then, I've legally changed my name to Christopher Young. It was my middle name."

"Tell me about you," I inquire, genuinely curious to learn more about him and what has transpired in his life since our last encounter in the courtroom.

"You didn't come back after recess," he begins, his voice laced with emotion. "That day changed my life. The judge explained that, given the nature of the crime, she was prepared to sentence me to jail time. But after hearing you speak, she had a change of heart." He pauses, his eyes reflecting the weight of his words. "I was sentenced to five hundred hours of community service. That's where I met Cass." Christopher motions to the man beside him, his gesture filled with gratitude. "Cass is a chef who also volunteers at the kitchen."

"The director of the kitchen knows my history," Cass begins, his voice heavy with the weight of his past. "So when he found out that Christopher was being court-appointed to our kitchen, he asked me to keep an eye on him." His gaze flickers to Christopher, a mixture of empathy and gratitude in his eyes.

"I was raised in Chicago by a single mom who was too busy whoring herself out for her next fix," he explains, his words raw with pain. "My older brother was involved with a gang, and I wanted to be just like him. By the time I was thirteen, I was a regular in juvie. When I was sixteen, I found myself on trial for involuntary manslaughter."

Christopher places a supportive hand on Cass's shoulder, silently urging him to continue.

"I got myself in way over my head," Cass continues, his tone somber, laden with remorse. "My girlfriend had just had our baby. She was killed in a drive-by." His words hang in the air, weighted with grief. "Being young and stupid, I didn't think when the guys asked me to drive. We stopped at a house. They went in and shot the place up and used me as the getaway driver."

"How did you end up in New York?" Leopold inquires, his tone gentle yet probing.

"The judge had some connections and had me transferred to a maximum-security juvenile center here in the city rather than sending me to an adult facility," Cass explains, a sense of gratitude evident in his voice. "That action, I'm certain, is what saved me. While I was there, I received counseling and an education. That's how I got involved in culinary arts."

"What happened to your baby?" I inquire, eager to understand more about Cass's journey.

"After I got out, I was on probation for two years. I got a job and a place to live and fought to get visitation with Zuri, my little girl," he shares, pride evident in his voice. "CPS helped me get parenting classes, and eventually, I earned full custody of her. "A few years later, I met Tasmin, the love of my life. We married, and she legally adopted Zuri."

"That's an incredible story," I respond, moved by his resilience and determination.

"Cass is eternally patient," Christopher reflects, his voice filled with gratitude, his eyes shimmering with emotion. "I wasn't the easiest to deal with at first, but Cass came back day in and day out. He waited patiently until I stopped acting like an ass," he chuckles softly. "Then, he and Tasmin petitioned the court to allow me to move into their home rather than stay in the youth shelter. He and Tamsin went above and beyond, stepping in as the parents I never had. They made sure I went to school every day and graduated from high school," he continues, his tone reverent. "That's when I decided to go to the Culinary Institute of America."

"Mr. Genovese," Christopher says, his gaze meeting mine with sincerity. "I never forgot what you said that day." His words hit me like a tidal wave, causing a lump to form in my throat and tears to well in my own eyes. "I'm not perfect, but each day I've tried to make a positive difference, no matter how small, in the world around me. It's what Zuri and I have taught our little girls to do as well."

"Zuri?" I falter, my voice betraying a mix of shock and disbelief as I look between the men.

"I fell in love with his daughter and married her," Christopher reveals, his tone filled with emotion. "We have two little girls. Isla just turned three, and Seraphina is ten months old." With a gentle motion, he lifts his phone and extends it to me.

I blink back tears as I study the image of Christopher, his wife, and their daughters. "You have a beautiful family."

"Thank you," Christopher responds, his voice cracking with emotion. "I was worried about how you'd react when you found out it was me buying your restaurant. I hoped you wouldn't reconsider the sale."

"Backing out hasn't even crossed my mind," I declare, my voice steady despite the emotional weight of the moment. "I firmly believe that what we often perceive as chaos and confusion is just a part of a larger, unfolding story. When it feels like I'm stumbling in the dark, I've learned to be still," I say, intertwining my fingers with Leo's. "To wait for the unseen force that guides my next steps." I cast a meaningful glance between Leopold, Cassius, and Christopher. "Every joyous moment, heartache, and twist serves a purpose. As long as we allow it, fate will ensure we reach our perfect destination."

The room falls into a momentary silence as I gather my thoughts. "I don't know by what stroke of fate you learned that my restaurant was for sale," I begin, my voice carrying a mix of awe and respect. "But I do know that you are the one who's been raised up for this time. I'm proud to know that you're the man who's destined to carry on the legacy of *Italiano Desiderio*," I say, feeling a swell of gratitude and admiration for the determined young man seated across from me.

Christopher pushes his chair back and circles the table until he stands before me. I rise, and he reaches out, pulling me into a tight embrace. "Thank you, Mr. Genovese," he says, his voice trembling with gratitude. "Thank you for seeing something in me —for believing in me when no one else did."

"It's been an honor, Christopher Young," I reply, my voice thick with emotion.

As I hand over the key, a sense of bittersweet emotion washes over me, mingling with the tears that threaten to spill. In our tearful exchange, there's a sense of comfort in the promises we make to stay present in each other's lives.

As Leopold and I stepped into the conference room earlier today, I never anticipated that the buyer would hold any particular importance. It never occurred to me that it might be someone from my past, especially not the boy who left a lasting impression on me all those years ago.

Over the years, I revisited the image of that boy from years ago, hoping he had found his way in the world. To now stand face-to-face with the man Christopher Young has become fills me with profound awe. Knowing that I played even a small part in shaping his journey touches me deeply.

Leopold

Tony and I have been living in Northmeadow permanently for a little over a month. The renovations to the bed and breakfast are finally complete. With Charlotte's help, we've managed to decorate and furnish the guest rooms and central areas of the bed and breakfast. Our private living area is still a work in progress.

Despite all the unscheduled trips to Missouri, we managed to keep our ownership of Water's Edge a secret from Natalie and Alex, one that will be revealed this weekend.

Charlotte extended invitations to everyone under the guise of celebrating Natalie's birthday, which we will do. However, nestled within the festivities, we've prepared a couple of surprises of our own to share with our guests.

Tonight, we have dinner plans with Star and her new submissive, Jackson, as well as Owen and Astrid, who've been enjoying their stay in our newly renovated third-floor rooms—the very first guests to experience them.

"Would you care to have dinner with us before you leave, Charlotte?" Tony offers, extending the invitation.

"Are you sure that wouldn't be an imposition?" Charlotte responds, her tone hesitant.

"We'd love to have you," I interject, wrapping my arm around her in a reassuring gesture.

Over the past few years, our bond has grown remarkably close. Charlotte has become like a mother to me, and I cherish her dearly.

"I already set you a place," Tony adds with a warm smile, indicating his readiness for her company.

"This pasta is delicious," Owen compliments, breaking the silence. "Astrid and I worked up an appetite with my rope and flogger this afternoon."

Charlotte's fork slips from her hand, clattering against her plate, freezing everyone in place.

"Anthony," she addresses Tony quietly, her tone laced with curiosity. "How do you all know each other?"

Tony takes a deep breath, steeling himself for the explanation. "We all frequent the same BDSM club in New York," he admits bluntly.

"Fire and Ice?" she asks quietly.

"Yes, ma'am," he confirms.

"The same Fire and Ice where Natalie met Alex?" Charlotte's questions come in quick succession.

"Yes, ma'am. That's the one."

"It's not a dance club or bar?" Her disbelief is evident.

"No, ma'am, it isn't," Tony affirms.

"And you go there, too?" Charlotte turns her attention to me.

"I do," I confirm with a slow nod. "It's really not what you think—"

She holds her hand up, halting my words. "I love you, Leopold, like a son. And Natalie is my daughter," she says before lifting her wine glass for a long sip. "But I don't want to know any more about what any of you do—" Charlotte surveys the table, her gaze steady on each of us. "Behind the closed doors of your bedrooms." Then, as if brushing off the moment, she resumes eating, her fork returning to her plate.

"I love you, Mama Charlotte," I say with a smile, planting a kiss on her cheek before laughing softly.

"I love you too, my dear," Charlotte responds warmly with a gentle pat on my hand.

As the tension dissipates, a wave of relief washes over the table, and we all resume eating, the atmosphere lightening with each passing moment.

Anthony

As the afternoon sun bathes the scene in warmth, a sense of anticipation fills the air. Maxim, Irina, and Svetlana's late-night arrival adds an element of intrigue to the gathering, especially with Brandon's unexpected presence after a year-long separation from Svetlana.

Dimitri, one of Maxim's guards, is here with Jessica. They were in town to visit Maxim and Irina's adopted daughter, Amelia, who is just pulling in with Viktor. Amelia recently wrapped up a cross-country tour with her rock band and is in town for a few days. Their playful puppy, Nadiya, adds a touch of joy as she frolics around, relishing the attention.

"They're coming," Stanley whispers urgently. "Quiet everyone."

The group gathers beneath the gazebo, anticipation palpable in the air as they await the arrival of Alex, Natalie, and their children. As the family rounds the building, a chorus of "Happy Birthday" erupts, breaking the silence with joyful exuberance.

Rose's laughter rings out as she rushes to Viktor, her favorite, who scoops her up in his arms and showers her with kisses.

Tears well in Natalie's eyes as she takes in the surprise celebration.

"I don't know what to say," Natalie admits, her voice wavering with emotion as she gazes around at the gathering.

Leo pulls Natalie into a tight hug. "Your mom made this happen," he says, nodding towards Charlotte.

Charlotte stands beside me, beaming.

"Thank you both," Natalie expresses her gratitude, her voice choked with tears. "I can't believe everyone's here."

There's no time like the present to continue with the surprises.

"Leo and I have an announcement to make," I say, moving to stand beside Leopold and intertwining our hands. "We'd like to tell everyone that we're now the proud owners of Water's Edge Bed and Breakfast." Our guests break into cheers and applause. "We thought it very fitting for our first event to be a birthday party for Natalie. Especially since we would've never found this place without her."

"You guys bought it?" Natalie's jaw drops in disbelief.

"We did," I confirm, a proud grin spreading across my face.

"We fell in love with the area when we were here for Natalie's wedding," Leo adds, his eyes alight with excitement. "Mrs. Wilson let us know she was looking to sell the place so she could retire, and we were looking at getting out of the city and slowing down. So, we took the leap and purchased it."

"Charlotte has been instrumental in helping us make some changes," I mention, giving Natalie's mom a grateful smile.

"How long have you been keeping this from me?" Natalie turns to Charlotte, a hint of amusement in her voice.

"For a very long time," she says and laughs.

"And you all knew and didn't tell me?" Charlotte admits with a laugh.

"Guilty," Owen confirms with a laugh, earning nods of agreement.

"We're going to be neighbors," Leo remarks with a grin, his excitement contagious.

"There's more," I announce, my voice trembling with

emotion. "Over the past year, Leopold and I have been going through the steps to adopt. we've found our son—a little boy from Colombia who stole our hearts the second we saw his picture." Gasps of surprise ripple through our friends as they absorb the news. "It's been a rollercoaster of a journey, waiting for all the pieces to come together, but they finally have." I attempt to speak further, but the overwhelming emotions leave me speechless.

"We're flying to Columbia next week," Leo announces, his voice tinged with excitement. "There's a mandatory one-week cohabitation period before we go to the Columbian family court to formally adopt him. And since Nana Charlotte will be looking after him while we're running the B&B, she's coming with us."

"Oh, Mom," Natalie exclaims, her hands flying to her face.

"I'm so honored to be a part of this journey with you two boys," Charlotte responds, her voice filled with emotion.

"How old is he?" Alex inquires, his curiosity evident.

"He'll be one next month," Leo answers with a smile.

"Leopold and I are so grateful for the love and support you've all always shown to us," I express with heartfelt gratitude. "We can't wait until you all meet our son."

Many cultures lay claim to the legend of red thread. It's said that two people who are destined to meet are connected by a single red thread. This thread may stretch or become tangled for a time, but eventually, the thread of fate will bring you to the person connected to the other end.

That's why you'll find a drawing in each room of our bed and breakfast—a simple sketch of two hands clasped together by a single red thread.

Our journey, intertwined by these red threads, has led us to this moment—a gathering of the most unlikely family members bound together by fate.

No matter the time or distance that separates us, the thread that binds us to one another will never be broken.

Epilogue

ANTHONY

Charlotte opted to stay back at the hotel. At the orphanage, they requested only Leopold and me to attend. We find ourselves in a modest room with bare walls and a sparse collection of chairs. Leopold's legs fidget restlessly, anticipation mounting with each passing moment, knowing that at any instant, the door will swing open, and we'll lay eyes on our son for the very first time.Several months prior, we received a request from the orphanage to send photographs and personal items of clothing. Their aim was to acclimatize our son to our presence and scent, thus easing the inevitable uncertainty he'd face upon meeting us.

The doorknob squeaks as it slowly turns, and with bated breath, we watch as it cracks open. Yessenia, the adoption coordinator, steps into the room, cradling a little boy in her arms. He has long brown curls and big blue eyes.

I reach over and grip Leopold's hand tightly. We were instructed to remain seated and silent until Yessenia introduces the child to us. Right now, that feels like an impossible feat.She smiles brightly as she settles into the chair opposite us, the little boy nestled against her. "I explained to him that we were coming to meet the men from his pictures," she says softly, attempting to turn him to face us, but he resists. Instead, she adjusts her position so he's oriented towards us. "He just woke from a nap."

While we wait for him to adjust, we take the opportunity to learn more from Yessenia about his usual routine, his favorite foods, and anything else that might help us understand him and make his adjustment smoother.

As we converse, the child's eyes connect with Leopold's. In a poignant whisper, he utters, "Dada," evoking a surge of emotions that words cannot fully express.

Yessenia's voice is gentle as she praises him. "Very good," she says, her tone filled with warmth. "And who's that?"

His gaze, so innocent and pure, meets mine, and I'm consumed by a tumult of emotions, each one a testament to the depth of love I already feel for this precious child. "Papa," he says, his voice soft but clear.

"That's right, your Dada and Papa," she says tenderly, turning him to us. My gaze shifts to the toy he clutches tightly against his chest—a little red fire truck. "He refused to leave without this. It's his favorite toy."

"Kameron, do you like firetrucks?" Leo asks softly.

He nods shyly in response, his blue eyes meeting Leo's with a mixture of curiosity and timidity.

Leo looks to Yessenia for confirmation before sliding off his chair and settling onto the floor, offering his arms to Kameron. "Would you like to play down here?" he asks softly, a hopeful smile on his face.

Kameron, who hasn't yet taken his first steps, snuggles into Leopold's welcoming arms.

In a tender moment, Leopold holds Kameron close, his gaze filled with adoration. "I'm so happy to finally meet you, Kameron," he whispers lovingly.

Tears cascade down my cheeks as I witness our son, Kameron Matthew Genovese, play with his Daddy.

Adoption, poignant in its beauty, emanates from profound

loss. Amidst my tears of joy are tears of sorrow and gratitude for the courageous young woman who gave our son life.

"Play," Kameron states with determination, squirming in Leo's arms.

Leo laughs softly. "Yes, Kameron. We can play." He steals a glance at me, tears pooling in his eyes.

I pull out my phone, capturing the precious moments of their first interactions as father and son. I watch with tears of joy in my eyes, recording every smile, every laugh, every touch. After a few minutes, I set the phone aside and join them on the floor, enveloped in the warmth of our new family.

Yessenia's voice breaks the tender moment, bringing our attention back to reality. "It's time," she says softly, handing Leo a small cloth bag containing all of Kameron's belongings. With a gentle kiss on the baby's head, she leaves us alone, allowing us to savor this precious time as a new family.

As we walk out of the building with Kameron's head on my shoulder and his firetruck cradled against him, I feel a surge of overwhelming emotion. Beside me, Leopold's hand finds mine, our fingers intertwining naturally.

Outside, the setting sun casts a warm, golden glow over the city streets, illuminating our path forward. A gentle breeze whispers through the trees, carrying with it the promise of a fresh start.

I turn to Leopold, pressing a tender kiss to his temple, my heart overflowing with so much emotion. "I love you, *cuore mio*," I whisper, my voice barely above a murmur yet carrying the weight of a lifetime's worth of moments shared between us.

Leopold's gaze finds mine, shimmering with unshed tears. "And I love you," he replies, his voice soft and filled with emotion. "And Dada loves you, too, Kameron." Leopold leans in to place a tender kiss on our sleepy little boy's cheek, sealing the moment with love and warmth.

Together, we take our first steps into the next chapter, knowing that as long as we have each other and our precious son, we have everything we need to build a life filled with love, laughter, and endless possibilities.

The End

Sometimes home isn't a place.

Sometimes, it's a person.

Continue with *Home is Us*, an emotional M/M romance about love, healing, and finding the one person who feels like home.

Looking for something darker?

Aoife Quigley refused to choose between power and love.

So she took both.

Enter the world of *Bound by Darkness*, a dark romance filled with obsession, betrayal, forbidden love, and dangerous ambition inside the Irish syndicate world.

Find Tara's Books Here

About Tara

Bestselling author Tara Conrad writes where passion meets peril, crafting dark, spellbinding romances that blur the line between devotion and destruction.

Inspired by the haunting brilliance of Edgar Allan Poe, her stories reimagine Gothic tales with modern sensuality and power.

Within her pages, heroines rise unbroken, villains fall beautifully, and the darkness always tells the truth.

When she isn't writing, Tara travels with her husband, meeting readers who have found pieces of themselves in her worlds.

She believes love isn't always light. Sometimes, it's found in the dark. 🖤

Acknowledgments

George- Without you—your support, your encouragement when I was ready to quit, your celebrating my victories, and most of all, your Love. There's no one I'd rather be on this journey with. I love you forever and a day.

To my children- Thank you for all of your Love and support. Each of you has played such a big role in bringing this series to life and helping me realize my dreams. I love you all bunches!

To Baby E- Thank you for being Nana's helper. This past year has been one of the best in my life. I can't wait to have many more adventures together.

Simon Dornet- Thank you for taking a chance on a new author and a new series. You brought my characters to life and for that, I'm eternally grateful.

To the 'real' Sarah- We met at one of the worst periods in my life and have become friends in quite an unconventional way, but I wouldn't trade it for anything. I'm glad I was able to honor you and what you do for others in some small way.

To my readers: I don't know where to start. Two years ago, each of you took a chance on a brand-new author and the cast of characters she created. I'm humbled that you've fallen in Love with the Fire and Ice World and everyone in it. There were some laughs and plenty of tears. There were bumps in the road and twists you didn't see coming. And in the end, there was healing.

The end—two words that are bittersweet. These characters have been such a big part of my life for so long now. I'm not quite sure how to say goodbye to them. I hold on to the knowledge that they each found their happily ever after.

So, as we close the book on Fire and Ice, I hope that you'll come back for the new worlds I have planned.

You can keep up to date by signing up for my newsletter: https://subscribepage.io/FireandIceBooks

And also, by joining my readers' group on Facebook: https://www.facebook.com/groups/571538573826855

Much love,

Tara